FAKE
FLAME

FAKE FLAME

ADELE BUCK

Recycling programs
for this product may
not exist in your area.

ISBN-13: 978-1-335-04161-6

Fake Flame

Harlequin Enterprises ULC
22 Adelaide St. West, 41st Floor
Toronto, Ontario M5H 4E3, Canada
www.Harlequin.com

Printed in U.S.A.

For John, aka Mr. B—my very own romance hero

One

Eva was in her office when the music started. At first, she didn't pay attention, immersed in the paper she was grading. Then, the back of her neck prickling with dread, she recognized the tune. "Wonderful Tonight."

Darren used to say, "They're playing our song," when he heard it anywhere. It wasn't even a tune she *liked*. Just the one the band had been playing when he'd first asked her to dance back at Juliet and Mike's wedding three years ago. But Darren had decided that it meant something, that song. That it was some sort of sign from fate or God or the universe that they belonged together.

Well, if he still thought that, he could just go fuck himself.

Grabbing her office keys and ID off her desk, she stomped out into the hallway, pretty sure actual steam was coming out of her ears. Slamming her hand into the crash bar of the door of Wooton Hall, she emerged onto the quad and stopped dead.

There was Darren, playing Eric Clapton's asshole ballad on

an actual *baby grand piano* on the grass. That was bad enough.
Worse, there was a giant hand-lettered sign taped from the
open lid of the instrument, wafting gently in the spring breeze.
It read, I'M SORRY, EVA. PLEASE TAKE ME BACK. I'M
PLAYING OUR SONG FOR YOU.

Eva realized her mouth was open and she shut it with a
sharp click of her teeth.

"Oh, my God, that is so romantic," someone in a small
group of undergraduates a few yards away enthused.

Romantic? No. This was emotional blackmail. This was co-
ercion. This was Darren being a manipulative little assweasel.
In the past two months, she'd donated the flowers he sent her
to the local hospital. She'd blocked his texts and sent his email
to the spam filter. She'd taken a Sharpie to the handwritten
letters and written RETURN TO SENDER on every en-
velope before shoving them back into the mailbox, unopened
and unread. And that was just the beginning of his onslaught
and her endless iterations of *no*.

He looked to the side, still playing, and caught her eye.
And that fucker winked at her. He *winked*.

Eva took a deep, cleansing breath, and then another one
for good measure. Then, she turned on her heel and stepped
carefully back into the university building. Her first stop was
Celia Petrov's office. "Hey, Cee, can I borrow a lighter?"

Celia, a professor of Russian literature and someone who'd
never been able to kick her pack-a-day habit, looked up at Eva
and grinned. "Joining the ranks of the wicked?" she asked,
rummaging in her pen drawer and then tossing a pale pink
Bic over to Eva's waiting hands.

"Something like that," Eva muttered as she caught it. She could still hear that damn tune. Darren had run through it once and was starting again. What was that quote about doing the same thing over and over and expecting different results? "Thanks," she said, saluting her colleague with the lighter and turning back into the corridor. Trying the door to the maintenance closet, she pumped a fist when it opened. "Score." It took only a few moments of scanning the orderly contents before she found what she was looking for. She grabbed it and, after closing that door quietly, walked back out onto the quad, positioning herself a few feet from that ridiculous sign and raising her hands. Darren's playing abruptly stopped, his eyes going wide.

"Eva, what are you doing?" His voice was a wary croak.

"Exactly what it looks like. If you don't stop this shit, I'm going to use this lighter and this roach spray and make a fucking bonfire out of this piano."

Sean was reading *David Copperfield* when the bells went off. He and the rest of the squad abruptly stopped what they were doing and slid into action, running out to the garage bay to gear up and hustle to their ladder truck. He put his headset on, catching the dispatcher saying something about a fire at the university. Well, that at least was very close.

"Any structures involved?" Thea asked dispatch as she steered the truck out onto the street, siren blaring, heading for the emergency.

"I don't think so. Not yet. Possible arson, though. The

caller is pretty flustered—I think it's a kid—but fire was definitely mentioned."

Burning a college building? Sean had seen a lot in the course of his career, but this was some next-level bullshit.

But when they pulled into the access road that enabled them to go to the center of the quad at Montgomery University, there were no gouts of fire, no billowing smoke.

No. Instead, there was a beautiful redhead with flaming cheeks holding a dainty pink lighter and a can of something. Whatever she was trying to do was obviously not working because she was visibly frustrated, yelling something at a dude standing by a piano that was draped with what looked like a hand-lettered sign. The dude had his hands up like she was a gunslinger in a stickup. He was speaking, too, but his voice was low and calm as if he was trying to talk her off a ledge.

Piling out of the ladder truck, Sean could see that there was no actual fire. Reading the sign, his heart sank into his stomach. No, this might be an incendiary situation, but it was a romantic one, not a blaze. Sean and his team looked at each other for a few seconds and then Felix said, "I think this is a situation for diplomacy instead of hoses."

"You take the guy. I'll talk to the woman. We'll keep the hoses in reserve," Sean said. Having four sisters came in handy sometimes. Felix nodded curtly and stepped forward, catching the guy's attention and motioning for him to follow.

"Ma'am?" Sean called and the woman turned a pair of cool blue eyes on him. Yeah, she was mad all right. He gestured at the sign. "You're Eva, I take it?"

"Yes." She said it like she couldn't unclench her jaw.

"Wanna follow me over there and tell me what's going on?"

In response she raised up what looked like an industrial can of bug spray.

He flipped the face shield down on his helmet. "There's no need for hostility, ma'am. I just want to keep this situation from getting out of control."

"Then tell *him* to keep the fuck away from me for good." She pointed at the piano guy, who was twirling his index finger next to his ear. Sean could clearly see his lips form the words *crazy bitch*.

Oh, joy.

"Ma'am, I'm going to need you to just come away with me for a sec. You'll be in full view the entire time." A little more distance between these two seemed like a really good idea, as well as making sure she knew she'd be safe.

A little of the fight seemed to drain out of her at that moment and she moved to the shade of a nearby tree. Also a good idea. Redheads with her kind of pale skin sunburned like hell and it was a warm, sunny day. When he reached the tree, he held his hand out for the can and flipped up his face shield after she gave it to him. Crossing his arms over his chest, he looked at her for a few moments. The flush had left her cheeks but she still looked mad as hell.

In the gentlest voice he could produce he said, "Want to tell me what's going on?"

Oh, this giant man-child of a firefighter wanted to hear her side of the story, did he? Her glance flicked over the name badge on his—yes, predictably enormous—chest. *Hannigan.*

Oh, an Irish firefighter. How original. Now that the face shield was up, she could see his eyes were green, too.

Great. She was being grilled by a walking bar of Irish Spring. A total cliché. Even worse, a gorgeous walking cliché with a cartoon-worthy square jaw and paradoxically soft-looking lips. He raised one eyebrow—something she'd never been able to do, and that somehow set the capstone on her annoyance, making it a full and complete structure of its own.

"You want to know what happened? Fine. I broke up with that asshole two months ago." She gestured at Darren, who was talking with maddening calm to another firefighter. "And instead of taking the L and slinking off to a hole somewhere, he's been ramping up a series of *romantic* gestures until he actually got I don't know how many people to help him get an entire *baby grand piano* put on the quad in order to play the song that he's always said is *ours* but I never liked in the first place."

Wow. That was entirely more detail than she'd intended to give. But it felt kind of good, being able to talk about it. Since Darren was also a professor, she'd mostly stayed silent about their split, trying to take the high road. She'd seen all-too-many situations where women were labeled as the "bad guy" after a breakup, no matter what kind of shit men pulled. Now, since she'd lost it so publicly, she guessed all that circumspection was pointless.

Hannigan looked into the distance and rubbed his chin, his sandpapery stubble audible even over the gentle noises of the few students on the quad. He turned an inquiring gaze her way and she steeled herself for whatever was going to come next. An invasive question like, "Why'd you break up?" or worse, maybe a, "Sounds like a great guy. Aren't men supposed to do romantic gestures?" Or even the maddening, "What do you women want anyway? We just can't win." Typical male solidarity.

Instead, he said, "Do you think you need a restraining order?"

Oh. Wow. So he was going to take her seriously for a hot second? "No. He's not a stalker. He's just incredibly annoying and a grade-A gaslighter and liar."

Hannigan nodded. "Sounds like he's also a manipulative asshole."

From the way Eva's jaw dropped open, she was *not* expecting commiseration.

"Right?" She waved a hand at the piano, the sign now flapping vigorously in the freshening breeze. "He couldn't win me back—sidebar, such a gross idea—in private, so he's got to co-opt strangers into pressuring me to accept his 'romantic—'" huge air quotes "—gesture. Ugh."

"Sounds like this guy doesn't know you very well."

She closed her eyes at that, chuckling to herself. "No. And the sad thing is, I kinda thought he did at one point. Shows what I know."

The way her head was angled, he now saw that there was a strand of silver in her hair, threading through the red. Oh, damn. She was like a rage-filled amalgamation of Bonnie Raitt and Amy Adams in a cardigan and sensible flats. If he'd met her anywhere else, he'd be asking if he could get her number. But no. You don't take advantage of someone's vulnerability like that. At least, he wouldn't.

"Okay, so tell me what you were thinking when you rocked up with the pink Bic and the—" he examined the label on the can "—industrial roach spray?"

She sighed, rubbing her forehead and looking at the ground. "I don't know." Her voice had a frustrated snap to it, like a plucked rubber band. "I was angry and I just wanted him gone."

Sean's senses sharpened at that. He wasn't a cop and didn't want to be one, but he was interested in keeping people safe. "Gone permanently?"

She looked at him like he'd missed a step. "Yeah."

He needed to get this right. If he got things wrong, the cops might need to be involved. "So you wanted him dead?"

Her freckles seemed to pop off her face as she paled. "What? God, no. I just want him out of my life. Go cheat on someone else, jackass, leave me alone."

Ah, there was the reason for the breakup she didn't want to convey in that initial rush of narrative.

"Okay. So we've established that you didn't intend to harm…" He trailed off, not remembering the guy's name.

"Darren," she supplied.

"Darren. Okay." He already hated this guy who'd hurt Amy Raitt. Or was it Bonnie Adams? No. It was Eva. But he still had a job to do.

"I just wanted him to leave me alone. And actual conversation didn't get me that. So it seemed like making a flame-thrower out of a lighter and roach spray would send that message." She cringed and scrubbed her face. "God. It seems so foolish now."

"But you were driven to the edge." A suspicious eye emerging from that face scrubbing made him raise his hands. The last thing he wanted was to add to her obvious distress. "No judgment. People can be driven to the edge. It's a thing."

She laughed faintly at that, her hands dropping to her sides. "Yeah. It's totally a thing."

Sean sighed. "Okay. I'm glad the police didn't get involved." Her eyes widened in alarm. "Right. You'd probably be okay. Pretty white woman and all that, but next time think before you threaten arson, okay?"

Impossibly, her face got even paler, the cinnamon freckles practically 3D. "Oh, shit. You're right." She covered her eyes with her hands. "I am the worst."

The worst? Hah. "Nah, I think cheating Darren is actually the worst. But think before you fly off the handle next time, okay?"

She peered at him from between her fingers again. "Why are you being so nice to me?"

Two

Hannigan paused at the question, his square jaw set a little more firmly. "Well, I have four older sisters. They tell me stuff about how hard it can be to be a woman."

She stared at him. Was he a *unicorn*? "And you actually listen. That's rather remarkable."

He looked at the grass of the quad at his feet, seeming embarrassed. "It shouldn't be."

"You're right. But unfortunately, it is. The bar is so low it's in the Mariana Trench." Most men, even if they did listen, seemed to discount how bad things could be or accuse women of outright fabrications. Anything to not have to see the world through anyone's eyes but their own.

Lifting his head, he said, "Getting back to your more immediate problem, I hope your job will be safe when this story inevitably gets around."

Her spine straightened. "I have tenure," she replied, registering the surprise in his eyes.

"Impressive."

"Which isn't to say I won't get a stern reprimand from the dean or something for making the university look bad with my unhinged behavior. But I can handle that." She could, but she still felt a pang of sick dread in her stomach at the thought.

"What are you a professor of?"

He was seriously interested? "English literature and pop culture."

An honest-to-God grin spread over his face at that. "Cool. What's your favorite book?"

Eva paused, the turn in the conversation making her head spin a little. "Well, in terms of classic literature I'd have to go with Austen's *Persuasion*. But on the pop culture side it keeps changing. Authors putting new stuff out all the time and really doing interesting things, you know? Picking favorites in a constantly changing landscape seems like an exercise in futility."

"Cool. For Austen, I think I'm more of a *Pride and Prejudice* man, but maybe that's because I have four older sisters."

She barked out a surprised laugh. "Does that make you Lydia? You don't seem flighty to me." She shook her head. This conversation was possibly the most surreal thing that had ever happened to her.

He chuckled at that himself. "Never thought of it that way. I'm not planning on running off with an army deserter, at any rate."

"Yeah, I can see that not being a good look for you," she mused, rubbing her chin in a mock-thoughtful way. "Do you have a favorite genre book, though?"

"You mean like science fiction or something?"

"Sure. Or fantasy or romance or mystery or thrillers or horror…"

He made a face. "Read a lot of sci-fi when I was a kid. I'm trying to make up for lost time now. Classics. Trying to be well-read, you know?"

Interesting. "Okay, but there's more to being well-read than the old-school literary canon."

He looked like he was about to respond when a voice across the quad called, "Sean!" His head went up and he lifted a hand in acknowledgment to the colleague who'd been talking to Darren, a young Black man who was giving him a "wind it up" gesture.

"Be right there," he hollered back. Turning back to Eva, he said, "I gotta run. It's been nice talking to you. Lay off the homemade flamethrowers, though, okay?"

She laughed weakly, feeling more foolish than she had in a long time, and yet still wishing they could have prolonged their conversation. "Well, I couldn't even figure out how the lighter worked, so I wouldn't have made a very successful flamethrower-creator anyway. I thought you just pressed your thumb on the button and bingo—flame."

He chuckled and they started to walk together in tandem across the grass as if they'd somehow mutually agreed to prolong their conversation as long as possible. "They've had safety features for a while now. I'd tell you how to use one, but I'm worried you'd use that knowledge in a way you shouldn't."

Eva flinched at that. She'd been reckless. Worse than reckless. And, as they drew level with Darren, she saw how she'd catastrophically miscalculated.

Because he looked at her and winked. Again. Her stomach gave a sick roll. Apparently, she was in for more of this bullshit.

Sean saw the wink. It was like an evil eel slithering through the slime that was this situation. The jackass had thought his "bitches are crazy, am I right?" act had worked. Okay.

He could work this situation, too. He straightened up to his full six foot three and said, "I'd advise you to leave the lady alone." All four of his sisters would have crashed down on him for the macho posturing, but honestly? It kinda felt good.

The guy—Darren—blinked up at him, then sneered. "What's it to you?"

"She tells me you've been hassling her. Says she doesn't think it rises to the level of needing a restraining order, but I dunno. If she's driven to do something this drastic..." He let the statement trail off, punctuated with an eyebrow raise.

Darren shot him a smug look. "Show's what you know. Her doing something this drastic means she still has feelings for me."

"Standing right here, and yes, I have feelings. Of loathing," Eva said, then pointedly turned her back and stalked off into a building with "Wooton Hall" carved into the stone over the doorway.

Darren chuckled, condescension oozing from every pore. "She's supposed to be an expert in pop culture and she can't recognize a grand gesture when she sees one? And no, she won't be getting a restraining order against me, regardless of what I do. I'm also a professor here."

"Doesn't mean you can't also be a total fucking creep,"

Sean said, keeping his tone mild so that the insult would land even harder.

"Well, she's a crazy bitch," Darren shot back, obviously needled.

Rage spiked through Sean at the slur. This asshole seriously needed to leave the poor woman alone. "Right. But you want her back so badly you're ready to pull this stunt? You're the one who doesn't seem very stable to me. Maybe you need to go in for an evaluation. Because it's seriously creepy to make a scene like this." Reaching out, Sean ripped the sign off the piano, crumpling it into a ball and throwing it to the grass at Darren's feet. "I mean it. Stay away from her."

When Eva got back to Wooton Hall, she realized her hands were trembling. Adrenaline maybe. Or maybe it was just straight-up nerves from that incredibly out-of-pocket thing she'd just done. Something so completely out of character that if she hadn't still been holding Celia's lighter, she might have wondered if she had hallucinated the whole ordeal, surprisingly well-read and kind extra-large firefighter included.

Reaching her office, she flopped into her desk chair and sighed, rubbing her temples with shaking fingers.

"Professor Campbell?" A small voice came from the doorway. Eva looked up and attempted a smile.

"Xiuying, hi. What can I do for you?" She waved at the pair of guest chairs in front of her desk.

The undergraduate sank into a chair, letting her flowered backpack slide to the floor. "I just wanted you to know that someone was trying to film that whole scene on the quad. I got up in front of them and mostly spoiled the shot, though. At least, I think I did."

Eva suppressed a manic laugh. Perfect. She was probably going to be the character du jour on TikTok now. *Unhinged lady threatens to turn a piano into a cinder. See it now!* Seven zillion views.

She took in a long, careful breath. "Thank you," she said. "That was very kind of you."

Xiuying fingered a strand of her long, dark hair that lay across the front of her shoulder. "You were really upset. And nobody should invade your privacy like that—I mean, ever, but in this situation, it just seemed really bad. And it really didn't seem like you. Then I thought about how you talked about that boom box scene when we discussed *Say Anything* in class—you know about how Lloyd Dobler is being manipulative, maybe, and not romantic?"

"And you saw a Lloyd Dobler situation on the quad?" Eva had never considered that her classroom discussions would yield such tangible and personal results. *So much for having a useless degree, Dad. One point to me.*

Xiuying nodded. "Was I right?"

"Two hundred percent. Unfortunately."

The undergraduate sat up a little straighter, her narrow shoulders squaring. "Well, then I'm glad I spoiled that stupid guy's attempt to film it. I just thought you should know it's out there, maybe."

"Thank you again. I do appreciate what you did for me," she said as the young woman stood, shouldering her backpack again and shooting her a tiny smile.

Xiuying gave her a thumbs-up. "Solidarity, yanno?"

Eva smiled back, her heart warming at the unexpected support. "I do."

When they pulled back into the fire station, Felix slapped Sean on the shoulder. "Kinda nice to get called out for nothing but a pretty woman getting pissed off at a serious waste of space."

Sean shot him a sidelong glance. "I take it his 'bitches are crazy' explanation didn't fly with you, either?"

Felix shook his head, nose wrinkling in disgust. "What did she say to you?"

"Bad breakup and he's not riding off into the sunset like a good little asshole."

"Well, he's definitely an asshole, but she's also gorgeous. Even I can see that."

Sean put his helmet on the shelf and rubbed his hand through his sweaty, close-cropped hair. "Going to tell Kevin you found a woman attractive when you get home?"

Felix smirked. "We're solid. He'd just laugh and kiss me."

"Ah, young love."

Felix punched Sean's shoulder as they got out of their protective gear and hung it up. "Piss off." But he was grinning.

Sean thought further about the scene on the quad. They'd managed to connect at least a little bit even in the midst of all her stress. Then that asshole Darren had made it clear that he wasn't finished. His gut tightened. "You think maybe I should check up with her in a few days? See how she's doing?"

Felix wagged a finger. "Ahhh, I knew there was something

there. She went from threatening you with bug spray to laughing at something you said to her in approximately zero seconds. I clocked that whole cozy little scene from across the quad."

Sean raised his hands as if surrendering. "No, seriously. No ulterior motives here." *Liar.* He hadn't wanted their weird little conversation to end, especially when she started taking him seriously in a way few people ever had. "I just want to make sure she's okay."

"Right. That's why you practically squared off with that fine example of human garbage before we pulled out. You're so invested already it's seriously funny."

"Felix is right," Thea called over one shoulder as she hung up her coat. "You're smitten."

"Well, it felt like the least I could do. Some guys just never get the hint."

"That guy needs more than a hint. He needs a clue-by-four to the skull," Thea muttered as she stalked toward the kitchen.

"Seriously," said Felix, agreeing. Then he turned, snapping his fingers and pointing at Sean. "But if you *were* dating her, then maybe that could be the same thing as a blow to the head."

A stuttering, shocked laugh burst out of Sean. Yeah, he was drawn to her. But he'd only just met her. "You're suggesting I ask the woman out to help her with her ex-boyfriend situation? How does that work?" It made him sound like a creeper—someone who would take advantage of her distress and vulnerability.

"Or you could offer to *pretend* to be her new romance. Follow me." Sean trailed after Felix, who dug around in his messenger bag in the bunk room. "Here," he said, pulling out a book and putting it into Sean's hands. "There's your instruction manual."

Sean looked from the book back to Felix. "This is an instruction manual?" On the illustrated cover where two men gave each other coy glances on a backdrop of a deconstructed British flag, a legend clearly read: *A Novel.*

Felix nodded, brown eyes shimmering with glee. "Yup. It's a book about a couple of guys in England who both—for their own purposes—need partners. So they agree to fake date. Like I said, an instruction manual for your situation. It's also poignant and funny as hell."

"So it's a romance novel." His next-oldest sister Caitlin consumed them by the pound. He'd tried a few when he was a teen and desperate for something new to read. He'd liked them in the past, but then his dad had shamed him for reading "girly" books and…well. The memory of that humiliation still made him want to drop the book and back away from it. Paradoxically, he also felt ashamed of being compelled by the recollection. Caitlin herself had been scathing about his dad's sexist attitude and he had to admit she was right.

Felix shot him a lopsided grin. "Come on, be the enlightened man I know you can be. Just give it a try."

Three

It took two days for the summons to arrive. A brief email from the dean's assistant asking Eva to drop in at two that afternoon. Dean Treadwell was usually more solicitous, asking if a specific time worked for a faculty member, not demanding their presence like this.

She must be pissed.

With dread sitting sourly in her stomach at the idea of having to discuss her personal life with the dean, Eva presented herself at the dean's suite at exactly two o'clock. "You can go right in," Treadwell's assistant said, waving his hand at the open doorway to the inner sanctum.

Right. With a brief little nod, Eva tried to settle her nerves and strode into the office, closing the door behind her. Dean Treadwell looked up over her reading glasses, then removed them, allowing them to dangle from the bejeweled chain around her neck as she pointed wordlessly at a guest chair. These chains were the older woman's sole eccentricity. She had one in every color and for every occasion. Otherwise, she essentially looked like an academic version of Miranda Priestly with her sweep of iron-gray hair and classic, elegant wardrobe.

"Eva, what the hell happened on the quad on Wednesday?" Her tone was hard to parse. Eva'd been expecting full-out rage, but there was a thread of something else in the dean's voice. If she was angry, it was a controlled sort of anger.

Taking a deep breath and sinking into the chair with a straight spine, Eva paused to collect her thoughts and said, "This is rather embarrassing. I broke off a long-term romantic relationship with Darren Perry in the music department a couple of months back. He has been pursuing a reconciliation, not taking no for an answer, and Wednesday was the showiest, most public expression of that. I was—well, I was pretty frantic about it all and I am sorry to say I overreacted."

Dean Treadwell frowned, picked up a pen and made a note. "Okay." She put her pen down and looked straight at Eva. "Are you all right? Because yes, you definitely overreacted and I am still astonished there isn't some incredibly embarrassing video going viral on social media. I wasn't here on Wednesday and only heard about it from Bill Ellers this morning."

Wait. Was Eva...not in trouble, somehow? She took in a deep, somewhat shaky breath then let it out slowly. Bill Ellers, only the biggest gossip on the faculty. Great. "Um. I think I'm okay. Thanks for asking. And yes, I think we can attribute the lack of any damaging video to the fairly light population post-exams and the actions of one of my students. She apparently blocked someone trying to record the incident on their phone."

"An enterprising young lady," the dean commented.

"Um. Yes." Eva tried not to cringe. This could have been so much worse. She couldn't believe there weren't multiple students who found the whole thing entertaining enough to record.

"And I suppose it's also good to know that the response time from the fire department is so prompt."

Remembering Sean Hannigan's comment about how much worse it would have been if the cops had been called—Eva's face flamed. That firefighter—Sean—he'd gone out of his way to be kind and decent to her when she'd been nothing less than unhinged. "Yes. I'm sorry that it happened and I can assure you that it will not happen again, Dean Treadwell."

A small, wintry smile flickered over the dean's face. "Oh, it most certainly will not. I will speak to Professor Perry. At the very least about having a large and expensive piece of university property transported outdoors where it might have been damaged by weather or..." She paused a moment to look at Eva, who wanted to shrink into herself at the memory of her flamethrower moment. "Have you taken legal action against him?"

Eva gathered her thoughts. If both Sean and the dean had the same idea... No. The vision of some judge telling her she was an overreacting hysteric because Darren had sent some letters and flowers and played a song was beyond humiliating. "You mean like a restraining order? I don't think the things he's done will appear threatening to a judge. I'm afraid it would just be a waste of time and money."

"Very well. You're free to go. But be careful."

Grateful for the reprieve and bewildered by the dean's unexpected show of support, Eva slid out the door and speed-
walked back to her office.

The next week Eva was entering final grades into the university's system when there was a light tap at her door. She
looked up, expecting a student, and was surprised to see a tall
man with a square jaw, light brown hair cut close to his scalp
and serious eyes leaning in her doorway, massive arms crossed
on his chest. *Wow.* A shot of pure lust shivered through her.

"Can I help you?" she asked, trying to pull herself together.
He seemed familiar somehow, but this was definitely not one
of her students. And thank God for that. She'd never want to
react this way to a student.

The man scratched his nose, not entering and looking a
little nervous. "Hi. I'm Sean Hannigan. I guess you don't remember me—"

"Oh!" Shock blazed through her. "Yes, sorry. It just took
me a minute, with no uniform or helmet." Not to mention
the baggy coat had obscured the contours of that truly spec-
tacular chest, which was currently sporting a tight T-shirt.
And now that she looked, she noticed that the logo over his
left pectoral read *MCFRS*. Montgomery County Fire and
Rescue Squad.

Sean grinned at that, seeming pleased at her sudden rec-
ognition. "Yeah. I wanted to stop by and see how you were
doing. Is it okay if I come in?"

She shook her head as if she could rattle some sense into
it and waved at her guest chairs. "Sure. Sorry, where are my
manners? Have a seat."

"If you're not too busy?" He stood by the chair apparently ready to leave if she was, in fact, too busy. There was something very endearing about all this careful politeness in that heavily muscled package.

"Not at all. Just finishing up some post-semester admin."

He settled his tall frame into the chair and rubbed the back of his neck. "So you okay? After that fiasco on the quad, I mean."

He was checking up on her? How incredibly sweet. "Yes, absolutely."

"Good. You haven't heard from your ex again, huh?"

She hadn't, in fact, and had been mildly hopeful that Darren had finally decided that she wasn't worth the effort anymore. "No, not yet at least."

He sat up a little straighter, his gaze sharpening. "So you think he might show up in your life again?"

Grimacing, she said, "He's shown no sign of letting up before now. So it's certainly possible." She hated waiting and wondering what Darren would do next almost as much as she hated his impossible persistence. It left her keyed up and off-kilter. Which it was probably intended to do. The bastard.

"I'd say probable," the giant occupant of her guest chair rumbled. "Guys like that see women as possessions and they'll keep trying to regain what they see as 'theirs.'"

As summaries of the personalities of men like Darren went, this was depressingly accurate. She felt an overwhelming exhaustion at the idea of having to deal with him again. "Maybe he's tired of expending the energy."

Sean shook his head. "Nah, usually they only stop if one of two things happens."

"What's that?" she asked, almost amused at his analysis of her terrible ex-boyfriend.

He held up one long, thick index finger. "One, if he finds another woman he wants to possess."

She shuddered. "As much as I want him to leave me alone, I do not wish that on anyone else. What's two?"

His middle finger rose and Eva had a shivery feeling down her spine. Those *hands*. They gave her all-too-many ideas. "If the woman is 'claimed' by another man."

Eva seemed unusually fixated on his hand. Was she alarmed by his size? Some women were. His sisters had spent quite a lot of time educating him about how he could have the best intentions in the world—or none at all—and scare the ever-loving bejeezus out of someone just by his presence. He lowered his hand, clasping it with the other in his lap, trying to look less imposing.

"So you're telling me to get a new partner?" Eva groaned. "I wouldn't even know how to go about doing that. It's so hard to meet people in your forties and I can't bear the idea of using apps."

Sean's eyebrows slid up. "You're forty?" he blurted. He would not have expected that, sexy silver streak in her hair or no. But you also weren't supposed to comment on a woman's age. Did her mentioning it first make it better? He didn't really think it mattered. Embarrassment crawled up the back of his throat like bile.

Eva smiled gently. "Yeah. I'm forty-one. But I appreciate the vote of confidence."

"That's only five years older than me," he said, then realized saying that was probably not the most choice example of game on the planet. "Sorry," he muttered. "I get flustered around pretty women."

Pale pink mantled her cheekbones. "Thank you. Unless you mean you saw one of our undergraduates shortly before you came in here and were still reeling."

Her teasing, far kinder than his sisters would have been, grounded him somehow. He snorted. "No. I meant you. But to get back to the problem with Darren the dirtbag—"

She clapped her hands at that. "Oh, I like it. Alliterative."

He coughed, thrown off his non-game again, then saw a newly familiar book cover on the shelf behind her head. "Hey, my buddy just loaned that book to me the other day."

She twisted to peer at her shelves, but the sheer quantity of books there meant she couldn't possibly have the slightest clue as to which one he was indicating. He stood and rounded her desk, tipping the paperback out of its place on the shelf. She stood, too, maybe alarmed at his sudden approach. He showed her the book, realizing that he'd come far closer to her than he'd intended. He could smell some sort of elusive fragrance from her perfume or shampoo. It made him want to lean over and inhale but he controlled the caveman impulse as her gaze scanned the cover.

"Your buddy lent this book to you?" she asked, her voice a little faint.

"Yeah. Felix. The one who talked your ex down last week."

"Your *firefighter* buddy recommended a *romance* novel to you." She seemed to have trouble processing that notion. Fair, given what most people thought they knew about firefighters, he guessed.

"He said it's really good."

Her clear blue eyes lifted to meet his. "It is. It's a fake dating story. I'm going to assign it to my contemporary romance literature class in the fall."

"Yeah." He took a deep breath to gather his courage, and said in a rush, "See, that's what I came to talk to you about. To maybe, I don't know…help you out with that ex-boyfriend situation by pretending to be your new boyfriend?"

The word *boyfriend* seemed to shimmer in the air like a mirage. Eva blinked fast enough to conjure a tiny whirlwind.

"Your friend suggested you *fake date me*? He does know the difference between books and real life, right?" She was still fixated on the notion that a firefighter had said and done these things. She felt like she'd slipped sideways into an alternate dimension.

"Yeah. I mean…" Sean rubbed his forehead. "Sorry. I'm a meathead. I'm not used to—"

"Stop," she said, the situation landing square in her educator's wheelhouse. "You are not a meathead. You're clearly a thoughtful person who is intentional in his actions. Slow down and tell me what you think this arrangement would entail." She'd read plenty of novels with a fake dating trope and could easily make the leap to what someone with a similar history would think. Not that she'd ever actually *do* what he was suggesting. Because she lived in the real world where people didn't do ridiculous things like that.

But she was interested to see where Sean Hannigan, some-one who may never have cracked the spine on a romance novel until recently, would go. And, if she was being one hundred percent honest with herself, the whole package gave her a little thrill. The chance to make Darren feel like a chump? The chance to be near this endearing and—let's face it—incredibly handsome man? Yeah. Full body shivers.

Sean rubbed the back of his head and a blush crawled up his neck. "Here's the thing. Your ex and I had words after you left the—" He waved his hand in the direction of the quad.

"Scene of the crime?" Eva couldn't suppress her smile even though the memory was still mortifying.

He chuckled. "Yeah. That. Anyway. My squad mate, the guy who lent me this—" he gestured with the book "—he said maybe I could help you with your issue by pretending to be your boyfriend. You know, be the guy who 'claims' you." He grimaced. "Sorry. I know, that's gross."

"Have you actually read that book?" she asked, sidling closer, wondering where she got the courage to do so. Maybe it was that he really did smell like Irish Spring now that she was near enough.

He shook his head. "Just a few pages. Enough to know the main character's landed himself in a big mess."

She chuckled. "Yeah. A big mess. Hopefully, I'm in a bit of a smaller mess that doesn't require something so drastic." He was sweet. Now that she'd indulged in her little fantasy, she needed to let him down easy on this silly plan.

At that moment loud footsteps could be heard in the hallway and then they both turned to see Darren in her doorway, red faced and pointing a finger at her. "You told the fucking *dean* that I wouldn't leave you alone?" he said in a voice of pure rage.

The sudden adrenaline spike that rushed through her threatened to turn into instant nausea. Through gritted teeth, she said, "Well, the fact that you're here *in my office* doesn't exactly disprove the statement."

He waved a hand like he was warding off a fly. "I can't believe you would go to *the dean*."

"I didn't. She came to me. Your stunt could have gone viral or something."

"*My* stunt? You threatened me with a homemade fire thrower." She wished she had that can of roach spray back in her hands. Even without the lighter it would have made her feel safer.

"Which I wouldn't have had to do if you'd done as I asked and *left me alone*. Instead, you had to stage a huge, embarrassing scene."

Darren rolled his eyes as if she was being ridiculous. "Come on! It was a romantic gesture."

Her hands balled into fists. "That wasn't romantic. It was an attempt at manipulation. And you're a gaslighting fuckboy."

"Bitch."

At that moment, a large hand came to rest gently on her lower back, sending tingles up her spine and making her startle. God. It was like Darren hadn't even noticed Sean. She'd almost forgotten he was here, she'd been so focused on Darren and his rage.

Sean's deep voice was almost a growl. "Don't you *ever* talk about my girlfriend like that."

Four

Eva's spine stiffened under his hand. *Ohh, I am in so much trouble*, Sean thought. She'd been amused, yes. Intrigued, yes. But had she actually agreed to his scheme?

She hadn't.

Darren looked him up and down, a scornful expression twisting his face. "You?" he scoffed. "Right. Eva'd no more date a muscle-bound gym bunny than she would someone who couldn't read." He blinked theatrically, then snapped his fingers. "Oh. Unless you're a charity case. Maybe she's teaching you literacy skills." His eyes slid to the paperback still in Sean's hand. "With romance novels. Figures. Next step up from a Sesame Street book."

Sean, filled with rage at this jackass's words, was gearing up to respond when Eva surprised the hell out of him by sliding her arm around his waist. "Take your disgusting insinuations about my *very literate* boyfriend and your unwelcome opinions about literature out of my office, Darren."

"Literature," Darren scoffed. "Oh. Right. The grocery store spinner rack full of stories that give women unrealistic expectations is so *literate*."

"Unrealistic to you, maybe," Sean said, savoring the sideways glance Eva shot him and Darren's infuriated glare. "Some of us know how to please our partners. In *every* way." He slid the hand that had been lightly pressed to her back to her waist, pulling her closer to his side.

Oh, his sisters would *kill* him for this caveman routine. He nearly laughed aloud as Eva leaned her head against his shoulder. He liked that. She was tall enough that her head rested right at the place where his biceps and shoulder muscles met. God, she just felt so *good*. She fit against him like she was meant to be there.

Darren gaped at them long enough that Sean almost pointed out that he was catching flies. Then the other man's eyes narrowed and he pointed at Sean. "You're that fireman. I remember you from the quad. You've been sniffing after her like a dog from the jump."

Sean ran his palm up Eva's spine, feeling the cool, silky fall of her hair against the back of his hand. "Your loss, my gain," he said as she looked up, meeting his gaze squarely and giving him a tiny, conspiratorial smile.

God, at this rate, he almost didn't want Darren to leave if his presence was going to have her looking at him like that, touching him like that.

Darren snorted. "Well. When you get the boy toy out of your system, let me know and maybe I'll even take you back." And with that parting shot he turned on his heel and stomped out of Eva's office.

* * *

As soon as the sound of Darren's footsteps faded, Sean pulled away, putting about a foot of space between them. Perversely, even though Eva had been irritated by his presumption, she was even more irritated by how he seemed to actively recoil from physical contact with her.

She'd always thought that the whole "big man" thing was kind of bullshit. But having his hard body beside her, ready to protect her from Darren's anger, had been hotter than she'd ever expected.

For a few seconds it had felt so *real*.

"Well, that didn't work," she muttered, flopping down into her office chair as Sean resumed his seat in her guest chair. Across her desk. Approximately a million miles away from her.

"Only because he thinks it won't last," Sean said. Why did he have to sound so calm, so *reasonable*? This was objectively a surreal situation bearing little to no relationship with reality at all. "We just have to keep it going."

"How?" That single syllable sounded waspish, even to herself.

"I don't know just yet, but I'm sure we can think of something." He gave her a crooked, almost rueful little smile. Like maybe he'd regretted embroiling himself in her shit. And who wouldn't? Her life was an utter mess.

She pinched the bridge of her nose between her thumb and forefinger, willing back the headache that threatened. "There is a cocktail party coming up—the dean always celebrates the end of the spring semester. It's kind of a required thing, so I was going to have to deal with Darren at that." And it would be good to be able to go with Sean on her arm, to not have to constantly be the one taking the high road, to ignore, to deflect—and to do it all on her own.

"See? I knew you'd think of something." Sean leaned forward, forearms on his knees, nodding encouragingly. And suddenly, all Eva could see were those forearms, defined and strong. She could almost still feel the way one had wrapped around her, tugging her close, sheltering her. "Eva?" His voice recalled her to the present moment and she blinked, meeting his eyes again, slightly dazed.

"Sorry. Yeah. But that's just one cocktail party. What else can we do in the meantime? It's not like I want to go out of my way to parade you around like a brand-new accessory."

He wrinkled his nose at that. "Yeah. No. Let's just take it as it comes, okay? We're sure to think of something else somewhere along the line. You especially. You're obviously really smart."

"Okay." She wasn't sure how she felt about his faith in her. He was a bit younger than she was. Was that it, maybe? Or maybe that he seemed more impressed by her job than he should be? "What exactly do you get out of this?" she asked.

He grinned, easy and confident. "I get to spend time with a smart, pretty lady. I don't see the downside for me."

She held up a hand at that. "Whoa. Let's not get this twisted. If this is fake dating, then it's *fake*." On one level, she still couldn't believe she was agreeing to this. On another, Sean's easygoing, matter-of-fact manner made everything seem much simpler than it was in truth. As if this out-of-character leap into adventure for her was an utterly ordinary weekday activity for him.

The grin stretched, broadening until she could practically see his molars. "Roger that. Loud and clear. But I still intend to make it look good."

Damn. Sean was having to pour every ounce of self-control into this. Because the fact of the matter was, he could easily be a goner for this woman. Fiery, smart, and had he called her *pretty*?

Dear Lord, but that was an understatement. She was beautiful.

He also was willing to bet that fiery nature of hers would translate seamlessly into passion if she let it. He could just see that red hair rippling over his coverlet as he worshipped every inch of her with his fingers, his mouth, his dick. The thought was a mistake. He shifted uncomfortably in his seat, willing that organ to settle down before it gave him away.

He thought of Darren, that overconfident, annoying blowhard. Yeah, that did it. Instant boner eraser. "So since your ex seems to have zero boundaries and less self-control, how do you feel maybe about taking some self-defense lessons?"

Her gaze sharpened. "First you suggest a restraining order and now self-defense? What do you know about Darren that I don't?"

He shrugged. "Not necessarily anything. But first responders see all kinds of domestic situations—bad ones—and he gives me a nasty vibe. I'm just saying it wouldn't be the worst idea in the world for you to have some basic techniques in your back pocket." And he knew just how she could acquire those techniques. Plus, it would enable him to touch her again.

She sighed. "Now I have to go find a self-defense class on top of everything else? Great."

"Nah."

She frowned. "I'm confused. You just said I needed lessons."

He pointed at his own chest. "I can give them to you. Easiest thing in the world. I used to teach a class at the Y."

Amusement flickered across her face. "Is there anything you *can't* do? I assume you walk little old ladies across the street when you're not busy putting out fires."

"Don't forget saving kittens from trees," he replied, amused by her vision of him as some sort of supercharged Boy Scout. "Anyway, on your feet. I can show you one of the most basic self-defense moves in less than five minutes."

"Seriously? Now?" She shook her head.

"On. Your. Feet," he said, getting out of his chair and shooting her a stern look. Oh, that did it. Her eyes went wide, pupils spreading black across the Caribbean blue of her gorgeous eyes.

This could really be fun.

That low growl shouldn't have sent a pulse of longing through her. It shouldn't have made her legs clench together, compressing her sex until it throbbed. She got to her feet, a little unsteady and wobbly in the knees.

"C'mere." He beckoned her around her desk with one of those big hands of his. Oh, first the forearms, now those hands. She could imagine him touching her most intimate places with those thick, long fingers. She swallowed and stood in front of him.

He grasped her wrist, his hand warm and strong. "Pull it away," he told her, that note of command still in his voice. She blinked. "Pull your arm away," he repeated. Was there a smile lurking behind those serious eyes?

Pull it together *and pull it away.* She yanked her arm up and away from him. Or she tried. He barely budged.

"You're stronger than you look," he said, his grip tightening a little, sending shivers up her arm. "Try again." She did, with no better results.

Her teeth gritted. "I can't. I might be stronger than I look, but you're obviously stronger than I am by a lot." What was the point of this? To make her feel small and helpless?

"Yeah, but strength isn't everything. You're tugging in a way that makes it easy for me to keep hold of you." God, his voice was a low rumble. Pure sex. At this rate, she didn't *want* to pull away from him. "What do you think the weak point of my grip is?"

She examined his hand, trying to focus on the task at hand rather than the X-rated scenes that coursed through her brain. "I don't know. It looks strong in general."

He tapped the place where his index finger overlapped his thumb. "What about here?"

"What about it?"

"Try pulling free by moving in that direction," he said.

"Here goes nothing," she muttered, and yanked her wrist. It flew free, cool air caressing the skin that had been warmed by his hand. "You let go," she said, her voice accusing. He was just playing with her now and she didn't like it.

He shook his head slowly. "No, you just took advantage

of the weakest point of my grip. Think of it this way—if you were prying loose a link of chain, would you go for the solid metal or the place where it was soldered? It's almost impossible to keep hold of someone if they pull where the fingers meet. Here, you grab me." He presented his wrist to her and she wrapped her fingers around it without even thinking.

"My fingers don't even meet. Your arm is too big," she said, her face heating.

"Yeah, but if I pull this way or that way," he demonstrated by moving his hand into her grip. He was strong enough that she kind of flailed like a marionette instead of remaining still like he had. "I still would have a harder time getting free than if I did this." He demonstrated the same maneuver he'd taught her moments before and her hand was suddenly empty. "Works even better if you twist or rotate your arm while you're doing it."

"Let me try again," she said, intrigued in spite of herself. It wasn't every day when someone taught her a new skill, and she was enjoying both the novelty and the weight of Sean's undivided attention.

He presented his wrist and she wrapped her hand around it. This time, he twisted his forearm as he whipped out of her grip, and she could see what he meant about how that made her even more helpless to hold on to him. "So that's it?"

"That's just the most basic move," Sean told her. "After you get free, you can either inflict some damage on your opponent or run. Or preferably both."

"Let me guess," she said, amusement rippling through her. "Knee to the balls?"

He shook his head. "While that can be effective, it's also expected. You want to try to do the unexpected thing. Stomp on his feet, drive your fingers at his throat or eyes."

"Then knee him in the balls?" Her amusement was turning to pure glee now.

He winced. "Um, sure. But then you beat feet and get the hell out of there while he's holding on to the family jewels. The point isn't to do lasting damage. It's to create an escape route for you." His phone chimed and he pulled it out of his back pocket. "And with that, I have to get going. I have a shift."

A pang shot through her. She wasn't ready to let him go, even though she knew she had to. "Wait." Eva grabbed a pad of sticky notes and a pen off her desk, scribbling her number on the top sheet and handing it to him. "Text me so I know how to get in touch with you."

He took it, folding it carefully and putting it in his pocket. "Will do. You stay safe, pretty lady."

And then he was gone, leaving her feeling buzzy and warm in every place he'd touched her and some of the places he hadn't.

Five

When Sean arrived at the firehouse, Felix gave him a long, considering look. "So did you see her? You must have. Your smile is so big, the term *shit-eating grin* needs to be redefined."

"I did," Sean said, not even trying to tamp down the glee he felt and knew was oozing out of his pores.

"Was it a hard sell?" Felix asked. "Honestly, after I suggested it, it started to sound more than a little weird."

Sean moved to the kitchen, Felix following. Lunch had just been cleared away and he and Felix were on the rotation for cleanup. Without needing to confer, Felix started to rinse the plates that were stacked in the sink and handed them one at a time to Sean, who placed them in the dishwasher. "Well, I honestly kind of almost blew it. She was looking pretty skeptical about the whole thing as we talked. Seemed to think it was kind of funny, but definitely nothing to be taken seriously."

"So did she go for it? What happened?"

"The jerk came to her office and started yelling at her.

Something about the dean and her getting him in trouble."
He hadn't thought Darren could be more of an asshole. He'd
been wrong. What had Eva seen in that guy anyway?

Felix rolled his eyes and dropped some cutlery into the
machine. "What an ass. He staged that whole silly scene and
it's her fault he gets called on the carpet for it?"

Sean lifted one shoulder. "Yep. That's the kind of dude he
is, apparently. Nothing is ever his fault."

"The worst. So what happened then?"

"Well, I slipped into protective boyfriend mode." Heat
crawled up his neck as he remembered how easily his inner
caveman came roaring out when Eva's safety was in question.
The heat redoubled when he remembered how good she'd
felt cuddled up against him.

Felix gaped. "You did? Without getting her buy-in first?
How did she take it?"

Sean rubbed the back of his neck while he waited for Felix
to finish with a bowl. "She handled it surprisingly well, actually, though all things considered, if she'd denied that I was actually her boyfriend the whole scene might have gotten odder
than it did. So yeah. It was an impulse move on my part, but
kind of a dick move, too. If I'm being honest." His unusually
impulsive action had nearly done him in. He was going to
have to be much more of his normal, careful self from here
on out if he wanted to keep spending time with her.

"But she rolled with it. That's good. How did the ex take
the news that she'd moved on?"

"Not well." Sean described Darren's scorn, his insults and
the petulant way he'd stormed off afterward. That still both-

ered him. Darren seemed like far more of a potential problem than Eva wanted to admit.

"Well, that sounds awkward. How'd you leave it with her? Is she instantly going to fake break up with you?" Felix's dark eyes twinkled with humor.

Sean shook his head. "Nope. She's got some sort of cocktail party thing she's got to go to for work. I'm going to be her date for that so she doesn't have to face the ex on her own."

Felix punched him in the arm. "Good man. That would be a nightmare scenario, for real—having to go to a party where you know your ex is going to be there? And go alone? And have to deal with the possible gossip of your colleagues?" He gave an extravagant shudder. "No, thank you."

Sean hadn't really given it that much thought, but Felix was right. There were a lot of layers to that event, a lot of ways it could fall out badly. A little flame of pride flickered in him at the thought of helping make it the least little bit easier for Eva.

Eva pulled her car into the garage and cut the engine, leaning her head back for the space of one deep sigh. Then she grabbed her bag and got out, already hearing the fusillade of toenail clicks and jingling tags. "I'm coming, my beloved, I'm coming," she said as she opened the door to the house. Timmy, her four-year-old spaniel mix, danced and whined and wiggled on the threshold.

"Good boy," she said, sinking to her knees and running her hands over his silky sides. He gave a little groan and leaned into her as she massaged him in earnest. He'd been in a horrible accident prior to his time at the pound and though he was entirely healed, he did love to have his muscles worked over. He gazed up at her, one hundred percent doggy devotion in his liquid brown eyes. He licked her chin and she gave him one last pat before reaching for his leash on a hook by the door. Snapping it on, she set out down the street, waving at her newlywed neighbors, Kari and Rob. The single community on the street had been mostly sorry to see him taken off the market, but Eva thought they made a nice couple. Turning the corner, she saw Krystal was just shutting her door with Luther, her giant mastiff, sitting patiently by her side.

"Evening," Eva called to Krystal, who grinned broadly at the sight of Eva and the much smaller Timmy.

"How's my favorite little runt?" Krystal said as the four of them began to move down the street, the dogs greeting each other with sniffs and wagging tails.

"He's fine. How's my favorite giant?"

Krystal barely had to lean over to thump the huge dog's broad back. "This lump is just fine." The two women had acquired their dogs around the same time and began running into each other during morning and evening walks. The random encounters turned into intentional ones as they traded puppy training tips and watched their dogs grow— Luther into the hundred-pound behemoth he now was and Timmy into fifteen pounds of charm and soft fur. Eva had sprung for a doggy DNA test and learned that Timmy was mostly Cavalier King Charles spaniel, with some terrier and poodle tucked further back into his family tree. Along the way, Krystal and Eva had become fast friends as well. They waited while Luther took his time inspecting a tree before lifting his leg on it, looking as always a little embarrassed by the audience. Or maybe that was just the natural expression in his whiskey-colored eyes.

"How's higher ed?" Krystal asked as they moved out again.

"Interesting. Well, the semester isn't interesting. The semester's over. But life is interesting."

Krystal's dark eyes slid sideways, considering her. "Is Darren finally leaving you alone?"

Eva laughed, surprised. "No. But remember that scene on the quad where I behaved like an actual lunatic?"

A tiny smile tipped Krystal's lips up. "No, I remember Darren acting like a damn fool as usual and you reacting proportionally."

"You're too good of a friend," Eva said. She didn't get close to many people, but Krystal was special. "Do you also remember the firefighter?"

Krystal sucked her teeth, her cheekbones popping under her dark brown skin. "The hot firefighter?"

Heat flooded Eva's face. "I never said anything about him being hot."

"Honey." Krystal shook her head. "You didn't have to."

"So what happens next?" Felix asked as he and Sean went to do inventory on the emergency medical supplies.

"You mean besides the cocktail party thing? By the way, how do I handle myself at a cocktail party thing?" Was he going to embarrass himself at this thing? Worse, was he going to embarrass Eva?

Felix shot him a level look. "You pretend it's a cookout

but with less comfortable clothes. You make small talk, you sip a drink, and in this case, you remember that you're pretty arm candy for a pretty lady. You do have a nice suit, right?"

"Yeah." He'd had to get one to be his sister Caitlin's best person at her wedding. She'd insisted he not just get something off the rack from Men's Wearhouse and had taken him to a higher-end shop where they not only sold him a suit, but also tailored it to perfectly fit his broad chest and trim waist. That purchase now looked more like an investment than the extravagance it had seemed at the time.

"Good. But my question remains. What are you doing besides the cocktail party? Fake dating's all well and good but you kind of have to do it in front of the asshole to get him to take the point."

Sean nodded and checked the listing for gauze bandages on the clipboard. "Yeah, we're kind of playing that by ear. I started teaching her some self-defense techniques. Not to show off in front of the asshole, but just in case the asshole does what assholes do."

Felix nodded, his face going thoughtful. "Maybe you could do more with that."

Sean lost count and turned to his friend. "What do you mean?"

"Well, she's a professor of pop-culture studies. I'm guessing she's got a lot of marginalized students and she probably cares about them. Those are vulnerable kids."

"Okay…" Sean said, still not knowing where Felix was going with this.

"Why don't you expand that offer to her students? I'm

guessing the campus gossip grapevine would get back to the asshole in no time flat if you did something like that."

Sean nodded to himself, tapping his pen against his upper lip, excited by this. He would prefer to have Eva on his own, but he did like the idea of helping students she cared about. "Yeah. That could really work."

"What do you mean I didn't have to?" Eva's voice was tight with suppressed laughter.

"Honey." Krystal pointed a manicured finger at Eva's face. "You have zero game face. Do not play poker, do not pass Go, do not collect any dollars. That man is fine as frog's hair and nobody needs to tell me because those blue eyes of yours give *everything* away."

Eva hated the way her pale skin gave her away with blushes. Like it was doing now, she knew from the feeling of crawling heat on her neck and cheeks. But her *eyes* gave her away, too? This was too much. "Um…"

Krystal shrugged. "Also, he's a firefighter. Ipso hot ergo propter hot."

A helpless laugh stuttered out of Eva just as Timmy squatted to poop. He gave her an aggrieved look, which only made her laugh harder. Before bagging his droppings she had to wipe the tears from under her eyes. "Okay, that was the funniest bit of fake Latin I've ever heard."

"What can I tell you? I make the funny happen."

"You do. You're positively wasted at the SEC. You should have been a standup."

Krystal chuckled. "Nah. I like being funny in a stealthy

way, you know? Like, nobody expects a securities lawyer to be anything but dull. I mix things up."

"I'll just bet you do." They paused again for Luther to do his business and, as she did most days, Eva thanked her lucky stars that Timmy was a smaller dog, producing smaller...output. But she also knew that Krystal had left her ex-husband because he'd been violent and she'd gotten Luther as more than just a pet. His presence was definitely a potential deterrent to anyone wishing her harm.

"So what about the hot firefighter?" Krystal returned to the thread of their conversation. She was unerringly good at that, never allowing a digression to derail her.

"Oh, he stopped by my office again today. To check on me and, well... To offer to be my fake boyfriend so maybe Darren would leave me alone." She said the last part in a rush, almost afraid she wouldn't be able to get the ridiculous words out.

Krystal stopped walking. "He did what now?"

"I know, right? Straight out of a romance novel. And it was his idea, or his coworker's." He'd seemed so sweetly enthusiastic about it, though, no matter whose idea it was.

"This just gets weirder and weirder. I hope you let him down gently."

"Well..."

Krystal stopped, folding her arms across her chest. "Shut up. You did not agree to this weird scheme."

"I was going to let him down gently but then Darren showed up, hollering abuse and Sean—hot firefighter—stepped in and defended me as my *boyfriend*—"

Krystal just laughed at that. "Red, you're going to be the death of me. How long is this charade going to go on?"

Eva shrugged. "He's going to go to the faculty cocktail party with me in a couple of weeks, so at least that long." Then she'd have to let him go as gently as she could. He was darling, but she couldn't afford to get attached. He needed someone at least as young as he was, and Eva was definitely not that.

"Well, that's good that you'll have someone to buffer any interactions with Darren, then."

"And he's going to be teaching me some self-defense moves, just in case Darren ups the ante with his behavior." And she'd get a chance to touch him again. And have him touch her...

"Excellent notion. I took self-defense classes after the divorce and it was a good way for me to reclaim my power."

"It's a little concerning that so many people think Darren might become violent," Eva said as they turned back toward home. He'd never shown any sign of behaving like this while they were together and the contrast made her belly shiver.

"He's been acting like twenty kinds of fool since you caught him cheating. And you never know with men who are that entitled. They're capable of a lot."

Six

Exhausted after his shift, which had contained one car crash requiring the Jaws of Life and one kitchen fire that was, thankfully, easily put out, Sean dragged himself home for a shower and well-earned rest. But before he could get either, his next-oldest sister Caitlin called him.

"Cait. What's up?"

"Baby brother, it's been too long since we've heard from you. Just checking in."

"I've been busy. And I haven't been a baby for a very long time." As if his sisters would ever stop putting him in his place. In his teens and twenties, he'd been frustrated by it. Now it was merely a minor annoyance, something he just had to accept wouldn't change.

"Yeah, yeah, I know. But you know that Mom will forever treat you like you're still in diapers."

"Doesn't mean you have to do the same thing," Sean grumbled.

"Fine, fine. But you're going to be on the hook for the monthly family dinner, you know. You can't keep ditching."

"I don't ditch. I have a schedule that Mom and Dad refuse to recognize. I can't just take off whenever I want to." Sean's dad had been self-employed before he retired and never seemed to get it through his head that not every position worked nine to five. "Accidents happen at all hours. Fires happen at all hours."

"I know that." Caitlin sighed. As the two youngest with only two years between them and a more significant gap between Cait and their next eldest sister Maeve, Sean and Caitlin functioned like a sub-team within the larger family unit. An art teacher at a private high school, Cait had also confounded family expectations. According to their parents, the Hannigan children were supposed to do three things: go to Mass every week, get married to a person of the opposite sex and have several children as soon as possible. The three eldest were pretty much perfect in that regard.

Cait and Sean? Not so much, though it was possible that Cait and her wife would have children someday. "You planning on having kids?" he asked, knowing that the seemingly out-of-the-blue query would make sense to Cait.

"Ugh. No. Because adorable moppets turn into teenagers and I see those bastards every day already."

Sean laughed. "Man, you're going to get it in the neck from Mom and Pop."

"I know. But you're not exactly off the hook yourself—they're going to keep up the pressure for you to find some-

one and get married. Your schedule helps keep you out of
the dating pool somewhat, but it can't protect you forever."

"Well… I did kinda meet someone." When Caitlin got
over her exaggerated expressions of shock, he explained about
the situation with Eva.

"Oh, my God. I think I adore her," Cait said after he was
done. "She threatened to *torch* the piano? That's seriously badass."

"Yeah, and it was quite a coincidence that she had the same
book Felix lent me right there on her bookshelf." He hadn't
gotten to the bit yet about Darren showing up in her office to
rage at her. The memory made his teeth clench. And his fist.

"You giant nerd. Forget about this fake dating nonsense.
You've caught feelings for her, haven't you?"

"Cait, I barely know her." *But I do want to get to know her
a lot better.*

"Yeah, but you're the biggest romantic softie ever. Don't
tell me you didn't have to fight all kinds of chivalrous urges."

"No, I didn't." Because he *hadn't* fought them. He'd let
them rip right from the jump, using his size and possessiveness to posture and crowd the smaller, slighter Darren.

But Cait was sometimes too shrewd for her own good—or
for his. "Ohhh. You acted like a big ol' caveman, didn't you?
Did you beat your chest?"

"No, not really." Dammit, his sister could still make him
feel all of six years old and forty pounds, the once tiny kid who
had attracted bullies like a magnet. "But I kinda jumped the
gun on the whole fake dating thing because her ex showed

up in her office all abusive and horrible and I told him to stop treating my girlfriend like that."

The next few seconds contained something Sean had never heard from his sister: stunned silence.

"Okay, let's do this." The *this* in question was Eva's summer seminar syllabus, but as much as she appreciated alliteration, she always dreaded this task. When she'd begun her second year of teaching it had seemed like it would be easy: copy last year's, change the dates and the details, and hey, presto: new syllabus.

The reality was very different. First of all, she didn't believe in teaching the same exact class year over year. That path led to stale class content and bored students. While the sprout of the new class always sprang from the seed planted the year before, she introduced different texts, which led to different questions, which led to different discussions. All of which made for a vibrant, fun semester, both for her and for her classes.

But man, it was a lot of work, requiring lots of passes over the document to make sure everything was just the way she wanted it. And also, she had to check the dates at least three times. Calendars seemed like they should be the easiest thing on the planet to wrangle. And yet, no. She needed to be aware of holidays—and not just the ones the university officially celebrated—she wanted every student in her class to know they were important: that their learning was something she was invested in, and that meant carving out ways of ensuring that some of her students weren't caught out because their religious practice had a celebration or holiday service.

In the end, it was worth it. But in the beginning, it always looked like an impossibly steep mountain to climb. "Journey of a thousand miles starts with a single step," she muttered to herself as she opened a new Word document and copied and pasted the basics—her contact information, her office location and the rest of the minor details that thankfully didn't alter year over year.

Just as she was considering her digital calendar and starting to create a structured outline, her phone rang. She sighed when she saw it was her mother on the other end. "Hi, Mom," she said.

"Hi, honey. Your father checked your academic calendar and it says that classes have been done for over two weeks. Why haven't you contacted us about coming down for a nice, long visit?"

Eva suppressed a shudder. "Well, I was grading and that takes a lot of time. And now I'm preparing to teach a summer seminar."

She must have been on speaker, because her father's voice boomed out, "What's the use of having an academic job if you don't get summers off?"

"Hello to you, too, Dad." She didn't say that one of the major reasons why she always taught at least one class over the long break was so she didn't have to go to Florida. In the summer. "I couldn't come for a long visit anyway," *even if I wanted to*, she didn't add, "because it would be unfair to Timmy to leave him for that long."

The dog, hearing his name, lifted his head from his paws and gave her what looked like an anxious look. *Don't worry,* she mouthed at him, even though that was a ridiculous thing to do. He couldn't possibly understand her. But he did put his chin back down and let out a sigh, his black-spotted sides heaving.

"I swear, you care more about that dog than you do your own family," her mother fussed.

"No," she said, drawing the syllable out in the hopes that speaking slowly would artificially grant her patience. She hated the way even the simplest conversations with her parents could stress her out, the way her mother especially would always put the worst construction on her words. "But I am responsible for him. And I take that responsibility seriously."

"Don't understand having pets," her father grumbled. "It's not like they're good for anything."

"Timmy is a comfort to me," she said, her patience starting to fray the way it always did when dealing with her parents.

"Well, if you settled down with someone, maybe you could develop some healthier relationships with *people*," her mother said in a voice that was supposed to be sweet and reasonable but was really just passive-aggressive.

"I am seeing someone," Eva said. And for several long seconds, her parents had not a blessed thing to say back.

"So wait. You actually *did the fake dating dance* in front of the ex?" Caitlin was audibly suppressing giggles now.

"There was no dancing," Sean said.

"You know what I mean. Like those dude birds who do

the elaborate *look at me* thing in front of the lady birds. It's as much a message to the other dude birds."

"Not sure that's entirely accurate, but whatever. I just told the guy I didn't appreciate how he was talking to my girlfriend, and he said something about how I'm an over-muscled and under-brained guy and she wouldn't stay with me long and stomped off." He didn't much care that Darren had called him names, but he hoped Eva hadn't taken the other man's words to heart.

"Some asshole called my little brother stupid?" Cait's voice was practically a growl.

"Now who's being a caveman?" Sean asked.

"Cavewoman. And it doesn't have the same cultural significance, so—" His sister blew a raspberry. "Anyway, you're the most annoyingly well-read person I've ever known who didn't get a four-year degree. So it's cool that she's a pop-culture studies professor. Maybe she'll even expand your reading beyond that one romance book."

An idea started to take shape in his head. One that could connect them even further. "Yeah. Maybe I can get her to recommend some books to me." The idea of them reading together on some cozy sofa popped into his brain and it warmed him straight through. He'd love that kind of domestic scene with Eva. Nothing big, just everyday closeness. Perfection.

"Don't make it like a class, though. It's shitty to expect people to do their job for you for free."

"No class. Got it. I ain't got no class anyway."

"Ugh."

"I can hear your eyes rolling, *little sister.*"

"Just because you grew up to be so big and buff doesn't mean I can't still take you out, annoying boy."

"That's annoying man to you. Oh, and I'm going to be teaching her self-defense. And Felix suggests maybe I offer *that* as a class for her students."

"That's not a half-bad idea. I knew I liked Felix."

"Anyway, it seems like we might have the beginnings of a plan." He loved the way this was shaping up, like a more complete picture than the bare sketch they'd had before.

"Just be careful, though." Caitlin's voice went all serious, unlike his usually irreverent sister.

"What do you mean?"

"I know you, you giant squishmallow. Underneath all that protective gear and heteronormative beefcake, you get hurt easily. And I don't want you to get hurt."

Sean infused his voice with all the overconfidence he didn't feel. "No worries. I got this."

Eva's mother rebounded from her apparently stunned state. "You're not going to try to work it out with Darren?"

Ugh. It figured that her parents would just *love* Darren. He was that kind of liar: very plausible to snobby parents. They considered her career as a pop-culture professor to be low class, whereas Darren could get her parents tickets to symphony concerts and operas, so his job was just dandy. It fit with their image of who she should be, which was a reflection of them. *Doctor's daughter*, not a person in her own right.

"No, Mom. Darren lied to me." She hadn't talked directly about the cheating because Mom's pearls had already been

clutched way too dramatically from some of Eva's more ris-
qué utterances in the past. The damn necklace might just pop
apart one of these days.

"Well, did he say he was sorry?"

Eva's teeth met with an audible click. "Darren and I are
finished, Mom. And I'm finished talking about him." *Are we
done here?* she wanted to ask. But knew better.

"Well, that's too bad. We were looking forward to seeing
him when we came up in a few weeks."

"Wait—what?" Why had they harangued her about visiting if they were just going to fly up here?

"Yes, some of your father's former colleagues at the hospital
are having a little reunion weekend. It will be so much fun!"

Considering her father's interventional cardiologist colleagues had been, to a man (yes, they were all men), boorish
braggarts, Eva failed to see the fun side of things. No wonder
her mother wanted her to still be with Darren. Her parents
and their friends were in a constant state of what looked like
all-out war to Eva but they probably considered it "friendly"
competition. Who could claim the biggest bragging rights.
And having a childless daughter who was still single in her forties with a career they didn't think much of didn't give them
any ammunition.

"And of course, we'd like to have dinner with you. It's too
bad Nana's house doesn't have more room—we'd love to stay
with you." This was such a typical ploy, she almost didn't register it. Her grandmother had left her the tiny two-bedroom
house and Eva'd done the second, smaller bedroom up as her
office. Even so, there was barely room for a futon in there, let
alone the luxury king her father would demand.

"I'm sure you'll be much more comfortable at the Marriott," Eva said in what she hoped was a soothing tone.

Her mother sighed audibly. "Yes. I suppose you're right."

"Anyway, I have a lot of work to do. Send me the dates you're going to be here and we'll figure out an evening to have dinner."

Her mother rang off without any more fuss—her dad had probably wandered off at some point, bored and at loose ends like he had been since he entered retirement. He was one of *those* retirees—someone who'd had an active and personally fulfilling career who hadn't wanted to give it up. But tremors in his hands had ended all that, and her mother had always dreamed of retiring to Florida.

Eva couldn't think of anything she'd enjoy less.

But at least they'd sold the giant house that had to be cleaned weekly by a small army—a ridiculous enough home for three people, but when she'd gone to college and moved out, it had become an absurdity. And by the time her parents moved, it was a positive albatross.

She glanced around her tiny office. If she'd chosen this little house instead of inheriting it, she might be accused of overcorrecting.

Her laptop's inbox chimed and she saw her mother had already sent their travel plans, down to the flights in and out of Baltimore and a suggested date for dinner. She shook her head, remembering the guilt trip her folks had tried to lay on her at the outset of their conversation. It was practically Pavlovian: get Eva on the phone, try to get her to do something.

She tapped her chin and considered her phone, then picked

it up. Having admitted she was "seeing" someone, it would be odd if she didn't at least invite him to the family dinner. She tapped out a quick text with the information, feeling an odd squiggle of pleasure when she saw three bouncing dots immediately.

Seven

Sean could feel the ridiculously wide grin that split his face in two as he read Eva's text. Dinner with her parents? Sure, why not?

Eva: They'll be awful, fair warning.

Sean: Awful how? An awful lot like you? Because that'd be awfully adorable.

Eva: Cute. No, they're snobs. Sorry to say. They don't approve of my job.

Sean: They don't approve of you being an actual tenured college professor?

Eva: Nope. Dad was a big-time doctor. Pop-culture studies? Heresy.

Sean: So no approving of firefighters with associate's degrees, huh?

Eva: Afraid not. Going to say no, now that you have the whole picture?

Sean shook his head as if she could see him. Nope. I'm in. I don't care what two strangers think of me. Sticks and stones, right?

Eva: Brave man.

Sean: I run *into* burning buildings for a living, remember?

Eva: Yeah, but you haven't met my dad.

Sean: I look forward to it. Wanna come to a family thing with me later this month?

Eva: Absolutely. That way I won't owe you the world's hugest favor.

Sean: I'll send you the details. We're on for tonight, right? Project Get to Know You?

Eva: I'll be there.

Sean: Good. Later, pretty lady.

Eva just sent a blushing emoji at that. Sean chuckled and set his phone down, picking up the novel Felix had lent him.

"Is the book that funny?" Thea said, entering the dayroom where Sean was stretched out on a sofa.

"It's pretty funny in places, but I was laughing about something else," Sean said, opening the book and willing nosey Thea to keep out of his business.

Too late. "Ohhh, is this about that lady from the callout the other week? Felix and I knew you were smitten with her. *You love her, you want to date her, you want to kiss her...*" Thea singsonged like Sandra Bullock in *Miss Congeniality*, a movie the firehouse had streamed a few weeks ago with a break in the middle to put out a small fire some jerk kids had set in the woods.

Come to think of it, Thea kind of resembled the movie character, at least in personality. Ambitious yet goofy, no "girly shit" as she would say. She also didn't give a crap about appearances, and her relationship with her hairbrush was, well, casual.

"Careful, or I'll start calling you Gracie Lou Freebush," Sean warned, keeping his eyes resolutely on the page in the hopes she'd drop the whole thing.

"Might be worth it," Thea mused, theatrically stroking her chin.

"Worth what?" Felix asked as he came into the room and offered Thea the bag of cheddar popcorn he carried with him.

Thea dug in and shoved some popcorn in her face, talking through her mouthful. "Being called a horrible nickname from a Sandra Bullock comedy if I get to tease Sean about his *massive crush.*"

"Careful there, Gracie Lou Freebush. You won't be crowned Miss Manners if you talk with your mouth full." Sean sometimes felt like he was hanging with his sisters when he verbally sparred with her. It was familiar. And a little disturbing sometimes. He had enough sisters, after all. As much as he was amused by Thea, he didn't need another.

Thea stuck her butt out and made a fart noise, then left the room. "Maturity, thy name is Anthea Martinelli," Felix muttered, shaking his head. But there was a smile lurking in his expression, too.

"Eh. She reminds me of Caitlin sometimes. It's homey." Sean made to open up his book again, but Felix cleared his throat in an overly theatrical way. "What's up now?" he asked, looking up and putting a finger between the pages to mark his place.

"Did Thea say, *massive crush*? Because we knew you had an attraction to Eva, but this seems like it's moving a little fast. Have you even seen her since she agreed to my wacky scheme?"

Sean should have been fine with this question. He had enough years of experience with nosy sisters, after all. But something about this coming from Felix made it different. There might be few secrets in the firehouse, but Felix seemed *worried*, which wasn't normal. He rubbed the back of his neck, thinking about what to say about how he felt about Eva. Every short text communication they'd had since she gave him her number seemed to have a thrilling layer of flirtatiousness spread over the top. It was just so *easy* to be himself around her.

Felix pointed at him. "Uh-oh. That's your tell, dude."

Sean froze. "What is?"

"Whenever you are uncomfortable, you rub the back of your neck or your head or something." Felix's eyes had gone all troubled in a way he really didn't like.

The alarm went off at that point and Sean got to his feet, dropping the book to the coffee table as he hustled to get geared up.

Saved by the bell. Literally.

Eva shifted on the tall bar stool and tried not to check her phone for what felt like the thirty-fourth time that evening. Sean had texted: a callout had run long and he had to shower and change before he could meet her.

He wouldn't stand her up. He wouldn't. She told herself that over and over.

But she also didn't know him, and her glass of white wine had been as sweaty as she felt for about twenty minutes now, and the bartender was giving her a sort of pitying look she didn't like. Then her eyes shifted over Eva's shoulder and widened, a broad, flirty smile spreading over her face. "Hey, what can I getcha this evening?" she said, winking and tossing a cardboard coaster on the bar.

"Tap beer." That *voice*. It just rumbled through her like a sonic boom, resonating in her chest and stomach and lower still.

"We have…" The bartender started rattling off selections as Eva turned and caught Sean's eye. He raised a hand to the bartender and she trailed off.

He shot her the barest of apologetic looks and a grin. "Just whatever's not too hoppy. I have to apologize to my best girl here first." He picked up Eva's hand and she thought he was about to kiss the back of it in an old-fashioned move. But no. He turned it over and pressed his lips—his *soft* lips—to the center of her palm. Sensation zinged through her and she shifted on the bar stool again, this time in involuntary reaction to…*that*.

Who knew the palm of her hand was an erogenous zone?

"Sorry, baby," he said as he lifted his gaze to meet hers.

Nobody had *ever* called Eva *baby*. If anyone had asked her if she approved of that as a pet name before tonight, she would have scoffed and called it infantilizing. But now? It was like the entire world had been dumped upside down and shaken like a snow globe, all disorientation and whirling confusion.

And somehow, she liked it.

"Thanks," he said to the bartender as she set a pint glass on the coaster. "Let me settle up and we can move to a booth." When the bartender mentioned that she'd already paid for her wine, Sean shot her a sidelong look. "Paying for yourself because I'm running late? That hurts." He threw down a bill on the bar and knocked it twice with his big fist. "All set here. Come on, gorgeous."

With that, Eva was towed off her stool to a booth in a dim corner of the pub, feeling more than a little flushed, her heart pounding. She slid onto a banquette and blinked with surprise when he came in after her, one big thigh resting alongside hers, the heat from him penetrating through his jeans and hers. Firefighter? This man was fire itself.

"This okay?" he asked. "Easier not to be overheard this way."

Eva's heart seemed to give a little kick, as if it was resuming normal rhythm. Right. Yeah. This was about practicality. And about practice. Looking like a real couple in front of other people. That was the entire reason they'd planned to meet up this evening. There was no reason whatsoever to feel a spiraling sense of disappointment.

No reason at all. She swallowed her sauvignon blanc and her feelings and gave Sean what was probably the wobbliest smile in the universe.

"So sorry I'm late," he said, seeming to misunderstand her disappointment.

"No! Don't be. I mean, if I was late the most valid job-related reason would be a crying student in my office. But that isn't exactly saving lives or anything."

"Well, saving lives wasn't the source of the delay today," Sean grumbled. "We had a minor porch fire—already pretty well contained by the homeowner—and some asshole had parked his Tesla in front of the hydrant."

Eva's eyes went a little round at that. It was cute. He was so used to having people around him know enough about protocol that they would think this was old hat. "What do you do in a situation like that? Call a tow truck?"

"Ha. No time. No, we smash the windows and thread the hose through."

"You don't go around?"

He took a long sip of beer, then relaxed, his arm resting on the seat back behind her shoulders. "Nah. Screws with the water pressure and that can cost lives. Besides, anyone who parks on a hydrant should know they literally might get hosed. So we put the fire out and were getting the area cleaned up, gearing up to go, when the car's owner shows up and has a screaming meltdown at us."

Her eyes, if possible, got even bigger. "Was he also eight feet tall and green? Because I've seen you guys in your fire-fighter suits and I'm not sure I'd scream at you under any circumstances. You're intimidating."

God, he loved this woman's sense of humor. "Turnouts, not firefighter suits. And no, he was tall but nowhere near eight feet. And his face was pretty bright red, not green at all."

"So he was mad."

"Yeah, screaming and hollering about suing the department, the homeowner, anyone who witnessed the windows being broken, the whole nine yards. We didn't want to leave until he'd calmed down. The house in question was owned by a little old lady who was understandably shaken up. The guy had her in tears." He'd wanted to frog-march the guy away from the old lady's house and shove him into traffic. The entitled jerk had reminded him of Darren, now that he thought about it.

Her eyebrows drew together and her expression went impossibly sympathetic. "Oh, poor thing."

"Yeah. The guy was a piece of work. But he got his attorney on the phone in a hot minute—which tells me he's the kind of guy who sues everyone at the drop of a hat—and even the ambulance chaser told him he didn't have a leg to stand on. So he called an Uber, we finished up and here I am. Late."

"In a hot minute, huh? Is that your departmental motto?

Also, don't worry about being late. Better late than never."
She squeezed his forearm and practically stopped his heart.
He'd known after sliding in next to her that he was probably
taking their little act too far. She had to be getting uncomfortable with his flirting and physicality, which was why he'd
backed off. But he liked her so much, it felt natural to want
to be close to her. Her reaching out to touch him? Oh, his
sister was not wrong about that squishmallow part of him.

"Um..." He cleared his throat, trying to get his brain back
online. "No. We don't have a motto."

"Too bad," she said. God, her fingers were warm on his
skin. He wanted them to move. To stroke and explore. Maybe
Felix was right to be worried. He did have it bad for her. He
forced himself not to move, if only to prolong the contact. "I
think *in a hot minute* is a pretty good motto for a firefighter
squad."

"Might give our dates the wrong impression, though."
The words flew out of his mouth before he knew what he
was saying. Heat crawled up the back of his neck and sweat
beaded his hairline. "Wow. I'm sorry, that was not cool. I
didn't mean—"

He was interrupted by her crack of laughter, her hand
leaving his arm to cover her mouth as she laughed, her eyes
sheening over with moisture. "No, that's fine. You're awfully funny."

"Funny-looking, my sisters all say."

"I'm guessing that's because they're your sisters. It seems
like teasing is a thing siblings are contractually required to
do to each other."

"Well, I never signed a contract, but there's definitely some serious history, at least in my family." Like the way even Cait, his closest sister, annoyingly still saw him as some overgrown child no matter what he did.

"So they picked on you? Because you were the youngest?"

"Yeah, some. But it was mostly just in fun. But when other kids bullied me? Oh, that was when the harpies would fly."

Eva was confused. Other kids bullied Sean? Six-foot-and-more-than-a-few-inches Sean?

He must have registered her befuddlement because one corner of his mouth kicked up. "I was a pretty small, stringy little kid. I didn't really get a growth spurt until I was fifteen. Then I shot up like a weed and was a tall, stringy kid. I finally started lifting weights when I was a junior in high school to try to fill out a little."

Eva choked on her wine. "A little?"

He leaned in as if to share a secret with her. God, he smelled good. That just-showered man scent. "Yeah. Almost twenty years of lifting and working a very physical job took it a ways past *a little*."

"If you say so." Eva had never really been someone who was attracted to muscles. In her experience, they'd all too frequently come attached to cocky jerks. But Sean was funny and didn't seem to take himself seriously at all. On top of being kind and a good listener, he carried himself like he had nothing to prove, and that was powerfully attractive.

"Oh, by the way, Felix had an idea I wanted to run past you. How about in addition to teaching you self-defense classes, we open up the opportunity to a group of your students, too?"

She inhaled sharply, her mind racing. "That's a *wonderful* idea." All too often she'd gotten a window on the lives of some of her students—not that they always told stories about their experiences, but the way they reacted to various books or media told her that too many of them had experience with some form of abuse. She couldn't and wouldn't invade their privacy, but this? This was something she could offer that could be of real help.

His answering smile lit up his face. "Really? I'm glad you like it. Felix thought you might have some vulnerable people in your classes."

"He's one hundred percent correct. Thank him for me, please. And thank you."

They discussed logistics for a few minutes until a waiter came by with menus. "What are you in the mood for, baby?" he asked, sliding easily into the boyfriend persona. Or had he ever slid out of it? His attention on her since he came in had been unwavering, though somehow not unnerving. Sean had an ease about him that she envied. And there was that pet name again. *Baby.* It sent a little shiver up the back of her neck, almost as if he had touched her there.

To take her mind off him, she scanned the menu. "Shepherd's pie, please."

"Sounds good. We'll have two of those. And a side of fries." He handed their menus back to the waiter with a grin.

Eva decided to experiment with being the girlfriend. She

poked him in the shoulder. It was rock hard. "Fries and shepherd's pie? How many potatoes can you eat?"

"Woman," he said, sending his voice into a lower register and contorting his face with apparent disbelief. "I'm a big Irish boy. I can eat *all* the potatoes."

Eva suppressed a giggle.

"What about you? Red hair. Irish girl?"

She shook her head. "Scots. Well, mostly. Clan Campbell."

"Och aye?" he said in a ridiculous, broad Scots burr.

This time she really did giggle. Good grief, it was like she was possessed. She never giggled. "That's a terrible accent."

"Never claimed to be an actor. But that's cool. If your family was *English*, that might be another story."

"Wait, your American family has strong feelings about the United Kingdom? For real?" She'd seen plenty of anti-British sentiment in Irish media, but hadn't ever seen it in her own country.

"When I tell you my dad is Irish, I mean he's *Irish*. County Clare. Came to this country in his twenties with his plumber's tools and a pocketful of change—he'll tell you himself. Self-made man, buying real estate, fixing it up, moving on. Married a nice girl from South Boston and followed some investments down here to raise his family. What about you?"

Eva blinked, imagining the four sisters, Sean, their parents, presumably more than a few grandchildren... It was a lot. Her family situation might be quiet and sterile and *small*, but she was used to it. "Um. Just me. Parents grew up in Bethesda, high school sweethearts, Dad was an interventional cardiologist until he retired a couple of years ago."

"Wow. Only child, huh?" He got a bit of a faraway look in his eyes as if he couldn't quite picture what that would look like. "Did you love it or did you hate it?"

She shrugged. "Neither? I never really wanted siblings. When I'd go to friends' houses it seemed like a lot of conflict and negotiation. In some ways it was easier just being the only. But the weight of expectations was a hundred percent on me, so that was sometimes hard, too. Basically, like anything else, there were trade-offs."

That crooked smile tilted his mouth as he looked down at her. "Yeah. I know something about that, too."

Eight

Sean pulled his truck up in the driveway of Eva's little house and checked the knot of his tie in the rearview mirror, his heart pounding like a teenager taking his first girlfriend out on their very first date. The pub dinner had been fun—more fun than he'd expected, because Eva was surprisingly down to earth when you got to know her. They'd swapped more stories about their childhoods and early adulthoods, learning the kinds of things about each other that couples knew. Eva's favorite color was blue and she couldn't abide peanuts. She wasn't allergic, she made it plain. She just didn't like them.

"Sounds un-American, but you gotta be you," Sean had teased. He'd learned other things about her that evening, some of them things she didn't have to tell him. Her relationship with her parents was strained, that was evident. She'd fiddled with the napkin in her lap when she talked about their forth-coming visit, her nerves on subconscious display in a way that made him want to smooth away that worried groove between her eyebrows. But that would have been going too far.

But first, they had to get through the faculty cocktail party. "Darren will be insufferable," she had warned. Sean didn't care. He could take all the shots that twerp fired at him. He just wanted Eva to be comfortable, protected.

He got out just as Eva's front door opened and his heart nearly stopped. She wore a sleeveless dress in a deep, midnight blue. It crossed in the front, showing the faintest shadow of cleavage, and the skirt swirled just below her knees. Her hair trailed down over her shoulders in waves of purest fire. "Wow. You look beautiful," he said as she stopped in front of him.

"You look pretty amazing yourself," she said, touching a fingertip to the knot of his tie. His throat went tight as if she'd touched his skin. "You ready to face the dragons?"

He chuckled, but it came out as a strangled sort of sound. "If they're dragons, they're not the kind that breathe fire, so I think we're good."

"I thought fighting fire was your wheelhouse?"

"Yeah, but it's my night off."

Her gorgeous eyes danced with laughter and he remembered what he was supposed to be doing. Turning, he opened the passenger door of his truck and handed her up to the high seat. "What a gentleman," she murmured.

"Got the old wreck detailed and everything," he said, relishing the way her eyes skimmed over the polished exterior and sparkling glass. "Nothing but the best for my girl."

After shutting the door, he jogged around the front of the truck and climbed in, hitting the starter and backing carefully out of her driveway. "Anything else I should know about to-night?" he asked. Their date the week before had been pure fun. They'd both "practiced" their double-act as a besotted couple, but the stakes had been nonexistent. This was their first big gamble, seeing if Darren would buy it enough to slink off. For Eva's sake, Sean hoped it worked.

For his own, he hoped it didn't. He wanted an excuse to stick around.

Eva arranged her wrap and her bag on her lap, just to have something to do. Sean's *old wreck* was a shiny, new electric truck, humming nearly silently along her street. "Anything else you should know?" she repeated. "No, I don't think so. I mean, you know who Darren is, so that will help. I'll point out the dean and introduce you to some of my colleagues that I'm friendlier with. Then we'll just spend our two drink tick-ets on severely mediocre wine or beer and eat a few passed ap-petizers. It'll be stingy because…academia, but after the dean makes a speech—blessedly a short one, if my past experience is to be trusted—then we can hang around for another ten minutes and then go home."

"Sounds pretty simple," Sean said as he spun the wheel, turning them toward campus. For some reason his calm pres-ence had the opposite effect on her. Her stomach was flutter-ing and quivering with nerves. She couldn't even think about those appetizers or she might feel actually sick.

God, what kind of a wreck would she have been if she'd had to come to this thing alone? In all her years of reading romance novels, she'd never have guessed that a trope could bring her so much real-life comfort.

All too soon, Sean was parking and handing her out of the truck. She moved to put on her wrap, but he silently took it from her fingers and settled it over her shoulders with so much attention and care that her fluttering nerves settled a bit. "Ready?" he asked.

She nodded and he followed her lead, walking beside her into the function room, low music playing over the PA system. Eva stopped at the check-in table and got their name tags and drink tickets. He offered his hand to take the tickets with a murmured, "White wine?" She nodded, the fact that he'd remembered her drink order from the week before warming her. He strode off and Eva scanned the room, looking for Celia or another friendly face.

"Still stringing the boy toy along, I see," a low and all-too-familiar voice murmured, unwelcome breath heating her ear. She stepped away from Darren, almost stumbling on her high heels in her haste to put some space between them.

Dammit. She should have gone with Sean to the bar. She fought to keep her expression neutral, maybe even a little bored. "I told you to leave me alone."

He shrugged, his eyes glittering with malice. "I'm faculty, you're faculty. This is a faculty function. I have every right to be here."

"Yes, but why you have to be tedious at *me* is another question." Eva wished she had something to do with her hands other than fiddle with the strap of her tiny bag. She suppressed that urge to fiddle, knowing it would only expose her nerves.

Darren's eyes narrowed and the malevolent glitter went out of them. Now he was just mad. "Tedious? You were with me for almost three years."

She forced a smile that she knew didn't reach her eyes. "Yes. And I regret every last day. Now—"

She didn't get the chance to finish her sentence. Sean arrived by her side, offering her a glass of wine and pressing a soft kiss to her temple. "Sorry it took so long, baby," he rumbled.

Was his voice deeper than usual, or was she imagining things?

She smiled up at him, this time her expression genuine. "Thanks." She took a sip, suddenly enjoying the game where before she'd just been nervous and upset.

Darren snorted. *"Baby?"*

Sean merely looked at him, his expression utterly blank until Darren flushed and looked away. Wow. She fought the urge to fan herself. Was this a superpower siblings gave you? Eva was terrible at conflict, either fleeing from it or freaking out entirely. And while her latest freak-out seemed to be panning out unexpectedly well, it wasn't exactly something she wanted to continue doing.

A server came by with appetizers. "Oh, Eva. Chicken satay. You'll like this," Darren said, grabbing a napkin and a skewer and holding them out to her.

Sean sighed. "Darren, the woman doesn't like peanuts. You oughta know that."

Before Darren could respond, the dean joined them. "Professor Perry, Professor Campbell. Nice to see you getting along so well." She glanced at Sean, and Eva jumped into so-cialization mode.

"Dean Treadwell, this is Sean Hannigan."

Sean stuck his hand out and the dean shook it, giving him a contemplative look. "Lovely to meet you, Mr. Hannigan. Glad you could come to our little end-of-semester celebration."

"I'm just happy to be where Eva is," Sean said without an ounce of insincerity or guile. *How did he* do *that?* Eva was straight up bad at lying, even about small things. But here he was, making everyone—almost including her—believe that he thought she'd hung the moon.

Darren snorted again, which turned into a cough as the dean turned her gaze on him. "Dr. Perry, I'd like to speak to you about some possible changes in the music department for next year…" And with that, she drew him away as easily as a child towing a toy boat through the bath.

Sean chuckled as he watched the dean scalpel Darren away from Eva. "That woman's good. I was afraid we'd have him on us like a barnacle all evening."

Eva sighed and sipped her wine. "Yeah, he's definitely not giving up. But I fear he's also making everything look ami-cable enough that the dean will decide there's no problem."

"Can you let her know that it is a problem?"

Eva grimaced. "I'm afraid that if I bring it up again, it's me that'll look like the problem—too fragile, overreacting, the whole nine yards."

Sean thought about something that'd happened to his el-dest sister Erin a decade before. Not a perfect analogy to this situation, but all too close to it. An echo of the helpless rage he'd felt at the time rippled through him. "So we just have to keep on keeping on," he said, placing a hand on the small of her back in a tiny show of possessiveness. The heat of her skin radiated through the silky fabric of her dress.

"I'm sorry you have to keep pretending like this," Eva groaned.

"I'm not." *And I'm not really pretending*, he didn't add.

"Seriously? I'd think you would be eager to be shut of me by now," she said.

Sean took a sip of his beer, playing for time. Was she kidding? "Why would I want to be shut of you?" he asked. "You're fun to spend time with and easy on the eyes." *Especially in that clingy, sexy dress*. The one he wanted to take off her. Maybe with his teeth.

"It's that simple for you?"

He shrugged. "I'm a simple kind of guy."

She shook her head slowly, her eyes never leaving his face. "But you're not. Not by a long shot."

Celia joined them then, her face alight with interest in one of the few strangers this evening would contain. "Eva, I'd heard you'd brought someone new," she said, eyeing Sean with appreciation.

"Let me guess, Bill Ellers is maintaining his title as the faculty's biggest gossip?" Eva nearly groaned. She supposed the focus on her was inevitable given the past couple of weeks, but she hated it. After battling her parents' efforts to make her a reflection of themselves, she preferred either to be entirely unseen or to be able to manage how people perceived her. To be the subject of gossip was to have no control over her image and reputation.

Her colleague merely grinned and thrust a hand at Sean. "Celia Petrov. Russian studies."

"Sean Hannigan. Fire and rescue," he responded with a twinkle, shaking the woman's hand.

"So it's true? You turned my lighter into a date?" Celia looked positively gleeful.

"Oh, so the pink Bic was yours, huh?" Sean shot Eva a mischievous sideways glance and she wanted to drop into a hole.

"Indeed it was. I thought Eva'd taken up smoking like me, but instead she merely wanted to exterminate some vermin. Where is the weasel anyway?" She glanced around the room but didn't seem to spot Darren.

"He's already made his play to annoy Eva and was neatly removed by the dean," Sean said.

"Good for her," Celia said.

"I didn't know you didn't like Darren," Eva said. In five years of being office neighbors with the Russian studies professor, she'd gotten to know and respect the woman, but they weren't that close. That she'd have an opinion about Darren was a surprise.

Celia shrugged. "I didn't really feel one way or the other about him until he pulled that stunt on the quad. If I'd found out about it before you, though? I honestly would have punched him in the head. I have a cousin whose ex proposed to her via the jumbotron at a Nationals game."

"Ex, huh?" Sean looked amused.

"Yeah. As a result of being publicly put on the spot like

that, he immediately became the ex. I have no patience with this kind of public pressure."

"Good for them," Eva murmured. It was nice to know that not only were there people in the world who felt the way she did, but one of them was occupying the office right next door.

At that moment, a utensil rang against a glass and the dean stepped up to a lectern set up at one end of the room. "Pray for brevity," Eva muttered under her breath.

Sean had to say he was enjoying himself far more than he'd thought possible. But just being with Eva was rapidly becoming one of his favorite pastimes. If he could annoy that jerk Darren at the same time? Bonus.

As Eva'd predicted, the dean's speech was short and to the point. She thanked the faculty for another great year, noted some of the achievements that had occurred, touched on admissions for the coming academic year and then told everyone to enjoy themselves. All in all, maybe five minutes. Go, Dean Treadwell.

After, it seemed like an awful lot of people wanted to come and say hi to Eva. He wasn't sure if she was just popular with her colleagues—which wouldn't surprise him—or if people were curious about his unfamiliar mug hanging around the place.

That wouldn't be a surprise, either. He knew what novelty could do in terms of attracting attention. And it seemed that the news had spread about how they met. He fielded questions about the fire department, his schedule, their training—basically, anything to do with being on the squad. They seemed surprisingly interested in the answers. In his turn, he listened to linguistics professors talk about how many languages they knew, history professors about global events he'd never heard of and everybody on the real subject of the evening: university gossip.

When they finally broke away from the party, Eva looked wrung out and more than a little annoyed. "I'm so sorry," she said as they approached his truck. "I thought for sure we could slip out a lot earlier than that."

"Don't be sorry. It was a new experience."

"I should have known that having you there would mean you'd become the topic of the evening. We're all like rats in a too-small cage. We know everyone else, know more than we want to about their lives and their work, and anything novel is like tossing feed into a fish pond: immediate feeding frenzy."

Sean made a show of checking his body for injuries. "I seem to have come out without a scratch. Damn. I'm good."

She swatted weakly at his arm as he opened the truck door for her. "Social carnage. The scars are invisible."

He shut the door and thought about how to proceed with her as he rounded the truck's hood and took his place beside her. Loosening his tie before he started the engine, he turned to her and said, "You really don't have to take things all that seriously. I had fun tonight. It was as new to me as I was to them. It was interesting." It was especially interesting to see some surprised faces when he made a reference to Dickens. *Hey. Not just a pretty face*, he'd wanted to say.

She swallowed, her throat convulsing as she stared through the windshield. "You sure?" she asked, her voice a tiny squeak.

"Because I thought it was kind of awful. I felt like we were on display, that you were on display. And I hated that."

He touched her chin, asking but not demanding that she turn to look at him. She responded, but not in the way he expected. She turned her face so that her cheek touched his fingers, an almost catlike caress. It made his heart rate kick up and a surge of desire arrow through his body. "I didn't feel on display. I felt like your colleagues cared about you. That they were rallying around you. That they were interested in me because they cared about you."

Her eyes finally lifted to meet his, her soft cheek moving away from his hand. "Really?"

"Yeah. Really." His voice sounded like gravel rattling through an iron pipe. "Anyway. Let's get you home."

Nine

Eva sat bolt upright in the passenger seat of Sean's truck. She felt a little exposed and raw after having practically nuzzled his hand. But he was so *solid*, so kind and reliable, that she'd indulged in a moment of weakness before she even knew what she was doing.

At least his truck didn't have an old-fashioned bench seat. She would have been tempted to slide next to him, to sit with their legs touching like he'd done with her in the banquette at the pub. How warm and near would he feel with just the thin fabrics of her dress and his suit pants, rather than two layers of thick denim? Would the heat from his leg actually scald her?

"That's a very nice suit, by the way." It was an inane statement, but at least it was neutral. The suit fit him so well it must have been tailored. With a physique like that, he would have looked like Herman Munster in an off-the-rack suit, but the jacket tapered nicely from his broad shoulders to his waist. She could only imagine what the pants looked like under that jacket.

Neutral? She thought his tailoring was a neutral topic? She was the one who was inane.

"Thanks. When my sister Caitlin got married, I was her best person. She insisted I get a good suit to stand up with her."

"That sounds nice."

"Yeah, except she got an even nicer suit that was even better tailored than mine."

"She got married in a suit?" His family seemed awfully traditional. A suit for a bride seemed out of character.

He shot her a sideways grin. "Yeah. Her wife, Nicole, wore a dress. There was some debate on either side about whether they'd both wear dresses or both wear suits or do the heteronormative thing. I think they finally decided on the dress and suit approach to appease my folks."

"And did it?"

"Nah. They still had a litter of kittens apiece. So much for heteronormativity all the way around."

A startled snort-laugh escaped Eva at that. "Are your parents better about their relationship now?"

He shrugged and tilted his head to the side. "It's kind of a moving target. They wished Cait wasn't gay, but they're happy she's in a loving relationship, but they wish if she wanted to get married that she'd marry a man because they think marriage is between a man and a woman…blah, blah. Being Catholic and not being able to have a ceremony in the church made it all the more complicated."

Eva, raised with the occasional visits to Congregationalist churches on major holidays but nothing more in terms of a religious upbringing, boggled at the complicated nature of his explanation. "Are they upset that she didn't get married in the church or that she couldn't?"

"Both? I don't know. I think my mother especially is pretty muddled about it. Like, she doesn't want the church to recognize gay marriage, but she also loves her kid. It's a mess."

Sean's seemingly easy acceptance of this didn't quite tally with standing up for his sister at her wedding. There were more undercurrents in this situation than she would have suspected previously. And for someone who described himself as *simple*, Sean had quite the capacity for nuance. "You're close with Caitlin?"

"Yeah. She and I are the youngest. There's a five-year gap between her and Maeve, and she's pretty tightly bunched with the Irish twins at the top of the leaderboard."

"Irish twins? I'm not familiar with that term."

"Erin and Bridget were born ten months apart. They were in the same year at school. Irish twins."

"Oh," Eva said, feeling a little like she'd just been swamped by a wave. She'd known families with more than one kid. Of course she had. But she'd never met someone with so many dynamics. She was drowning in novelty. Or maybe just drowning. She hadn't really thought explicitly about how the various personalities of that many people could create complications upon complications. So many potential alliances and conflicts.

It was honestly a little scary to contemplate.

Pulling into Eva's driveway, he wondered if he'd overwhelmed her with his family. She looked a little shell-shocked and pale.

Wait until she actually *met* them.

"Can I walk you to your door?" he asked, getting a recurrence of those first-time, first-date nerves he'd felt earlier in the evening.

"Um. Okay." But when he went to open her door for her this time, she was already sliding down from the seat.

"Hey there," he said, catching her waist as she dropped toward the driveway. "Those heels and this truck are a bad combo." He should let her go now, shouldn't crowd her.

He didn't move. Her dress was so silky, and the curve of her waist fit so nicely in his hands. Her blue gaze was locked on his face. The moment stretched as he dragged air into his lungs.

A dog began to bark wildly, apparently from her house. She turned to look at her front door, breaking the spell of the moment between them. "Timmy," she groaned.

"Timmy's your dog?" His hands were still on her waist. He really should release her. But he still couldn't seem to move. Her hands were on his biceps. When had that happened?

"Yeah. He's very protective of me."

"I think I like Timmy." After all, they had the same mission.

"Do you want to meet him? Do you even like dogs?" There was a compelling vulnerability in her expression that made him want to scoop her up in his arms and carry her into her house.

"I love dogs. I'd love to meet Timmy." *I'd love to spend more time with you. Alone. No audience, no faking.*

"Okay." She seemed to realize that her hands were on his arms and also did not know how to get from next to his truck to her front door. Well, that made two of them.

Think, thickhead. He berated himself, then took a deep breath and moved her gently to one side so he could close the door to his truck. Then he offered her his hand as if they were fourteen. She took it with a tiny, secretive smile and led him to the front door of her house where the barking and scrabbling sounds grew louder.

"I'm here, Tim. Settle down," she said as she turned the key in the lock and pushed the door inward. A small mass of silky white fur with black spots came barreling out, wiggling and barking and not seeming to know what he wanted to do with himself.

Honestly? Sean could understand where the pup was coming from. Eva made him want to wiggle and bark, too.

She squatted then and half petted, half massaged the little dog's sides. He calmed at that, emitting a little doggy groan and looking at her with eyes of liquid love.

"Looks like you have the magic hands," Sean said. Wow. He'd never considered that he might be jealous of a little spotted mutt before. He wanted those hands all to himself. On himself.

"He was hit by a car before I got him," Eva said. "I think he still gets stiff and sore, so he likes his massages."

"Aww. Poor pup." Sean squatted and held out his hand for the dog to sniff. It took a couple of moments, as Timmy's attention was squarely on Eva, but he finally noticed and gave Sean's fingers a sniff and a lick. Sean stroked the dog's silky chest, not wanting to rile him up again with more stimulating head pats. "He's a sweet little thing."

"Yeah, he's definitely little but sometimes I think he believes he's the size of my neighbor's mastiff. He's definitely more of a burglar alarm than anything like a guard dog."

Since the dog was calm now, Sean stroked his silky, feathery ears, massaging those lightly in his hands. He got the groan of approval for his trouble. "Awww. Good boy. You're just happy to see your momma home safe." *And I can absolutely relate.*

Eva was in so much trouble. This sweet, handsome man had just run the social gauntlet for her, pretended to be smitten with her and now he was being lovely about her small, ridiculous dog?

She was going to have to google *how to protect your heart* because she was in grave danger of losing hers. She'd thought she knew what she was getting into—even though fake relationships in books always ended up with the couple together, this was reality. Her life wasn't a trope; it was *hers*. She was in control. Or she'd thought she was.

Sean looked up from the dog to her, lines fanning out from his smiling eyes. "Oh, hey. My sister Caitlin thinks you should recommend some more books to me. Do you think you could?"

Could she? Like any reader, she loved nothing better than to recommend books. Her cheeks heated as she wondered whether he'd enjoy the sexy ones she loved best. "Um, sure. Why don't you send me some of your favorites and I'll be better able to tailor the recommendations."

"I can do that." He got to his feet then and she rose, too. They'd been crouched close together to pet Timmy and now they were practically nose to nose. His pupils were dilated, inky blackness spreading across the green. Timmy flumped onto her shoes and sighed, seemingly just content to have her home and incidentally pinning her in place. "I should probably head out and leave you in peace. But I admit I don't really want to go," he said.

"You don't have to if you don't want to." Where did that come from? She needed him to go away so she could calm down and stop crushing on him.

He rubbed the back of his neck. God, he was adorable. There was something about a man in a suit with his tie half-undone and that top button open. The tiniest sliver of vulnerability at the hollow of his throat. "Maybe I should make myself useful and check your locks. Darren doesn't have a key, does he?"

Eva froze in the process of bending down to make Timmy get off her feet. "Well, he did have one, but I got it back from him when we split."

Sean grimaced. "Oof. You have no way of knowing if he made another copy. I'd change it if I were you. Front door only?"

Oh, she hated this so much. The sexual charge abandoned her, only to be replaced with frustrated tension. "No. He had one to the door to the house in the garage, too. And the code to the garage door opener." She shooed the dog inside.

His eyebrows flew up. "You need to change that right now."

Ugh. She knew he was right. But the code was an old favorite of hers. *Which makes it a stupid code, you fool*, her inner voice chided.

"Okay. Fine. Let's change it, then." She wasn't exactly gracious as she went into the foyer and pulled her phone from her bag to bring up the app that controlled her garage door. She thought for a few moments before keying in the new code.

Sean, having followed her inside and closed the door behind them, visibly relaxed and she nearly laughed at his reaction. "You really care, don't you?" It was a silly question. He was a firefighter. By definition, they cared.

But his green eyes snapped to meet hers and she was lost. "Yeah," he said, his voice a rusty growl. "I really do."

Eva couldn't help it. She launched herself at him and kissed him.

Sweet Jesus, Eva was kissing him.

He didn't think this was possible—he had signed up for the fake relationship. To be the object: The Firefighter. To deflect her horrible ex.

But no, he was the subject.

And he was subjected to her. Oh, her lips were so soft. And oh, he loved kissing her so much. He wrapped his arms around her, pressing her to his body until he didn't know where she ended and he began. They were one being, pleasure incarnate. He'd never been so aroused from just *kissing*. Heck, he liked kissing a lot. It was fun. But this was something else, something on a whole other level.

Timmy whined and poked his nose between their legs. She groaned and pulled away, leaning back against his arms and looking up at him with hazy eyes. "I'm sorry. That wasn't fair of me. I don't know what I was thinking."

Thinking? Who wanted to think when they could be kissing? Or maybe getting naked? "Why was it unfair?"

"Because I didn't ask. Because I feel like I'm taking advantage of this fake scenario or blurring the lines." She stroked the short hair at the back of his neck with gentle fingers while her gaze roamed his face. "Because you're doing so much for me, and I feel like I'm taking too much."

A feeling akin to panic bubbled up in him. Was this it? Was she ending things? They'd barely gotten started. "You didn't steal those kisses," he said. "It was a fair exchange."

"Yeah, but what if it starts feeling too real?"

Too late. "We're adults. We can take care of ourselves." He could handle anything if he could just have more of those kisses, that closeness, the feel of her *wanting* him. It didn't matter so much that it was fake if it felt this real.

"Can we, though? I'm all jumbled up inside and I can't seem to think straight with you around. Yes, Tim, I know I need to let you out," she said to the whining dog as she moved out of Sean's arms. He followed her to a large den in the back of the house. There was a sliding glass door that led to a little patio and a fenced backyard. She opened it for Timmy and he scooted out, tail wagging. She rubbed her forehead as she watched the little dog sniff around and finally lift his leg at the base of a small tree. "I'm sorry," she said again. "I know I'm giving the worst kind of mixed signals and that's just wrong of me." She looked sideways at him as if she was afraid of what she might see in his expression.

He looped a lock of her silky red hair behind one ear. "No. You're fine. Here's what I'm going to ask you to do. Put a chair in front of your front door, okay? I don't like the idea that Darren might be able to get into your house. Then tomorrow I want you to call a locksmith and have it changed. The one to the garage for good measure, even though you've changed the code."

"You're being awfully nice to me again when I'm nothing but a mess," she said.

"I like you. It's easy to be nice to you. And for now, I'm out of your hair until Tuesday evening." Their first self-defense class. She wouldn't cancel *that*, surely.

She nodded. "Thank you. And I'm sorry I'm so muddled."

"Don't be." He made for his truck, his heart heavy. He should have been expecting that she'd commit to the fake dating being just that: fake.

But more than just his own feelings had started to feel real tonight.

Ten

On Tuesday Eva went to the small room in the gym complex she'd reserved for their self-defense class. When she stepped inside, she saw Sean was already there, and her heart gave a little kick at the sight of him. Like her, he was dressed in a T-shirt and a pair of gray sweatpants, but his casual attire seemed molded like a superhero suit on him. He was speaking to a few students who seemed to have the same opinion, but his head came up immediately on her entrance, finding her gaze with his own and shooting her a smile so sweet, so genuine, it nearly made her heart melt and dribble out of her rib cage.

She'd regretted her decision on Saturday the moment her door had closed behind him. She'd never had a first kiss that had felt so *right* before. And what had she done? Thrown it away like an utter ninny. She worried that her heart was in danger? Hell, the very reason why they were performing this little charade was because that organ had already been stomped on. Who cared about a little more pain, if she could feel the pleasure that his kisses had promised?

He approached her as she set her bag down in the corner of the room. "Hey," he said, his green eyes glowing with appreciation. God, he was the best damn actor in the world because that look seemed to promise he'd lay everything at her feet in a heartbeat. "Did you get the locks changed?"

She nodded. "Yes. The very next morning. Paid the Sunday callout charge and everything."

"Good girl." Oh, Jesus. Why did that rumbling reply and that easy grin feel like a hand gently caressing her most intimate places? If he called her *baby* again, she might just melt into a puddle of pure lust.

"Are we ready to get started?" Her voice was embarrassingly shaky but Sean seemed not to notice.

"Yeah." He clapped his hands twice and the side conversations around the mirrored room abruptly ceased, about a dozen pairs of eyes focusing on him with eager anticipation. He introduced himself and thanked Eva for inviting him to give the class, commanding everyone's attention seemingly effortlessly. Eva was impressed. Was there nothing this man *couldn't* do?

As he started to segue into their first demonstration: the hold-breaking technique he'd shown Eva before, one of the young women raised her hand. "Yeah?" he asked.

"Is it okay if I take video of the demonstration? Putting this on social media might help people who can't be here in person."

"Good idea. That is if Professor Campbell is okay with it." He raised his eyebrows at her and she nodded.

"Fine with me." She probably owed the TikTok gods a sacrifice for not going viral with her homemade flamethrower, after all.

He clasped her wrists, explaining briefly how she was going to get free, and Eva swallowed the sudden lump in her throat. She didn't want to break away from him. Instead, she wanted to lean into his grip, to welcome it. He seemed to sense her hesitation, shooting her a considering look and saying, "Whenever you're ready, Professor…"

Fine. She twisted and pulled her wrists the way he'd taught her before, dancing backward as if to remove herself from the reach of an assailant.

"Good. The important thing is to retain your own freedom of movement—not to fight back, but to remain free and mobile. You can't do that if someone has their hands on you or if they've pushed you to the ground. Now pair up and practice. Technique doesn't mean much if you don't have it ingrained. Shock will make you freeze up, so you want to prepare your mind and your body so you react almost automatically."

And as he circulated and help students as they started to practice, Eva could admit she knew something about her body reacting automatically. Because hers was absolutely on fire right now.

"All right, that's all we have time for tonight," Sean said to the students. Eva had faithfully played his sidekick and faded into the background as he helped students with the moves he'd taught them. But every time he touched her, he'd felt his blood hum with the awareness of her. Memories of their kisses on Saturday had invaded his thoughts even as he'd instructed her how to get free of him, with each hold bringing them into greater contact.

He kept one eye on her as various students came to him with questions. He was afraid she'd bolt from the room and he wouldn't see her again until…when? But she lingered, chatting with a young man who'd arrived late to the class and who probably needed some help catching up.

When he finally broke free of the last of the students, they were the only ones left in the room. "Hi," she said, shifting the strap of her bag on her shoulder.

The room seemed suddenly smaller and much warmer. "What's up?" he asked, his throat tight.

"I had a book for you—you asked if I'd recommend some more." Was it his imagination, or were her cheeks pinker?

"I forgot to send you my favorites," he said. He hadn't forgotten, but he hadn't wanted to crowd her, not even by appearing in her email inbox. Besides, he didn't want to send her email. He wanted to talk to her, even if he couldn't touch her except to demonstrate self-defense techniques.

"I know. I just…" She blinked and her eyes met his directly and he felt like all the air had been sucked out of his lungs. "It's one of my favorites."

"And you knew I'd like what you like?"

Her lips popped into her mouth, then twisted into a shy smile. "I hoped you would."

"Okay, then. Let's have it."

"It's in my office."

He couldn't help the slow smile that spread across his face. She had a book for him. That she'd chosen. But she hadn't brought it with her. She'd left it in her office. A room with a door. He wasn't going to take anything for granted, but that was a pretty compelling set of facts. He gestured toward the exit. "After you."

His asking her to precede him was possibly a mistake. She was wearing sweatpants, but they were the kind that were *fitted*. They clung to the luscious curve of her ass as she exited the workout room. He hustled to walk beside her because he wasn't sure if he could keep himself from drooling if he followed that gorgeous view all the way to her office.

She glanced up at him as they walked across the campus, a speculative glint in her eye.

He added that look to his mental math of the situation, always keeping in mind that he might be misreading her cues entirely.

When she scanned her ID to let them into the building that held her office, something in her demeanor seemed to relax. Was it the familiar surroundings or something else? Curious, he followed her to her domain.

She closed the door behind them and his pulse jumped. She was leaning against the door, looking up at him with a strange expression. Almost defiant. Almost vulnerable.

Whatever it was, it brought him to his knees. Literally.

She blinked in astonishment. "What are you doing down there?"

"Hoping," he said, laying his hands gently on her hips.

A smile almost trembled at the corners of her lips. "Hoping for what?"

"Hoping you'll let me taste you."

★ ★ ★

She'd thought Sean was an angel. Too good for this world. Too good for her.

But that face looking up at her? Utter devil. His fingertips curled at the waistband of her silky joggers, teasing.

Asking.

She realized then that she was in control. She palmed his cheeks, feeling the faint stubble, the strong jaw and cheekbones. Did she want this man to do what she thought he was asking to do? She'd spent the entire class getting more and more turned on by everything about him. His presence. His goodness. His care and attention. There was only one answer to his question.

"Yes."

His eyes slid closed and he pressed his forehead to her pubic bone for a long breath. Then he pulled off her sneakers one by one and tossed them over his shoulders. He tugged her joggers and underwear down and off, the cool air of her office teasing her heated flesh. And then. Oh, God. His tongue teased her clit, his hands gripped her hips and he pressed his mouth to her sex.

Oh, *God*. His tongue *owned* her. Her head thudded back on the door in complete abandon. Sean tasted her with *intent*. He dragged his tongue against her clit then flicked it, stoking then firing her, sending her toward the climax that seemed inevitable, then lulling her down to a restless ache over and over.

"Sean," she moaned, wanting to chase that climax. She looked down and caught his gaze. Mischief was in those green eyes. "Sean. Let me come."

He shook his head without breaking contact, the movement arousing but not releasing her from her tense spell. He
doubled down by lapping at her clit and gripping her thighs,
which had started to shake. He groaned as he slid one finger
inside her, that long, thick finger she'd been thinking about
since that first day he'd visited her here. She could now be
entirely honest with herself about that little fantasy. And dear
Lord, but the reality was better.

"Oh, God. More." She'd never in her life been this shame-
less, this free. He hummed again in evident pleasure and sent
a second finger to join the first, pumping gently as his tongue
continued to work her in that advance and retreat that made
her want to scream. With his free hand, he draped one of her
legs over his shoulder, opening her farther, and kept up his
relentless torture. Her hands skated over his silky hair, too
short to grip like she wanted to, to direct him, to make him
let her come like she needed.

He chuckled, possibly sensing her frustration, his hot breath
puffing over her pussy in an even bigger tease than before.

"Sean."

"Mmm. I like the way you say my name," he murmured,
almost inaudible with his mouth pressed against her, then
starting his assault again.

"Sean… Sean. Sean, Sean, Sean, Sean. Please let me come.
Please, Sean."

He placed a tender, teasing kiss on her clit at that and looked
up at her, breaking contact for the first time since he'd started.
"Oh, I like the way you beg me even better."

"Sean…" This time it was a groan as her eyes closed and her head thudded backward again, making him chuckle.

"Okay, gorgeous. I got you." He leaned forward again and this time the onslaught was constant. He licked, he flicked, he pumped his fingers, winding her tighter and tighter until she shattered in pulsating release, having barely enough awareness of where she was not to scream and sob. Instead, she trembled and shook, and he pressed his tongue flat to her clit as she rode out the sensations rippling through her body.

"Oh, my God," she said as he withdrew his fingers from her and licked them clean, which was possibly the dirtiest, most delicious thing she'd ever seen. Dragging her leg off his shoulder, she slid down the door until her bare butt met the prickly industrial carpet. Somewhere in the recesses of her brain, she felt like she should feel self-conscious. But she was too wrung out, too hungover on pleasure, to care. "What. How. Oh, my God," she repeated.

Sean felt like a king. Like a god. Eva was limp and sated, half-dressed and practically in a puddle and he'd done all of that. Swiveling to sit and lean on the door beside her, he pulled her into his lap, cuddling her and smelling the sweet scent of her hair as he caressed the lovely, bare curve of her ass.

She stirred restlessly, pressing her hip against the rampant erection that stretched the front of his sweatpants, then shifting away so she could palm him over the fabric. "Oh. I need to do something for you," she said.

He nuzzled behind her ear. "That *was* for me."

"You know what I mean," she groaned, squeezing him until his eyes nearly rolled back in his head.

"Yeah. But going down on you was…" He couldn't explain it. Couldn't put into words that king/god feeling he had from giving her that much pleasure. From making her say his name, making her beg. He could have a hundred orgasms and none of them would feel that good.

"Are you even *real*?" she asked, leaning her head against his chest, her hand still gripping his dick in a way that felt almost as cozy as it did erotic.

"Do I feel real to you? Because I feel very real to me. That…" He hissed as she traced his cockhead with her fingertip. "That feels very real."

"Mmm. Yes. Quite…real." She continued to move her hand, making him think of smooth, cool bedsheets, not scratchy carpet. Dim, seductive lighting, not overhead fluorescents. Jesus, if he didn't have a lapful of satisfied, drowsy, half-naked woman, he'd think he'd fucked the entire thing up. She deserved better than this rough, desperate seduction in her own *office*, for crying out loud.

Then her hand slipped upward and then down *into* his sweatpants and he swallowed hard as her soft, warm fingers wrapped around him and began to pump in earnest. He was so aroused from going down on her, he almost felt too sensitive, like her hand was too much. "God, Eva." His breath hitched as she gentled her touch, until it was teasing. *Oooh.* Evil. She was using his own technique against him. Strong then soft, teasing, then ramping him toward release, then teasing again.

"Payback's a bitch and so am I," she murmured in his ear,

then kissed him and he was lost. This woman's mouth. The softness of her lips, the wickedness of her tongue. He sucked on that tongue, trying to take control back, but her hand gentled on his dick again and he gasped, unable to control his reaction. "Mmm." She hummed against his lips, tightening her grip again as his hips rocked into her fist. "Yeah. That's it. Lose control for me. Come for me."

Her words sent him over the edge. He groaned and shuddered as hot bursts spattered against his sweatpants, across his skin. Her hand, slick with his come, slid a few more times up and down on his softening length as she kissed his panting mouth.

He sucked in air, then brought his hands up to her face, scanning her features with wonder. "God, Eva. What are we going to do once we've found an actual *bed*?"

Eleven

*B*ed. Oh, she wanted him in her bed. She wished they could teleport straight to her bedroom. But since that technology hadn't been invented, she had to do the next best thing. "I'm sorry. I made a mess of you," she said, pulling her hand out of his pants. It glistened with the evidence of his orgasm. She looked over at her desk where a large box of tissues sat. She could no more levitate that box toward them than she could teleport both of them to bed, but she did wish she could. "I don't want to move, but we should get cleaned up," she grumbled. His index finger—that big index finger that had utterly lived up to its potential—grazed her cheek.

"We should. Do you have somewhere you need to be?" God, his expression was so tender. It could split her in two, that look.

"Not immediately. I walked Timmy this evening and he should be settled down for the night."

"Come for a drink with me, then."

"Um…" She glanced down at his sweatpants, which now sported stains that practically shouted to the world what they'd been doing. "I think I made you unfit for public consumption."

He laughed, boosting her to her feet and swatting her bare butt. "Nah. I'm a Boy Scout, remember? I'm always prepared."

She rolled her eyes and moved over to the desk, yanking out a handful of tissues and wiping off her hands before she offered him the box. He toed off his sneakers and shucked his sweatpants off to clean himself up, then unzipped his gym bag and pulled out a pair of jeans.

Gracious. That body. Those *thighs*. She realized she was staring. She also realized he'd noticed. And he didn't seem to care.

"Okay, then. One drink. I guess we should talk about my parents' upcoming visit. You're definitely going to need to be prepared for that." She found her joggers and pulled them on.

He paused in shucking on his jeans. "What's to prepare for?"

"Well, I told you that they're awfully snobby. I don't know how much experience you have with people who are like that, but they can be, well, hurtful."

He zipped his fly, then stepped in front of her, cradling her jaw in his hands. She looked up at him and he stroked his thumbs over her cheeks. "Honey. I don't care what they think of me. Sticks and stones, right?"

One of her hands came up to cover his. "But they—and I really hate to say this because they're my *parents*—can be really awful."

"You think your parents, who don't know me, can be more

cutting than my four sisters who've known me all my life? I love those women but they can be fucking *brutal*. Especially when Erin and Bridget team up. They're like the Voltron of sisters."

She frowned. "Are those your 'Irish twin' sisters?"

He bopped her nose gently with one finger. "They are. But even without having them in my life, I know your parents can't hurt me. Unless they hurt you. C'mon. Let's wash up properly and go get a drink and you can prep me whichever way you like about meeting your parents."

As he settled Eva into his truck, Sean knew he was giving the entire show away. He was putting all his feelings out there on the line.

And he didn't care one bit. Maybe it was the endorphins of giving and receiving orgasms. Maybe it was how vulnerable Eva could be when she stopped guarding herself so fiercely. She still seemed kind of relaxed and dreamy from their hot encounter, leaning her head against the window and twisting a strand of that enticing red hair around her finger. The silver streak glimmered with each passing streetlight, and Sean's heart felt like it was turning over just glancing at her.

"You didn't give me the book you wanted to lend me," he said, returning his attention to the road.

"Oh, shoot. Yeah. I was a little distracted." Her voice veered close to a giggle.

"I made an English teacher stop thinking about books. I consider that a major accomplishment. Tell me what it's about."

She shifted, sitting straighter. "It's a political story. It's about a powerful Black political consultant and the childhood friend she keeps reconnecting with. She's just such a badass character and the way they're kept apart is heartbreaking."

"But they fall in love."

"Yes, they fall in love. It also reminds me of some of my favorite media. Like *Chamber of Lies*." He adored the way her face got animated when she talked about the things she was passionate about. He couldn't wait until he wasn't driving so he could give her his full attention.

"The TV show?"

"Yeah. Have you seen it?"

"A few episodes. It was good. Maybe I can get the squad to agree to a streaming marathon. Care to come and be a guest lecturer?"

"At firehouse screening night? Wouldn't you prefer just to watch what you want to watch?" There was that laughter in her voice again, warming him from the inside out. Making Eva laugh might be his second-favorite pastime, after making her come.

"Well, screening nights tend to get interrupted by callouts, so your lecture might end up being abandoned."

"Harshest add/drop period of any semester I've ever experienced," she said, her voice dry.

He barked out a laugh. "Well, it wouldn't be intentional. Emergencies wait for no lecture. Or movie or TV."

"True." He could see her in his peripheral vision, studying his profile. "Did you always want to be a firefighter? Like, was it your childhood dream?"

He shook his head. "Nah. I thought I wanted to be a doctor, like your dad."

Voice flat, she said, "You're nothing like my dad."

"Yeah. Turned out I wasn't much good at math and science. So that idea went out the window pretty early. I kind of stopped thinking about that question for a long time, then when I was in junior high, my class got a tour of the local fire station. I liked the idea of being a first responder, of helping people."

"You said you were bullied as a kid. Some kids turn into bullies because of that. You went the other way entirely."

He shot her a quick glance. "Yeah, Caitlin has said something similar. I used to wonder if there was a connection, but the more I think about it, the more I'm glad I could emulate my sisters defending me rather than the bullies who harassed me."

"In my experience, more things are connected than not," she said, gazing out the window.

"What's connected with you?"

She clasped her hands and stretched them in front of her. "Well, I'm pretty sure my horrible history with men has more than a little to do with my dad."

Ugh. Had she really gone there? Had she, a forty-one-year-old woman, ascribed her horrible romantic history to *daddy issues*?

Pathetic.

"Or maybe that's just a cop-out," she said as Sean pulled his truck into a parking space in front of a restaurant and bar that was far enough from campus that she probably wouldn't run into any of her students.

"Why do you think it's a cop-out?" he asked as he undid his seat belt.

"Because I'm an adult and I'm capable of making my own mistakes?"

"Hmm." He got out of the truck then, and met her on her side, taking her hand as he hit the remote lock. "Kind of going against your other theory, though, right? And why is my choice of career inevitably tied to my childhood trauma whereas your romantic history is just…there?"

Sean may not have been good at math or science—which was no shade to him; she was terrible at them, too—but he had a very sound grasp of logic. "I don't know. I just feel like I should be owning my own mistakes, not blaming them on my dad."

He opened the door of the bar and waved her inside. "Someone once told me that parents push our buttons so well because they installed them on us. It's all well and good to say that you should be one hundred percent making your own decisions, but you're still not making them in a vacuum. Your childhood might be behind you, but it's still back there. It still affects you."

Since it was Tuesday, they found two seats easily and she hoisted herself up on a stool, propping her elbows on the long expanse of wood. "Yeah, you're probably right. I just hate the thought that my history pulls my strings like some puppet."

Sean flagged down the bartender, who took their orders and quietly went away to fill them. No flirty attempts to get Sean's attention from this dude, thank goodness. "So you needed to prep me for the meet-the-parents dinner. Go ahead and prep me."

She sighed and rubbed her eyelids. "Okay, so I mentioned my dad is a doctor."

"Yeah? What else?"

"That's the thing. There isn't any more. That's his entire personality. Being a doctor—well, retired doctor now, which he hates—"

"He hates being retired?"

"Loathes it. Because being a *practicing* doctor is important. Being a retired doctor is…not. He doesn't save lives anymore and can't lord it over everyone." *Including me*, she didn't say. The fact that her father always needed to be the most important person in the room had been confusing to her as a child. As an adult, it felt pathetic. Juvenile.

Sean's eyebrows flew up toward his hairline. "What about your mom?"

"She's almost worse. Her entire personality is being a doctor's wife."

"How does that work?" There was laughter in his voice.

She should hate telling Sean this. It was shameful, how shallow her parents were. But she felt almost conspiratorial. She *liked* sharing these facts with him. "Well, she did work when he was in medical school—you know, the old story about the woman who put him through school. But at least he didn't leave her for a younger woman twenty years ago, so we have that going for us. But as soon as he started earning money, she stopped working and almost exactly nine months later had me."

"That's almost eerie."

She slapped the bar. "*Right?* So her entire life revolved around raising me, keeping house, having the occasional party for his doctor friends and their equally Stepford wives. And she played tennis. That's the one thing she was actually good at and maybe the only thing she did just for herself."

Sean thanked the bartender as he placed their drinks on the bar. "So how are they going to be awful to me this weekend?"

Eva took a long sip of her gin and tonic, then set it down with a thud. How had she ever thought that putting this perfectly lovely man in front of her parents was a good idea? "They're going to try very, very hard to make you feel small."

Sean cocked an eyebrow. "Um…. You might have noticed I'm not exactly small. I'm guessing I'm probably taller than your dad and outweigh him by…a lot."

She pointed a finger gun at him, winking. "Yeah. I think you know what I mean, big guy. Not small as in stature, but small as in as a person. To them, you're not one of the important people. No big, fancy degree, no big, fancy job."

He shrugged, amused. "He saved lives, I save lives. Tomayto/tomahto."

"Are you really that unaffected by snobbish people?" she asked. "I feel like I'm putting you right back in the position of being bullied and I hate that."

Sean took a deep breath and held it for a moment, thinking. "Look. When I was a kid, I was trying to figure out who I was. We all have to do that when we're kids. We're forming as people. But I'm not a kid anymore. I know who I am. My parents have their own issues, but I never doubted that they loved me. My sisters could be brutal as fuck, but I also know they love me. I have a good job that helps people. I pay my bills. I have good friends. What does the opinion of some-one who somehow managed to go to medical school and still feels inadequate enough to want to make other people feel small matter?"

She flinched a little at that and Sean reminded himself that he was talking about her *father*, of all people. "I'm sorry. That was a pretty harsh thing to say about someone I've never met. Especially your dad."

She covered his hand with her own. "No, that's okay. I was just…well. That was probably awfully accurate. I just never thought about it in those terms, but you're probably right. I just wish I wasn't setting you up for, at best, a dull evening."

Not for the first time, his fingers itched to smooth out the worried groove between her eyebrows. She was trying to pro-tect him now? That was too cute. "Oh, I'll make up for that by giving you an all-too-exciting time at my folks' house."

Her eyes widened. "How so?"

He turned his hand over so he could lightly clasp hers. He loved touching her, in every way—sexual, nonsexual—he loved it all. "Well, you already know my immediate family has seven people. Then you add my sisters' kids and the fact that none of us are especially quiet when we get around each other and, well. It's a lot."

She laughed at that, but she also looked a little nervous. "My upbringing was very, very quiet. So yeah. That does sound a little overwhelming."

"Don't worry. I'll get you some noise-canceling head-phones. You'll especially need them when my nieces' voices start to sound like they're trying to call dogs."

A smile spread across her face. "Oh, my. Shrill?"

"Yeah. They get excited and we have to herd them outside or risk permanent hearing damage," Sean joked. "Christmas is basically chaos."

"I can only imagine." Eva was now looking slightly dazed, and he figured he should ease off before he scared her away entirely. The contrast between his huge, noisy, chaotic upbringing and her small, quiet, sterile one yawned in front of him. Well, he could protect her from both his family and hers if needed.

"Seriously, though, my family is great in a lot of ways. Caitlin, my next-oldest sister, is really going to like you, I think. She approves of you expanding my reading."

Eva's expression softened, then she gave a determined little nod. "Well, then. I look forward to meeting her. We're just going to have to get past dinner with my folks first."

Twelve

Prior to getting ready to go out to dinner with Sean and her parents, Eva went for her evening dog walk with Krystal, the mid-June night giving a hint of the heat and humidity to come. "I just wish I didn't know already that this is going to be an absolute disaster," she said as she watched Luther lift his leg against a convenient signpost.

Krystal, having met her parents on an all-too-memorable prior visit, just gave her a significant look.

"I mean, Sean was absolutely right. My father has less than no reason to put people down. And why did I not ever figure that out before?"

Krystal sighed. "Because you're too close to the situation. Also, parents tend to be able to frame things for their kids in ways that make their own world view pretty powerful."

"True." Eva sighed in return, then stripped a plastic bag off the roll attached to Timmy's leash and squatted to clean up after him.

"I know it's a cliché, but try not to let them bother you," Krystal said, her eyes worried.

Eva nodded. "Yeah. I'll try."

Later, after she'd come home, fed Timmy and showered, she found herself facing her closet with a disproportionate feeling of doom. "Fuck it," she said and pulled out a silky blouse and a pair of linen trousers. It was a warm evening and she felt like being comfortable. Of course, her mother would be expecting a dress, but she just wasn't feeling up to it.

Dressed and made up and twenty minutes too early in the way she always was when she was due to get together with her parents, she wandered around her house, tidying the stack of books on her coffee table, watering her plants. Generally fidgeting in the slightly productive, slightly obsessive way that brought her straight back to her mother's disappointed gaze sweeping around her childhood bedroom even right after she'd put everything away.

So it surprised her to see Sean's truck pulling into her driveway ten minutes before she'd asked him to. She opened the door just as he was coming around the front of his truck, an appreciative gleam in his eyes when he saw her.

"Hello, gorgeous," he said as he brushed a kiss across her lips. *Wow.* He must have caught the surprise in her expression, because he grimaced and said, "Sorry. Didn't mean to presume."

"You're really taking the fake boyfriend thing all the way to the mattresses," she said, then winced because—yeah. If they'd had a mattress last time they were together, they totally would have taken advantage of that. And had that changed anything? No, it couldn't. She had to keep to their agreement, to not get impossibly tangled in this thing. It would be unfair to both of them.

"You have no idea," he said, taking her hand and leading her to the passenger door of the truck.

"I can let myself in and out of vehicles, you know," she said, but she was laughing a little, to let him know that she didn't *mind* so much as she wasn't used to this kind of chivalry.

"I know. But I like taking care of you." He winked and the wicked expression in his eyes was so similar to the look he'd given her as he knelt and gave her the most powerful orgasm of her life, she felt a blush heating her face. She didn't object again as he carefully closed the door and got in the driver's side.

"What's this?" she asked, pointing to a small box tied with a red ribbon on the center console.

"Little present for your mom. Chocolates."

Her eyes went wide. "Holy cow. You're the most full-service fake boyfriend anyone's ever had. And also, that's kind of genius because Mom will hopefully feel guilty about playing snobby head games and will be slightly less awful than usual."

"I have to confess that was a little in my mind," he admitted as he got on the highway. "But mostly it was because I wanted to make as good an impression as I can so that hopefully they'll be easier on you."

Eva sighed. "That ship, I'm afraid, has sailed."

Sean had his own issues with his family, but he hated that Eva's parents apparently didn't support her. Who could have such a kickass daughter and fail to recognize her amazing qualities?

Dr. and Mrs. Campbell, he guessed.

They reached the restaurant, a sprawling building that was decorated to look like some sort of high-end hunting lodge, in good time. But when they entered the lobby, Eva's hand in his, an older couple who had to be the Campbells were already waiting. Dr. Campbell must have been responsible for her blue eyes, and while Mrs. Campbell's red hair was now definitely courtesy of her hairdresser, the resemblance was definitely present. Sean didn't know a lot about clothes, but there was something indefinably *expensive* about them. Expensive and uncomfortable.

"Oh, there you are, Eva," her mother drawled as if they were late. Sean surreptitiously checked his watch. They were ten minutes early.

Let the head games begin.

Mrs. Campbell looked Eva up and down. "Would it have killed you to make more of an effort in your appearance? That streak in your hair is so *aging*."

Wow. Yeah. They were a lot.

Eva greeted her parents while ignoring her mother's words. "Mom, Dad, this is Sean."

"Nice to meet you, Dr. Campbell. Mrs. Campbell, this is for you." He handed her the little package, registering the older woman's surprise as she received it. "I hope you like chocolate."

"My goodness. Thank you." As anticipated, the gesture appeared to derail her a bit.

A hostess took that moment to intervene, gesturing with

a handful of menus that they should follow her to their table. Sean took the opportunity of being behind Eva's parents to let his hand rest on the small of her back, a tiny point of contact that told her he was there for her, supporting her.

Once they were seated and considering their meals, Dr. Campbell peered at Sean with barely concealed suspicion. "So Eva hasn't told us much about you."

"Probably not," Sean said cheerfully. "We haven't been seeing each other all that long."

"What do you do?" the older man asked, suspicion unabated.

"I'm a firefighter for Montgomery County."

"A *fireman*?" Mrs. Campbell said the word as if she thought that firefighter was some sort of made up, fictional occupation. "Don't take this the wrong way, but what do you have in common with our daughter?"

Was there a *right* way to take that? "Books," he said simply.

"Sean's a big fan of literature." Eva said, smiling at the waiter who brought a basket of bread to the table. "We bonded initially over Jane Austen."

Dr. Campbell blinked once behind his spectacles, owl-like. "A firefighter who reads Jane Austen." For the first time in his life, Sean felt like an animal in a zoo. He'd encountered surprise, sure. He knew what sort of stereotype boxes he ticked and how he'd get classified as a big meathead by a lot of people. But usually when he told people about his love of reading, their reaction was interest.

Dr. Campbell looked more like he didn't believe Sean.

Sean cleared his throat, reaching for his usual composure.

Eva hadn't been wrong about her dad. "And Dickens. And a lot of others. I was working my way through a lot of the English literary canon and was going to move on to non-English writers in translation, but Eva's broadening my reading in different ways."

Dr. Campbell flicked a glance at his daughter. "How is that? She's got the idea that pop culture is worthy of academic study."

"That's right. It's a lot of fun."

"Fun? Possibly. But I fail to see the merit of it."

"Dad, I get that you don't like my field of scholarship, but we really don't have to go over this again." Sean had never heard her voice sound so flat or small before. He hated it.

An uncomfortable silence settled over the table at that, with everyone studying their menus and avoiding looking at each other. When the waiter came to take their orders, Mrs. Campbell seemed to shake out of her stupor. "How did you two meet? I don't see you traveling in the same social circles."

"My team had a callout to the university. A situation on the quad." In his peripheral vision, Sean could see Eva's face turning rosy. Did she think he'd throw her under the bus by telling her folks about the specifics of that day? "Once everything was under control, I had a chance to chat a little with Eva. We hit it off."

"You hit it off," Dr. Campbell said. "I'm sorry, I'm just being honest here. I just don't see the compatibility."

Ugh. Eva'd always known that this would be the way this evening would go. But there was a tiny crumb of hope that maybe her parents wouldn't be, well, them. And how was it that her father could simultaneously think so little of her area of study and also think it was so far above Sean?

"Dad, Sean and I have a ton of compatibility so far. And also, it's very early. So maybe can you keep those kinds of observations to yourself?"

"Your father is just being honest," her mother said. "You're a college professor." As if she didn't know her own profession. She turned her gaze to Sean. "Do you even have an undergraduate degree, young man?"

Oh, she did not just *young man* Sean, a guy who could probably bench-press her mother without breaking a sweat.

Cheerful and unflappable, Sean shook his head. "Nope. associate's degree. But I make good money, my job has a positive impact on people's lives and I enjoy it."

Christ. Her mother didn't even have her undergraduate degree. She'd dropped out to support her dad when he was in medical school. But there would be no point in bringing that up. Her mother's internalized sexism wouldn't find the two situations at all comparable.

"A positive impact?" her father chimed in. "Seems like mostly what you do is mitigate damage."

"Why isn't that a positive thing?" Eva said, beginning to feel desperate and anxious. Her folks were doing the absolute rock bottom of what they were capable of tonight. "You think people's houses should just burn down and we should dust our hands and say, 'Oh, well'?"

Her father looked at her like she was being absurd. "Of course not. I just question the impact portion of his statement. Medicine has an impact, for instance."

"Dad, you're being ridiculous. Medicine also mitigates damage." *Also, he's a good person, which you absolutely are not. He's had more of a positive impact on my life in only a few weeks than you have in over forty years.*

"I saved many lives in my career, young lady, and don't you forget it."

"Sure. In your nice, safe cardiac cath lab, all clean and tidy and hardly exerting yourself. Sean also saves lives, but he risks his own to do it." In the aghast silence that followed from her parents, she said, "Sorry. *I'm just being honest.* You scrubbing up before a procedure isn't exactly the same as running into a burning building." Eva's jaw clamped shut. She'd never in her life spoken to her parents this way.

Their food arrived then, and Eva picked at her dish, appetite utterly gone. The table was silent and tense. Her mother's mouth was a flat line; her father stared stonily at his plate as he consumed his meal. Sean mostly seemed unfazed by the tension, except for the way he looked sideways at her, checking in on her. At one point he excused himself from the table and headed off in the direction of the restrooms.

But when he returned, he didn't sit again. "Well, I can't say this has been fun, but I've taken care of the bill and the tip. Eva, are you ready to go?"

It was like he'd read her mind. She had wanted to be gone for at least the last half hour. Her mother looked sharply up as she rose to her feet. "That's it?" she demanded.

"Say thank you for the meal, Mom. I've had enough." The relief that flooded through her made her muscles feel like water.

"*You've* had enough? Darren would never have behaved like this."

Eva let out a joyless laugh. "No, he would never have paid for everyone's meal. And Sean wouldn't cheat on me the way Darren did. So I have that going for me."

"I don't know what we did to deserve this behavior," her father said in his most withering *I've never been more disappointed* tone.

"I don't know what you deserve but you don't deserve Eva," Sean said, taking her hand in his. "She's too good for both of you. Have a nice evening."

"I can't *believe* they were that awful," Eva groaned as he handed her into his truck. "I am so, so sorry."

"You're not responsible for them. They're adults who've decided to behave that way. And you did warn me." Dr. Campbell had actually made him angry. Not with his dismissal of Sean, his work, or even his suitability as Eva's partner. No, what made him mad was the belittling way he treated his daughter, someone he should love and be proud of.

"They've never been *that* bad before, though."

"Well." He pressed a soft kiss to her lips. "Then you had no reason to think they were going to go quite that hard. Don't beat yourself up." He shut the door carefully as she buckled her seat belt, then moved to his side and climbed in. "What now?"

"Home, please." She groaned and tipped her head back, shutting her eyes as he left the parking lot and headed toward her house. "I can't even imagine what our next phone call is going to look like."

"Try not to think about it," he said. "Probably not an easy thing to do, but there's no point in dreading something out of your control."

"Thank you for, well... For being you, I guess," she said so softly he almost didn't catch it.

He shrugged. "I'm sorry if I overstepped, but I really couldn't stand seeing them treat you like that."

"They treated you worse."

"Nah. Their opinion about me means nothing. But they're your folks, and their behavior hurts you. That I didn't like. They could have taken potshots at me all day and I wouldn't have cared." But seeing Eva so rattled, apparently trying to make herself small in front of those two self-important jerks who didn't have the good sense to know that producing her was the best thing they'd ever done? Rage, an unfamiliar emotion, swirled through him.

"You're sweet."

I'm sweet on you he could have said. But it didn't seem the right time to make any sort of emotional declaration, what with Eva being so wrung out and vulnerable. He turned onto her street and pulled up in front of her little house, cutting the engine. "I had a nice time."

She snorted. "No, you didn't. That was awful."

He reached across the console and cupped her cheek in one hand. "The food wasn't bad. And I liked the parts where it was just you and me."

Her eyes searched his face as if she was trying to decipher some hidden message. She drew in a long breath, sighing. "How about some more of just you and me?"

Thirteen

The question hung in the quiet of the truck's cab for what felt like forever. Then Sean ran his thumb across her lower lip and asked, "You really mean it?"

"Why wouldn't I mean it?" she said. She knew she should keep him at a distance, knew she should protect herself and him. But the evening had left her raw and sad and desperate for more of how he made her feel.

"It was an emotional night for you. I wouldn't want you doing anything you regretted."

I'll only regret losing you when this is over, she thought. But what she said was, "I won't regret anything we do together, I don't think. In fact, I think I'd regret *not* enjoying you while I still can."

"Well, then. Let's go inside." His voice was husky and low, sending a shiver across her skin like he'd brushed her with a feather.

They got out of the truck and Eva let them into her house,

met by a bemused and sleepy Timmy, who sniffed Sean, seemed to remember him and then took himself off to his bed in the living room. Eva swallowed the lump in her throat and turned to Sean, who pulled her to him in a strong and enveloping hug. It seemed entirely too platonic, that hug, but she couldn't deny its comfort. His body was warm and solid, his back rising and falling under her palms with his breath.

"You okay?" he asked and she nodded, her cheek brushing against the soft cotton of his shirt, which smelled faintly and comfortingly of starch.

"More than okay," she said, and then his hands were sliding into her hair, tipping her head back for a searing kiss that made her pulse kick. "Kissing you is cardio," she murmured, feeling his smile against her mouth.

"Kissing you is heaven," he replied, his lips slanting across hers again, his tongue demanding entrance to her mouth. She opened for him, pressing her whole body closer, sliding her hands up his chest and wrapping them around the back of his neck. Then his arms tightened around her, and her feet left the floor. She squeaked and wrapped her legs around his waist, getting a pleased grunt from him as her hips lined up with his and…oh. The solid length of him pressed up against her felt so good she almost wanted to weep. He broke the kiss and murmured in her ear, his breath making her shiver. "Bedroom?"

"Upstairs." She pulled back a little, expecting him to put her down, but he just strode for the stairs. "Careful of your head," she said, laughing, as he entered her bedroom tucked under the eaves of the gabled roof.

Flicking the wall switch on and still not putting her down, he swept his gaze around the modest bedroom with its pale cream walls, sage green linens and hardwood floors. "Nice."

"Do you want to examine my decor or do you want to fool around?" she asked.

"Good point." He stepped around the bed and laid her down on her back, kissing her deeply while he toed off his shoes.

"Multitasker," she said, her voice veering toward a giggle. What was it about this man that just unstitched her every time?

"Motivated," he replied, kneeling on the floor to pull her shoes off and throw them into a corner. "Inspired." He unbuttoned her blouse, revealing the lacy demi-cup bra. "Mmm, enthralled," he said as he undid her trousers and pulled them off to see the matching panties.

She rose to her elbows as he got to his feet and stripped off his shirt. "Am I with a man or a thesaurus?"

He leaned over as he shucked off the rest of his clothes, his thick cock springing free. Then he leaned forward and kissed her, murmuring against her lips, "You are with a man who is motivated, inspired and enthralled."

She returned his kiss, sitting up so she could let the sleeves of her blouse slide off. "All right. That put me in my place."

Sean chuckled. "Yes, I've put you in your place. In bed. You've never looked better." The bra and panty set was going to absolutely put him in the ground. Somehow, they were the exact shade of her eyes. Seeing her topless for the first time, he was charmed by a smattering of freckles across her shoulders. God, he wanted to see every part of her, touch and taste every inch of skin. He tipped one bra strap off and traced the freckles with his tongue like he was playing connect the dots. She groaned and her head fell back, so he took advantage of her exposed neck and tracked up the side, placing openmouthed kisses from the juncture of her shoulder to the underside of her jaw and then just behind her ear, a spot that made her shiver.

"Oh, that's nice," she whispered.

"I'm going to have to do better than *nice*." Sean pulled back and got his pants from the floor, digging out his wallet and extracting a condom. Holding it up between two fingers, he said, "Nice and fresh, just opened the box today."

"You spoil me." A wicked smile curled her lips and she pushed back toward the headboard as he army-crawled up and over her body, letting his dick brush over the front of her panties as he went. She gasped and he pushed her legs apart with his knees, settling on his elbows and taking up his assault on her neck again. She rocked her pelvis, rubbing against him shamelessly until he clamped one hand on her hip.

"Now, now. No fair making me wild too fast." The bra strap he'd pushed down was still draped over her arm, and he used his nose to nudge the shallow cup under her nipple, reveling in her gasp as he sucked and did one slow, circular grind with his hips. "Harder or softer?" he said, pushing one hand behind her to unhook the clasp and take it off her entirely.

"A little harder." Her eyes were closed now, seemingly in absolute surrender. God, how he liked that. No. *Loved* it. He dipped his head and sucked the peak into his mouth again, tugging on it with more force and swirling his tongue. He was rewarded with a breathy groan, so he tried the same thing on the other side, appreciating her shivers and the slick rosiness of her skin where he'd sucked on it.

"My girl likes it a little rough?" He pressed a kiss to another newly detected freckle, this one on her sternum.

"Sometimes. A little." He looked up and her eyes were open again, her gaze held by his as if he was a snake charmer. Or maybe he was the snake being charmed.

"You tell me what you want. More. Less. Harder. Softer. You're in control here. It's all about you."

She was in control? Ha. One thing she'd learned was that Sean was very much in control almost all the time. And he was so genuine, so decent and so kind, she was fine with that. She welcomed it. It was lovely to be able to let the world fall away for a little while, to let someone she trusted take charge.

But what he was saying was important. Communication was important. And *oh, shit.*

"What's the matter?" he asked.

"We never had the testing talk. But I'm okay. I tested after I found out you-know-who was…you-know-what." She didn't want to bring Darren's name or his cheating into this room, this moment.

"I've been tested since I was last with someone. We're good." His eyes glittered with understanding and humor. "You're all tensed up. Now I have to get you all nice and relaxed again. Oh, *darn.* What a shame." He set his attention on her breasts again and it wasn't long until she was a puddle. A writhing, needy puddle, but a puddle nonetheless.

"That's better," he said as he pulled her panties down and

threw them aside. Testing her wetness with one probing finger caused her to groan.

"I think I might be obsessed with your hands," she said
as he added a second finger, pumping and rocking the heel
of his hand against her clit. He stretched out beside her and
teased her nipple with his mouth until she rocked her hips,
riding his hand, chasing her pleasure.

"Take it. Take what you need," he said, then blew a cool
stream of air across her wet, heated flesh, sending her fly-
ing, squirming and moaning. "That's it," he said, gentling
the movement of his hand but keeping up the pressure and
movement to draw out her orgasm.

When her shuddering ebbed, she raised a hand to his
face, cupping the severe angle of his jaw and appreciating
the wicked gleam of accomplishment in his eyes. "You are a
goddamn miracle, you know that? You're magic."

He waggled his eyebrows. "Wanna play with my wand,
baby?"

She laughed at that, helpless and wrung out. "You're also
terrible."

Pulling his fingers out of her, he sprawled out over her
body, his erection trapped between them. "Wanna be bad
with me some more?"

She feathered her hands over his hair, down the strong column of his neck, to his shoulders. "Yes. Very much."

He kissed her then, long and slow and decadent, stoking
pleasure to a new blaze inside her. Then he grabbed the condom from the nightstand, tearing open the packet and rolling
it slowly down, looking at her with hooded eyes as she watched
every movement. "Like what you're seeing, dirty girl?"

She nodded, licking her lips. Who was she becoming? Normally, the first few times she was with someone new, she was self-conscious and a bit tentative. But Sean brought out a new Eva, an uninhibited, almost reckless person she didn't recognize.

She liked that new Eva, if she was honest.

"What's your favorite position?" Sean asked.

"What does it matter? You already took care of me."

He wagged a finger at her, one of the ones that had until very recently been inside her. "Nuh-uh. Once is not enough for you tonight. I want to make you come at least twice and the idea of you squeezing my dick like you've squeezed my fingers really turns my crank."

His words almost made her dizzy. "Wow. Okay, then any position, but I need clitoral stimulation to get off."

"I figured." He grinned. "Then I guess we'll just keep you right where you are."

Eva looked like a goddess, her flaming hair flowing over the pillows around her gorgeous face. She reached her arms up and he leaned forward, allowing her to draw him down, their bodies flush. "Legs wider," he ordered because she seemed to like it when he got a little bossy. Yeah, there it was, her pupils flaring, eyes widening. But her legs spread, too. "That's it." He drew his cockhead up and down her slick, welcoming entrance, loving the way her eyes went a little hazy when he grazed her clit. "You ready for me?"

She nodded, her eyes meeting his and *God*, the tender feeling that ripped through him nearly undid him. He pushed slowly, relishing her body's welcome, the warm, wet embrace of her. When he was completely inside her, he gave a little grind of his hips, making her breath hitch.

"Is that what you want, sweetheart? Talk to me."

"Yeah. That. It's good." Her voice was low and breathy, sexy as hell. He did it again, a slow retreat, a slow thrust, a grind. All the while she traced patterns on his back, making electrical currents dance over his skin. He kissed her, closing his eyes as their lips and tongues played, inhaling the light, sweet scent of her skin, loving her taste.

Breaking the kiss, he rested his forehead on hers, continuing his slow grind, battling for control. He was not going to come until she did again. "God, Eva. You're so sexy." He could have gone on. *So beautiful and smart and funny and I could get lost in you if I let myself.*

Her hips had caught his rhythm, rising to meet him as he moved, swiveling as he ground against her. He loved that she sought her pleasure. Loved that she helped him get her there. She lifted her head, pulling him down to meet her as she initiated another long, lingering kiss, sucking on his bottom lip before she trailed kisses across his jaw and then lightly bit his earlobe.

He groaned. "I'm trying to make this good for you. You start playing with my ears and any control I have is going to go out the window."

"Mmm. Good to know." Her voice was husky, sultry, like dark chocolate and sin. She laughed as he shuddered, her breath fanning against his ear, stoking him further.

Well, he could play that game, too. He kept deep inside

her, pulsing his hips as he found that place behind her ear that had made her shudder before. She let out a startled, "Oh!" and he knew he had her, grinding his hips, kissing her neck and leaning on one arm so he could tug at a nipple with his other hand. Her body tensed, locked tight, then she shuddered with release, rippling and pulsing around him, sending his control out of the building. She gripped him with arms and legs as he pounded into her, his vision going white as pleasure ripped through him and he collapsed.

When he'd regained his breath, he kissed that special spot once more. "Am I too heavy for you?"

"Never." She tightened her starfish grip around him, making him grin.

Fourteen

Sean was aware of the unfamiliar fall of light before any-thing else, slowly drifting awake and feeling happier than he could remember being in a long time. Then a floral scent mingled with the earthier smell of sex tickled his nose and he rolled over, opening his eyes to find Eva, curled up almost like a child, both hands pillowing her cheek as she slept. Last night, after cleaning up and straightening the bedclothes, he'd cuddled her on his chest and they talked until they both drifted off.

The cuddling and quiet conversation was almost as good as the sex had been.

Almost.

As if his gaze had reached out and touched her, Eva's eyes fluttered open. "Morning," she said, her voice cloudy with sleep.

"Morning, beautiful." With one finger, he pushed back a lock of hair that had fallen across her forehead.

"I've seen myself in the morning. Not sure I would agree with that," she said, then yawned.

"I meant what I said, woman." He scooted forward and pressed his lips to hers in a single, fleeting kiss. "I have to get going for a shift soon, but do you have any coffee?"

"Do I have coffee?" She scoffed. "I'm an academic. Coffee is work juice. Coffee is life." She rolled to her back and stretched like a cat, then got out of bed and walked to the door where a robe hung on a hook. He let himself appreciate the curve of her bare backside and the graceful line of her spine until she shrugged the garment on.

After she went downstairs, Sean found his trousers and tugged them on, pulled on his shirt, then gathered up the rest of his clothes, folding them into a tidy bundle. Shoes in one hand and unworn garments in the other, he found her in the kitchen, a coffeemaker burbling contentedly at one end of the counter.

"I like the look," she said, pointing at his unbuttoned shirt.

"Glad to hear it. I'll do the stroll of pride into the station, then grab a shower and change into work clothes." He had spare clothes in his gym bag in the truck—he always did—but he was under a little more time pressure than he was comfortable with.

"Stroll of pride?" Her eyebrows went up.

"Yeah. Opposite of the walk of shame. Because I'm not ashamed of a damn thing." He bopped her gently on the nose with a finger and she rolled her eyes.

"Men. You all get to make whatever rules you want."

"Yeah, I know. It sucks. And I wish I didn't have to do

the stroll of pride or any other walking away from you today, but duty calls."

"Do you have time for breakfast?"

"No. I wish I did." He could see that scene unrolling in front of him, the cozy breakfast in her sunny kitchen, refilling her coffee, taking her back to bed...

She nodded, unaware of the way he was mentally rearranging both of their lives, and turned to rummage in a cupboard. Unearthing a travel mug, she filled it with rich-smelling, caffeinated goodness. "How do you take it?"

"That's perfect just like it is." He took it and just gazed at her for a few heartbeats. God, she was beautiful. A pang shot through him when he recalled that she wasn't truly his. But she kept making it clear that their agreement was definitely holding true. "See you Tuesday night for the next self-defense thing?"

"Sure thing." And with that, she rose up on her toes, grabbing the back of his neck and planting a quick kiss on his lips. "Be safe out there, okay?"

"Yes, ma'am." The grin on his face took him all the way to the station, past his catcalling, whistling coworkers and straight into the shower.

After he left, Eva fed Timmy before throwing some clothes on and taking him for his walk. Realizing upon their return that she hadn't seen her phone since the evening before, she found it in her purse. A notification on the screen said that her mother had called her several times the night before. One voice mail.

"Ugh." Eva heaved out a sigh and tapped to listen. Her mother's voice was sharp and displeased.

"Eva, this is your mother. I simply cannot believe how rude you and that…young man were this evening. Your father was deeply upset. And now you're not taking my call. I just don't know what to think. This is not how we raised you. Call me when you stop sulking."

Wow. This was one hell of a reframing job. Her parents had apparently managed to construct an entire alternate reality around last evening. She worried her lower lip with her teeth, thinking. She had about twenty-five percent battery life at this point. If she called her mom now, the phone might quit mid-tirade.

Well, okay. That could work.

She tapped her mother's contact info and only had to wait two rings before her mother got on the line. "Eva, thank goodness. I was starting to worry."

Years ago she might have been lulled by that opener. But she'd been the child of this woman for a few too many decades to fall for it. "Okay," she said.

"Your father is expecting an apology from you."

A surge of anger flowed through her. "Well, he can expect for a lot longer, because I have nothing to apologize for. You guys were the snobby ones who insulted my boyfriend. I'd say I expect an apology from you, but I'm not delusional."

There was a long beat of shocked silence from her mother. "I don't for one moment believe that that…*relationship* will last. You have nothing in common."

Eva didn't even try to hold back the bark of laughter that

roared out of her. Oh, they had tons of compatibility. And they'd proven it very handily last night.

"And did you say something about Darren *cheating*? What did you do to make him do that?"

Her laughter turned instantly back to rage. Inspired by the way she'd unloaded on her parents the night before, she took a deep breath. "Okay, Mom. I've really had about enough of everything. I am not responsible for Darren's infidelity. That's on him, one hundred percent. The fact that you would support his lying, cheating, gaslighting ass over your own daughter is just the latest thing *you* should be apologizing for. But because, as I said, I'm not delusional, I'm not going to hold my breath. I'm going to get off the phone now before I really say something I regret. Have a *wonderful* time with all of Dad's awful former colleagues. Goodbye."

As she briskly tapped the screen to end the call, Eva had a small pang of regret for the days where you could slam the handset of a landline down into the cradle.

Sean got to the second self-defense class and stopped just inside the door, blinking. They'd had about a dozen students before. But now there were at least two times that many. *Am I in the right room*? he thought. But yeah, he recognized several faces from the last session.

Behind him came a low whistle. He turned and saw Eva, blue eyes wide and staring. "What's going on?" she asked.

"Just got here myself. Seems like we're a popular destination these days."

The student who'd asked to record them the week before

bounced up to them then, face shining with glee. "You guys are like, *famous*."

Eva stepped forward to stand beside Sean, her face pale. "We're what?"

The student handed her phone to Eva. Sean bent over to look at the screen where the TikTok upload of the video she'd taken of them was playing. "See the comments?" the student asked, practically dancing.

Sean followed her pointing finger and his eyes nearly bugged out. The number under the comments icon was over a thousand. Eva glanced up at him, her expression questioning, then looked back at the phone and tapped the icon. Sean scrubbed the back of his neck as she scrolled. There was some variety to the sentiments, but mostly it was variations on:

Holy crap. They're hot.

CHEMISTRY FOR DAYS.

I need the movie about their love story like, yesterday. Inject it into my veins.

Cutest. Couple. Ever.

"Um…" Eva was more at a loss for words than he'd ever seen her. She handed the phone back gingerly, as if it was a bomb and she wasn't sure if she'd cut the correct wire. "That's… I don't know what to say."

"The internet loves you," the girl gushed, her gaze swiveling between the two of them.

Sean shook his head as if to clear it, then looked at Eva, laughing a little. "I really don't know what to do with that, but okay. I guess if people think we have chemistry maybe they're also learning about keeping themselves safe?" And if even perfect strangers thought he had chemistry with Eva, he must be even more obvious about how he felt than he'd thought before.

She punched him lightly on the biceps. "Way to see the silver lining, big guy. I guess we'd better get this show on the road?"

"Anything for our adoring fans." He winked at Eva and the student nearly swooned.

"You guys. Not fair. I wasn't recording!"

Eva held up a hand. "No personal recordings, Madison. Just the self-defense stuff. We don't want our privacy to be invaded."

The young woman pursed her lips to the side. "Okay. Sorry. I guess I got a little carried away at how great you guys are together. I totally ship it."

Sean, at a loss for what that meant, looked at Eva helplessly. "I'll explain later," she murmured.

Eva was wiped by the time they wrapped up the lesson. Sean? He was fresh as a freaking daisy.

"Thanks for a great session everyone," he called out, needing to raise his voice above the excited chatter of the students. The energy at this session was off the charts, starting out giddy, then getting more serious as they did a review of last week's moves and then continued to additional, more advanced maneuvers. Now they were giddy again. "Remember," he said, cupping his hands around his mouth. "The key to successfully performing any of these moves is practice. If you're rusty, you're more likely to freeze up, and every second counts, especially those early ones."

The student who'd taken video of them gave him a thumbs-up and started doing something with her phone—editing, probably—this kind of social media wasn't exactly in Eva's wheelhouse.

"Ready to go?" Eva asked, approaching him with a hesitancy she told herself was about possible cameras and not about the way all-too-real emotions seemed ready to bubble up inside her.

"Do we have a thing planned?" he asked, looking genuinely distressed.

"Oh, no. We didn't have anything planned. I'm sorry. I shouldn't have assumed—"

He cut her off with a raised hand. "No worries. I was just concerned I'd forgotten something."

"If you have somewhere you need to be or whatever..." Had she babbled this badly once in the last decade? She really didn't think she had.

He shook his head, grinning. "Nope."

"Okay, then," she said, a shy smile creeping across her face. How was he so perfect? Was it part of the act? Not liking that idea, she dug in her gym bag. "Oh, I have another book recommendation for you. Romantic suspense. This one has no fewer than two happily-ever-afters. And also a tragic World War II story." She handed over the paperback. "Fair warning, though. It's the beginning of a very long series and if you're like I am about potato chips..."

"Can't eat just one," he replied, checking out the back cover. "You're not just pandering to my male insecurities by giving me a book that stars Navy SEAL teams, are you?"

"Nope. These happen to be particular favorites of mine, I'll have you know. I'm really not sure how the author managed to keep all the story lines going the way she did. Over decades."

His eyebrows went up as he tucked the book into his bag. "Impressive. Now, want to go get a drink? I could murder a beer."

"Sure." She glanced around at the few straggling students who remained, but thankfully, nobody seemed to be paying much attention to them. While she wanted—no, more than wanted—to touch Sean, she had been unnerved by the social media comments about their chemistry. *Don't be such a fool. This is exactly what you wanted. The more people who believe this is real, the better the chances Darren will leave you alone finally.*

That was what she had to keep telling herself anyway, because this becoming really *real* was far too much to hope for.

Fifteen

They returned to the same quiet bar from their first meetup, with the same unobtrusive bartender, and settled onto stools. Sean took a sip of his beer, checking Eva out from the corner of his eye. She'd seemed kind of skittish this evening, so he'd been surprised when she asked to do something. She'd been quiet in the truck, but was definitely calmer now as she sampled her own drink. He hadn't let himself hope that she'd want to do something that wasn't for show, but now that they were here, alone—no cameras, no witnesses, he allowed himself to enjoy a tiny crumb of pure happiness.

"I have a question for you. I think I have some ideas about it, but I'm interested to know what you think," he said.

She lifted her eyes to his then, her expression surprised. "Shoot."

"So the whole concept of the *grand gesture*. It's kinda weird to me. What do you think?"

She gave him a tight-lipped smile and her head tilted speculatively. Somehow, he knew she'd shifted into professor mode. It was sexy as hell. "Why don't you tell me what you think first?"

He shifted on his seat. "Well, a lot of it seems like a performance. And if you're a performer, the audience is watching you, right? But if you're trying to apologize, to win someone back, shouldn't the focus be on them? Something about the whole thing just doesn't seem right." The whole public nature of it also didn't sit right with him, but he couldn't quite put his finger on why yet.

She nodded, setting her glass down in the very center of the cardboard coaster the bartender had given her. "Excellent point. Yes, a lot of times the characters who need to make a grand gesture seem to go for the *grand* while forgetting about the *gesture*. But a good grand gesture can be tiny. What it needs is specificity."

God, he loved bringing out this side of her. Seeing her eyes light up because she was talking about something she cared about. "What kind of specificity?"

"Specificity of the person they're making the grand gesture *for*. Without specificity, you're making a grand gesture *at* someone, and as you said, the focus is on the person doing, not the person receiving. And the person receiving is also often in need of an apology. So sometimes the grand gesture is a simple apology. A grovel."

"So what kind of grand gesture is a good one?"

She took a sip of her drink, considering. "It's rooted in the person it's directed toward. What they want. What, maybe, they were denied. Take the example of a historical novel where a character wasn't allowed to ride horses by their parent. The reasons don't matter. Fear, control, whatever. But they want that horse. They want to ride so badly. And when the love interest presents them with a beautiful, perfectly trained mare in the last quarter of the novel, that's a good grand gesture. Because it's about what they want, what they've been denied. What they deserve." Her mouth twisted a little and he wondered what she'd been denied.

"And what's a good example of a bad one?"

She took another contemplative sip. "Besides what Darren did, you mean?"

"Yeah, that whole thing was *definitely* about him and not you."

"Well, it is a good example of a bad one. But that's also just my take. I overheard people saying that they thought it was very romantic. Then again, they didn't know the context. Then again-again, to a reader who did have the context it might not matter."

"Why not?"

She shrugged one shoulder and gave him a weary smile. "For some people, the hero can do no wrong."

Sean's brows drew together. "How can anyone do no wrong? I mean, I guess I get it if it's your kid or your spouse or something, but a fictional character?"

Good Lord, but empathy was sexy.

"Well, I think a lot of it is just the patriarchy in general—you know, how men get bonus points just for showing up?" Eva examined Sean's expression, hoping he wouldn't get defensive, but his face remained open and receptive. "I mean, women have objectified actual murderers on death row. I've said before that the bar is in the Mariana Trench. But also, I think some readers just think about roles and not the characters behind those roles. They'll sometimes hate heroines who behave like they don't know they're heroines."

"How does that work?"

"Characters who are hostile or reject the hero out of hand when they first meet. I happen to love those kinds of characters when they're written with a real motivation for their anger. One of my favorites is this tiny little rage-nugget of a woman who moves to a town and absolutely rejects the handsome cowboy next door. Like, slams the door in his face when he's trying to be friendly. But you find out she's got really good reasons for not trusting anyone. Her prickliness makes a lot of sense once you get her backstory. And the book does a great job of having various characters show her kindness and break down some of those walls." God, she empathized with that character so much. She'd spent so much of her life just taking the bullshit that was slung at her—from her parents, from Darren—and she wished she'd taken a page from that character's book and stood up for herself earlier. Maybe she wouldn't be in this situation if she had.

But she also wouldn't be here with Sean now if she had.

"Various characters. So not just the hero."

She toasted him silently with her glass. "Point to you. One of the things that people who don't read in the genre miss out on is that, at its best, romance is about all of the relationships— family, found family, friends, coworkers—it's not exclusively about the main couple. Or sometimes more than a couple."

His eyebrows lifted at that and she nodded. "Relationships

with multiple partners can work. It's not for everyone, and it wouldn't work for me in real life, but I often read about successful relationships that wouldn't work for me for a variety of reasons."

"Sounds complicated."

"Of course it's complicated. People are complicated. And relationships have people in them."

"Sometimes more than two, I've heard." His eyes twinkled as he sipped his beer.

"How did we start on grand gestures and end up on ménage?" she muttered.

Sean's large hand landed on her thigh and squeezed, sending a rush of heat through her. "Stick with me, honey. We're going places."

Sean didn't miss the slight flare of Eva's pupils as he squeezed her leg. That tiny evidence of interest, of lust, was enough to make him want to haul her into his lap and make out with her right here on the bar stool.

Since he couldn't really do that, he said, "Hey, so there's a fundraiser we're doing for charity at the county fair this weekend. We might need some help with taking money, keeping the line in order, that kind of thing. You think you might want to volunteer? I know it's last minute, but—"

She put her hand over his. "You're already doing so much for me and you think I wouldn't volunteer for your charity event? Give me the time and the place and, if necessary, the T-shirt."

He flipped his hand so that they were palm to palm and

brought it to his lips. "Done. I'll text you the details. I wouldn't have asked, but one of my colleagues has kids and they've all come down with something, and..."

Eva's hand tightened on his. "You don't need to explain why you need help. Just tell me and if I can be there, I will."

Something in his chest seemed to grow warm and dangerously fluid at her words. The simple way she put herself there for him. This reciprocity was something new, something special for him. "Is this a grand gesture?" he asked.

Something he couldn't name flickered across her face. "Did I do something wrong? A grand gesture usually implies that the person doing it screwed up somehow and needs to make amends."

He squeezed her hand. God, he'd been in her bed just a few nights ago. And now touching her hand in public felt like an even bigger intimacy. It made this staged relationship feel spontaneous and real. "No. You didn't do anything wrong. I just want to make sure you know that you don't owe me anything."

"Um... Pretty sure I do. You pretending to be my boyfriend to fend off Darren, going to that awful cocktail party, meeting my *parents*. Best fake boyfriend ever. Ten out of ten, no notes. I totally owe you."

Fake. That word gutted him, grounded him. He had to keep reminding himself that she wasn't his. They could talk, touch, laugh, kiss. That didn't make any of it real. Time to change the subject. "So you promised you'd explain what your student meant by *shipping it.*"

A tiny smile curved her lips. "Ah. Yeah. So that's when

you see two characters on a television show or other piece of media and want to see them together."

"Like buying into a romance on screen?"

"Sometimes, but usually it's more about either one that's implied or one that the viewer wants to see. Like Mulder and Scully on *The X-Files* or Kirk and Spock on the original *Star Trek*."

"Old school."

"Oh, it happens in modern media, too. Lots of people very keen to see Steve Rogers and Bucky Barnes get together."

He felt his eyebrows go up at that. Clearly, there were lots of ways of approaching media he hadn't had a clue about before today. "But we're real. We're not some characters played by actors on a screen."

She tilted her head, acknowledging the point. "Yeah, but how we view media can color the way we interact with the real world. It can also have a bit of a dehumanizing effect when it happens. As you say, we're real. But I think the way Madison meant it is she's just rooting for us to get together in the way you do for people in real life. So more about language shifting from a very specific context to a more general one."

Well. He had to agree with Madison there. They enjoyed each other's company; they had chemistry for days; they just made *sense* as a real couple to him. He shipped the two of them like hell.

Eva had to get off this topic. The more they talked about their imaginary relationship, the more charming Sean got. His curiosity was both compelling and endearing. And it was every flavor of ironic that her student was "shipping" an imaginary relationship. They actually might as well be characters on Madison's television screen.

She finished her drink and placed the glass on the bar. "Anyway. We should probably call it a night."

Sean just nodded and lifted a finger for the tab, waving her away when it came and placing a couple of bills on the bar. "Let's get out of here." He took her hand as they walked out and Eva's stomach gave a little quiver of longing. Foolish stomach. Foolish quiver.

Foolish her for longing for more when Sean was just being an all-around fantastic guy. She should be grateful for what she had.

They drove back to the university in silence and Sean pulled in next to her car. She'd parked under a light in the faculty parking lot, but he still insisted on getting out and looking the car over. Then he stopped, rubbing his chin, looking at her passenger side front tire.

"You have a flat," he told her.

"What?" She hurried around to look at it, but yes. The tire was a pancake, puddled under the rim. "Well, shit."

"Can you pop the trunk so I can get the spare?" he asked.

She gave him a look that she hoped communicated the fact that she knew the spare was a dud and hadn't done anything about it. He opened his mouth, but she held up a finger. "Don't say it." She pulled out her phone and called roadside assistance. The attendant told her that a tow truck would pick it up sometime that evening and she didn't have to wait around.

"Can I bother you for a ride home?" Eva asked Sean as she tucked the phone back into her purse.

"Yeah. I think I want to make another walk-through of your house, too."

"Um... Okay." She wasn't sure what to make of his serious demeanor, of the way he scanned the parking lot as he let her back into his truck. "It's just a flat," she said as he took another circuit of her car. "I probably picked up a nail or something on my way in."

"Humor me," he said, his jaw tight.

"Oh-kay..." A sort of sick tension was gathering in her gut. She wanted lighthearted, curious Sean back. This version, stern and suspicious, made her nervous. Not about him, but about what was making him act this way. "What do you think is going on?"

"You didn't pick up a nail. There was a gash in your sidewall. Someone slashed that tire."

"What?" How could this be happening? What even was going on? He placed a hand on her elbow, gently leading her back to his truck and letting her in. "Do we need to call the police?" she asked.

He shook his head as he pulled out. "No. They won't really have anything to go on in terms of evidence, so it's pointless."

"True." Feeling both useless and helpless and liking neither emotion, she sagged back into the seat, blowing out an explosive breath. "You think Darren did this."

A tense nod. "I do."

"Why?" The question was practically a wail.

"Control, I'm guessing." Tension radiated off him in waves,

so she gave up trying to talk about anything until they got to her house and he did a thorough walk-through, checking every room, every window, every door. Timmy followed him, his feathery tail wagging as if this was an especially fun game for him. When he'd finished, he stood in her living room, fists on his hips. "Can I stay tonight?" he asked bluntly.

Anytime, her heart wanted to wail. *Stay forever; make this real*. But even her unease wasn't enough to quell her pride, so she just tightened her jaw and nodded. Besides, she'd been so wrong about Darren. What if she was wrong about Sean?

But then his face softened and he stepped forward and wrapped his arms around her. She melted into his chest, soaking into the comfort of his solid, warm bulk, and tried not to weep. Sean wasn't like Darren.

He couldn't be.

Sixteen

They didn't make love that evening, but Sean spent most of the night with his body wrapped around Eva like he could be a suit of armor for her, protecting her from everything in her life that caused her stress or anxiety. In the morning they walked Timmy together, her neighbor Krystal joining them.

"Nice to meet you," Krystal said, giving him a very slow, very obvious up-and-down perusal that made him want to laugh despite his tension.

Krystal's huge mastiff lumbered up to sniff him, his doleful, whiskey-colored eyes and wrinkly forehead seeming to beg for pets. Sean squatted, taking the drooly jowls in both hands and massaging.

"He's going to love you forever if you keep that up," Krystal said.

"This is the kind of dog you should have," he said to Eva. "Timmy's nice and all, but he's not exactly set up to do damage to anyone."

"Who needs damaging?" Krystal asked, her brows snapping together.

"One of my tires got slashed last night. Sean thinks it was Darren," Eva said, sounding weary. He'd held her until she fell asleep last night, but when he'd woken at around two in the morning, he could tell from her breathing that she hadn't stayed that way. Neither of them had had a good night.

"Christ, Eva. Do you need to come stay with me for a while?" Krystal asked. "Because you absolutely can."

Eva shook her head, sighing as Sean rose and they all set out in unspoken accord. "No. Sean had me change the locks and he also did a thorough check of the house last night. If it was Darren, which I'm not sure of—"

I am, Sean thought savagely.

"It has to be some sort of tantrum. He's not exactly a master criminal or anything."

"Honey." Krystal laid a hand on Eva's arm. "Almost none of them are. That doesn't mean you're safe."

Sean clocked Krystal's earnest face, the huge dog and the knowledgeable look in her eye. *Ah, shit.* This poor woman knew what Eva was going through. From experience.

As if she could read his thoughts, Krystal shot him a look that clearly said, *Watch out for our girl.*

Sean intended to.

Eva could scream at the way Krystal and Sean were fussing over her safety and security. In more normal times, both of these two would be charming and funny, making everyone laugh.

Now? They seemed to be bonding over the fact that her ex was the worst sort of jackass. Possibly a criminal one, not that they could prove that. She wished she could believe it was just some random, malevolent act, nothing personal. But she couldn't. When they parted at the end of their walk, Krystal's eyes were worried, and Eva hated being a source of stress for her friend.

"Let me make you breakfast," Eva said as she let them into her house. "Unless you have to run off again…" She hated the way her stomach seemed to twist around itself at that idea.

"No. I can hang around for a while. Hopefully long enough to take you to where they have your car. If they've been able to replace your tire, that is."

"Right." God, she'd tried so hard not to be a burden to this man who had already done her so many favors. Feeling more weary than she had since the split with Darren, she crouched to unclip Timmy's leash. Her dog, apparently sensing her emotional state, wagged his tail and tried to lick her face. "Thanks, sweetie, not now," she said, pushing his muzzle away.

"Hey." Sean's strong hand caught hers as she stood, then pulled her to him, an echo of the night before. God, the comfort of his body. Her hands explored his back muscles as he pulled her close. The words *I could fall for you* were on the tip of her tongue, but she resolutely kept them inside her mouth.

Now wasn't the time for that kind of truth telling. As much as they got along, their age difference was going to come into play at some point. This whole scary situation made her feel so tired, so *old*. And here he was, vibrant and full of life and making her feel like he was ten years younger, not five.

Taking a deep breath, she pulled back and gave him the brightest smile she could muster. "Breakfast?"

Eva was most definitely not okay and Sean wanted to pull Darren apart at the seams like a rag doll. But that wasn't on the table, so instead he followed her to the kitchen, sitting on a tall stool at her island and watching her perform. There was no other word for it. Her expression was oddly neutral. Her movements were quick and sure. She made him a perfect omelet and toast, putting the plate in front of her like a prize. When he didn't pick up his fork right away, she nodded at it. "Eat it while it's hot. I'll make another for myself in a minute." He dug in. The woman had a way with eggs, which were perfectly cooked and delicious, wrapped around a ham and cheese filling. Together with the sourdough toast, it was possibly the best breakfast he'd ever had.

Watching her move around her small kitchen, he imagined for a moment that this was his life, their life, together. This cozy domesticity might be his for the asking if he could get her to move beyond seeing what they had as a fake scenario. Because it sure as hell felt real to him and was feeling more real every moment they were together.

But now wasn't the moment to bring this up, not when she was under so much stress. Adding to it by declaring his feelings would only compound her worries. Finally, she sat next to him and quietly consumed her own breakfast. He got up to refill their coffee cups and tried not to stare at her, wanting nothing more than to wrap her up, keep her safe and out of the world.

Her phone chimed with a message and she glanced at it. "My car's ready," she said, her voice weary. She got to her feet and gathered their dishes, but stopped when Sean reached out a hand and laid it on her shoulder.

"Are you going to be able to take today off? You hardly got any sleep last night."

"If you know that then you didn't, either." Her expression went tight with concern. "That seems like it would be dangerous for you."

"It would be, but I'll go to the station and nap until we get called out. I'll be fine."

"What if you get called out right away?"

"Don't worry about me. I'll be careful. My squad is good. We look out for each other."

Her expression softened a little, easing the weary look in her eyes. "Good. I don't want to worry about you any more than I already do."

She worried about him? A tiny flame of hope flared in his chest at the thought. The very idea that he might be one-tenth as important to her as she was to him was like a shot of whiskey, warming him from the inside out.

But right now they didn't have time, even if she wasn't under so much stress. They had to get her car and he had to get to the station.

Sean did one more walk around her car, looking it over when they arrived at the garage. He even got a tire pressure gauge out of his glove compartment and checked all of them. Eva had to remind herself firmly that she couldn't get used to being taken care of like this. It was all going to go away, probably in very short order.

"Are you going to campus?" he asked her, brows lowered.

"I wasn't planning on it. I need to finish up my syllabus for the summer session class I'm teaching and I don't need to be there to do it."

"Okay. That's good. Be sure to lock your door when you get home."

She wished she could tell him he was being ridiculous, but the situation gave her a sickening feeling of *wrongness* and she couldn't summon the energy to not believe that this was happening to her. "I will. And Timmy might not be able to do damage, but he's very loud when someone rings the doorbell."

"Good. You might also research alarm systems." Her face must have shown how bleak she found that thought and he reached out and pulled her to him. "I'm sorry. I just know I'm going to worry about you when I can't be there."

She sighed, inhaling his comforting scent and rubbing the smooth cotton of his T-shirt on his back. "Don't worry too much. I don't think you should be distracted on the job."

"I can multitask."

"I know you're joking, but it seems like if you have a life-and-death job maybe you shouldn't?" she asked, tipping back in his arms to look up at him. A pang shot through her as she examined the planes and angles of his face. He looked rugged and handsome and rather absurdly young at the moment, even though his cheeks were unshaven and his expression was stern.

"Okay. I gotta get going. But maybe text me a few times over the next twenty-four hours?"

"You need proof of life?" Now it was her turn to have a joke fall more than a little flat.

One corner of his mouth hitched up. "I need proof of you. Sometimes I think you're too good to be true."

Okay, as a cheesy line, that needed work, but as a joke it was an improvement on what had come before. She was slightly relieved. Maybe their usual banter was returning. "Come back with your shield, *not* on it, Hannigan." She was all too clear on the fact that, between his fatigue and his dangerous job, that there was more than one way to lose this man.

He ducked and landed a swift kiss on her lips. "You've got it, sweetheart."

Sean *was* distracted over the next twenty-four hours. Distracted enough that Felix commented on how often he looked at his phone and Thea singsonged about him being in a tree and k-i-s-s-i-n-g. The shift was almost entirely uneventful, so at least he was able to catch a long nap. But the occasional text from Eva was like oxygen. She accompanied her messages with photos, walking him through her day visually. Her desk and laptop, with what he presumed was her syllabus on the screen. Her lunch of soup and grilled cheese. A little video of Timmy on his leash as they went for an afternoon walk.

And then there was the photo that he immediately saved to his photo roll. Because she'd sent him a selfie, squatting in her yard, with Timmy pulled up beside her, their faces side by side. Her blue eyes were direct and solemn in contrast to Timmy's perpetual bug-eyed expression and lolling tongue. But the more he looked at the photo—and, to be fair, he'd looked at it a lot since she sent it—there was a private sort of amusement and warmth underlying her expression that drew him in.

Christ, he had it bad for her.

"You look at that photo one more time and it might actually incinerate," Felix noted dryly behind him. Sean turned in the armchair he'd been relaxing in, taking in his friend's amused face. "Don't get me wrong. It's a very decent selfie of a very pretty woman. But isn't it imprinted on your retinas by now?"

Sean sighed and resolutely got to his feet, jamming the phone into his pocket. "Yeah. She's kind of imprinted on me in all kinds of ways."

"Is it still fake? What you're doing?" Felix asked.

Sean rubbed the back of his neck. "Yeah. She makes it pretty clear that's the deal in what feels like every other conversation."

Felix groaned. "I wish I'd never brought up the whole fake-dating thing. I should have known you'd end up getting your heart in a meat grinder."

The idea of not having what—well, whatever—he had with Eva seized him like panic. Was he setting himself up to be hurt? Yeah, probably. He still wouldn't trade it for anything. "I'm fine."

Felix looked at him like he was about to argue, then seemed to decide against that. "Okay. We're all set for the county fair thing this weekend, right?"

Sean snapped his fingers, remembering. "Yeah. And Eva's going to be helping out with the cash box. We've got some extra T-shirts, right?"

Felix's eyebrows flew up at that. "Oh, she's helping, huh? That's interesting."

"She's a good person." Sean wasn't sure why his shoulders had gone into a defensive hunch, but they had.

"I'm sure she is. But there are a lot of good people who still wouldn't volunteer to hang out on a sweltering day—Capitol Weather Gang says it's going to be an early scorcher—to help their *fake* boyfriend."

Sean's back teeth clenched. "What are you saying, Felix? Talk to me like I'm five."

His friend shrugged. "I'm just saying you may not be the only one who's overinvested in this thing."

"Didn't you hear what I said about how she talks about the fake-ness a lot?" It hurt that she had to continually remind him of it. He knew what the deal was.

Felix sent him a serene smile. "Loud and clear, cupcake. And maybe the lady's protesting too much."

Seventeen

On Saturday Sean arrived at Eva's house bright and early with a T-shirt that advertised the fundraiser. "I washed it, so don't worry. It won't be all stiff with chemicals and whatnot."

"Aww, thanks." Almost as a reflex, she brought the shirt to her nose. It smelled like Sean's laundry soap, sending tingles to her stomach. "I'll just put it on and we'll be ready to go." She retreated to her powder room to swap shirts, Sean's voice penetrating the door.

"Did you sunscreen up, woman? It's going to be sunny and hot today."

She laughed as she pulled the shirt over her head. "Sunscreen is my religion, my friend. Don't worry about it."

He muttered something that she couldn't make out, but when she emerged in her new garment, his eyes went smoky, sending even more tingles lower down. *No, don't tug me closer to that cliff. If I fall over, I might never come back.* She pasted a chipper grin on her face. "No time for that, oh, best fake boyfriend in the world," she said, grabbing a Nationals cap and threading her ponytail through the back before settling it on her head. "What's wrong?" she asked, noticing his brows had drawn together.

"Nothing. Let's get a move on."

She gave Timmy a final pat and told him to be good then followed Sean out to his truck. "So what's the deal for today?"

"Pretty simple. Five dollars a hug, all proceeds going to a children's cancer charity." *Aww.* Was there any image in the world more adorable than a hot man hugging a child?

"Wow. What about photos?"

"What about them?"

"Do you charge extra to have someone take their phone and snap a few shots of the hug as a memento?"

He nodded approvingly. "Nice idea. Maybe we'll have to do that next year. At this point, no. One hug, five bucks, no waiting."

Privately, Eva considered how much more she had gotten from Sean than mere hugs—though his hugs were nothing to sneeze at. And all for the low, low price of free. "I'm looking forward to meeting your colleagues," she said. She wondered especially about the one who'd originally recommended that first romance novel to him. She was both curious and grateful to that unknown firefighter.

"And they're looking forward to meeting you." He shot her a lopsided smile that sent her heart skittering before returning his attention to the road. "Felix especially, though Thea probably will be awfully curious, too."

"Is Felix the one who started all this?"

His chin dipped in a brief nod. "Yeah." Then his mood seemed to shift and he appeared pensive. While Eva felt like she knew Sean pretty well at this point, this apparent moodiness was something new. And concerning. She couldn't ask if something was wrong again; that would seem needy and badgering.

But something was definitely off.

"Has Darren pulled any other bullshit?" he asked. *Ah.* Maybe that was the issue. She hurried to put his mind at ease even if hers wasn't.

"No. The rest of the week has been decidedly Darren-free and therefore bullshit-free."

"Good." But the set of his expression didn't change. So maybe that wasn't the issue.

"I know you said nothing's wrong, but you seem kind of, I don't know…off."

His lips tightened and he seemed to be wrestling with something.

"I mean, I don't want to pry if it's too personal or anything, but if I can help in any way, I will."

If I can help in any way, I will. Oh, damn. She could help by being half as crazy about him as he was about her. The precipice of emotion loomed in front of him. Had he packed his parachute? Or was he going to land *splat* at the bottom? Only one way to find out.

Time for emotional BASE jumping.

He took in a deep breath and let it out slowly. "Okay, yeah. There's a problem. You keep saying this is fake. And yeah, I know that was the agreement. But it's feeling more and more real every day. And every time you say I'm such a great fake boyfriend I kind of die a little inside."

Out of the corner of his eye, he saw her shift, fidgeting with the seat belt. "You die a little inside?" Her voice was tiny.

He swallowed around the tightness in his throat. "Something like that."

"So it's not just me, then?"

"What?" He whipped his head sideways just long enough to see her pale face, then returned his attention to the road. "What do you mean *not just you*?"

"I've been trying so hard to say *fake* out loud to be sure I remembered where we were supposed to stand. I didn't realize I was hurting you. I'm sorry."

Hope, that foolish, wild, lumbering emotion, scrambled his chest. He reached out to clasp her hand. "Baby, no. It's okay." He squeezed and swallowed hard when she squeezed back. "That makes sense. I might have kind of done the same thing."

"Yeah. Maybe you did." Her voice sounded a little thick, as if she was fighting back tears. He pulled into an office complex parking lot, throwing the truck into Park and trying to gather him to her, both of them laughing when the seat belt held her in place. She unbuckled and he hauled her over the center console, feeling reborn as she straddled his lap and he gazed into her watery eyes.

"So we've both been trying to convince ourselves this was fake because we thought that was what the other person wanted and expected?"

She nodded, swallowing hard.

"So this is real, huh? For you, too?"

She smoothed her hand along his cheek. "Yeah. Turns out you're not the best fake boyfriend in the world."

"I'm not, huh?" Pure joy was bubbling up inside him because Eva was touching him. Touching *him*. Not fake-boyfriend-with-benefits Sean. Just Sean.

"No. You're the actual best boyfriend in the world. Nothing fake about it."

When they got to the fairgrounds, Eva's stomach did a little flip. Their first outing as a couple—a *real* couple, only minutes after they became one. It was a little absurd that this was freaking her out, but there it was. And she was going to have to meet a bunch of his coworkers at the same time.

Suck it up, buttercup, she told herself as she climbed down from the truck and followed Sean across the fairgrounds to the small tent with a table, a cash box, some chairs and a big sign that read *Hug a Firefighter for Charity: $5*.

"Sean!" She recognized the Black man from the quad. Fit, but shorter and leaner than Sean, he stepped forward and fist-bumped him. "And this is the lovely Eva. We haven't been introduced, but I do remember you." He shot her a dazzling smile and Eva's face felt like it was going up in flames. "I'm Felix, by the way."

"Um, nice to meet you. And yeah. Sorry about that whole getting your squad called out because I overreacted to my ex being a jerk."

Felix waved her comment away. "Pshaw. I'd far rather be

called out for a nothing burger like that than something where lives were lost."

"Well, when you put it that way, I guess I did you guys a favor," Eva joked, earning another bright smile. "But honestly, I'm usually a model citizen."

"And you're proving that by showing up to help us out today. Very model citizen of you."

Sean gave an exasperated growl. "Are you going to keep flirting with my girlfriend, or are we going to get things set up here?"

"We're all set. No need to get your panties in a wad. Eva, since you're going to be taking the money for the first shift, this cash box is your domain. We have a setup with the fair organizers that if we need change, we can send someone to the management office to get it. So if you start to get low, just let one of us know and we'll handle it."

"Sounds pretty simple," Eva said. "I might be an English teacher, but I can definitely make change in five-dollar increments. That much math is okay."

"Good sport," Felix said. "And let me know if you need a bathroom break." He pointed to a big Coleman cooler. "Bottles of water are in there. Keep hydrated, because it's going to be a hot one. And I don't just mean the women who'll be lined up to hug that big lunk."

Eva, who'd been focused on the logistics of volunteering, suddenly froze. Because there would be other women, not just cute kids. Hugging Sean. And she was going to have to watch it for four long hours. Those big arms and broad chest were *hers* to touch, dammit. Not anyone else's.

Suddenly, volunteering for this seemed like a terrible idea.

She realized Felix was studying her face carefully and she tried to smile, though the expression felt forced and unnatural and probably wouldn't fool a first-grader. "Sean's popular at these things, I'd imagine."

Felix rolled his eyes. "You have no idea. If we did one of those charity calendars and he was Mr. January, I don't think anyone who bought one would know what day it was come February. They'd just never turn the page. Forever."

"Ha." Yeah. Eva wouldn't have fooled a toddler with this act.

Felix sidled closer. "I thought your deal was fake. But you don't seem like it is."

"Yeah. It was. It isn't anymore."

"*Yesss.*" Felix gave a little fist pump and raised his palm for a high five. When her palm smacked into his, he said, "Great taste, my new friend."

"What tastes great?" A woman with a short crop of dark hair and huge brown eyes had arrived and was looking from Eva to Felix and back again.

"Sean, apparently," Felix said. And this time Eva smacked him in the shoulder while he ducked away, laughing.

Sean had never minded the hug-a-firefighter event. After all, it was a minimal effort for a good cause. And it beat those "put your cash in a boot" things where the squad hung out at a highly trafficked intersection and roamed around at every red light, trying to get their enormous boots brimful with cash. He always felt like he was going to get lung cancer from inhaling all the exhaust at those things. Not to mention they always seemed to be scheduled on the hottest, most humid day of the year.

But he could see that Eva, despite making bright conversation with his colleagues and the customers, wasn't particularly happy with seeing him hug other people. If they hadn't had their moment in the parking lot an hour ago, he might have even felt glad about that jealousy. But they had, and the idea that he was making her unhappy in any way fell very squarely in the not-good column.

When they had a lull, he slipped over to where she stood at the cash box and wrapped his arms around her from behind, kissing the top of her head.

"Giving me a freebie, huh?" she asked, and his heart nearly broke from the feeble approximation of her usual sassy tone.

"Anytime for you. You're not loving this, huh?"

She twisted slightly, looking up at his face, astonishment shining in her eyes. "I... No. It's embarrassing to admit, but I don't love seeing you hug other people."

He gave her a little squeeze. "I get it. If the roles were reversed, I'd be feeling very off about it. I'm sorry. I wouldn't have asked you to help out, but we weren't official then, and I didn't think you'd care."

She frowned a little, thinking. "That's the weird thing. I've never been jealous before. And I don't even think it's jealousy, exactly. It's more like, I don't know, a weird kind of possessiveness."

He would be an absolute liar if that statement didn't make him want to grin like the cheesiest bastard ever. God, but this woman was it. He knew it in that moment. He wasn't just thrilled to be in a relationship with her; he was falling in love with her.

"Only another hour or so. Then my arms are yours, one hundred percent."

"Considering the fact that I'm a huge fan of your arms, I'm going to hold you to that."

"*Hold* me to it? Puns? And here I thought you were a classy dame."

She smacked him lightly on the chest as someone approached the booth. "Get back to work, slacker. You've got charity money to raise."

And the smile she gave him as he walked away was so full of wicked promise, it made plans bloom in his mind like a garden.

Eighteen

"I think my feet are two sizes bigger from standing," Eva groaned as Sean pulled up in front of her house.

"Want me to rub them for you?" he asked, shooting her a sly grin that seemed to arrow straight down to her groin. When they'd finished their volunteer shift, they'd taken a walk around the fairgrounds, eating funnel cake and taking in the sights, including the pig races. Eva had forgotten how much she loved the pig—piglet, really—races. They were so silly and cute. Sean apparently felt the same, because his face went all soft like he found the tiny creatures adorable as well.

"You definitely don't want to get anywhere near my feet until I've had a chance to take a shower," she said as they got out of the truck. She could hear Timmy barking inside the house. "Oh, and I have to walk his royal highness before I can do that."

He stopped her with a gentle hand on her shoulder before she could unlock the front door. "Let me do that. You go and take a leisurely shower. I'll do a speed walk with the Timster."

She nearly collapsed in a puddle at the unexpected reprieve. It wasn't like walking Timmy was a burden or difficult or anything, but to have that task suddenly taken off her shoulders? In that moment it felt like the biggest luxury she could imagine. "You'd do that for me?"

"I'd do far more than that. I think you should know that by now," he told her, his eyes shining with sincerity, making her insides scramble.

"Okay. Thank you." She let them inside and clipped Timmy's leash to his collar. Timmy gave her a confused look when she handed it off to Sean and she crouched and gave him one of his massage/rubs. "You go and be good for Sean. Then later I'll give you your dinner." Still clearly confused, Timmy went quietly with Sean and she closed the door, leaning on it for a few breaths. She needed to mark this date on her calendar: the date everything changed.

Pushing away from the door she went upstairs, turned on the shower and stripped off her sweaty clothing, jamming it into her laundry hamper. Her shirt definitely no longer smelled like Sean's laundry soap. In the shower, she scrubbed what felt like every inch of her body and started to revive like a wilting plant being watered. Out of the shower, her hair in a towel turban, she moisturized and wrapped herself in her robe. Okay. Now she felt human again.

The sound of her front door opening and closing then the jingle of Timmy's tags and the click of his nails on the hardwood made her smile. This was so cozy and domestic, and nothing she'd ever thought she'd experience with Sean.

Then he was there, filling up the doorway to her bathroom, making her smile. "You look very fancy, lady."

She laughed, glee bubbling up in her like a fountain. "In my bathrobe and with a towel on my head?"

He stepped forward, stockinged feet making no noise on the tile. He must have taken his shoes off in the entryway. That small consideration sent a little thrill through her. "You look gorgeous in anything. But I like you best in nothing at all. Take everything off and take your sweet behind to the bed. I'll clean up and be right with you."

Heat bloomed between her thighs. That slight edge of bossiness? She would never have thought that would do it for her.

But like the way he called her *baby*, it did. It so did.

Sean took the world's fastest shower, erotic imaginings streaming through his brain in high definition. Eva was in the next room. Naked.

When he emerged, clean and dry and sporting an erection that could qualify as a load-bearing beam, he found her on her back, damp hair streaming across the pillows, looking at him with those gorgeous eyes that absolutely undid him every single time he saw her.

"You said you have plans?" she asked, tracing a finger over the top curve of one breast.

"More every second." His voice was rough, raspy and her pupils flared. "In fact..." He gripped his shaft and gave it a few long, slow strokes, gratified with the way her hips shifted as she watched him.

"You going to use that on me or are you going to stay over there by yourself?" Where had that sex-kitten voice come from? Wherever it had, he liked it.

"Well," he said, stalking over to the bed and stretching himself out on top of her plank-style so just the tip of his dick touched her. "I was thinking something like this." He dropped onto her and rolled so she was on top, enjoying the rich sound of her laugh. "Sit up, baby." She tucked her knees under her and sat on his abs, then gasped when he grabbed her butt and lifted, sliding down so he could look straight at her glorious pussy. She smelled delicious, too, like clean skin and aroused woman. He guided her down to his mouth and began a slow, teasing series of licks, relishing the shudder that went through her thighs. She moaned and he smiled, rewarding her with a little flutter on her clit. A gasp. Another reward.

Her hands thudded onto the headboard and she said, "Is that your way of saying you want me to be vocal?"

He hummed in approval and slowly pushed a finger in as he returned to the slow licks. She trembled and moaned and he sped up, hooking his finger forward.

"Oh, God. *Sean.*"

There's my smart girl, he thought, giving her another flutter and another finger. His dick throbbed with want, nearly painful. But he knew he'd get satisfaction later. By now she was moving, riding his mouth and his hand, so tense and glorious and *his* that he felt like the king of the universe. She was also chanting his name like it was some sort of ritual or prayer. He pushed a third finger in, pumping steadily, and clamped her hip with his other hand, giving her clit an all-out assault with his tongue that had her keening and shaking and shattering, the flavor of her release flooding his mouth. One final shudder rippled through her body and she slid her hips back, his fingers sliding out, to sit on his chest, then sliding farther until she could touch her lips to his.

"Oh, my God, you magnificent man. That was the best orgasm of my *life*."

Yes, ladies and gentlemen. Emperor of the universe.

She was a secret sex goddess. That had to be it. It was the only reasonable explanation for the fact that this man, this *delicious*, wonderful man, was hers. And had just laid waste to her body in the most astonishing way she had ever experienced. The aftershocks were still reverberating through her and she felt both wrung out and energized.

"Don't turn into a puddle on me now, sweetheart," he said, giving her butt a stinging slap that chased away the wrung-out feeling and sent a zing up her spine. "You gave me some ideas a few minutes ago."

"*I* gave *you* ideas?" she asked, her voice veering dangerously close to a giggle. What the hell was it about this man that he turned her into a *giggler*?

He nodded solemnly, grabbing her wrists and lifting them. "Hands on the headboard."

Ooh, that slight bossy edge. Her inner muscles clenched and she gripped the headboard, lifting her hips to let him slide out from under her. She heard the sound of a condom wrapper ripping and turned her head to treat herself to the sight of him rolling it on, letting a smile steal across her face as he looked up to see her watching. His eyes went dark and sultry, his hands slowing.

"Show-off," she said.

"When the audience is so appreciative it's hard not to," he replied.

"Fair. Because I am appreciative."

He leaned forward and dragged the tip of his cock through her folds. "So am I," he said, his voice a whisper that seemed to trail across her skin like a feather, making her shiver. Then he began to push inside her so slowly that she wanted to scream. But when she tried to lean back into him, he merely gripped her hips and held her still, continuing his gradual slide. Torture. That was the only reason why he'd do this. He'd had *three* fingers inside her, after all. She was ready. More than ready. When he finally bottomed out, he slid his hands from her hips up her back and she arched like a cat being petted. "My beautiful girl. Do you know how glad I am that this is real?"

The vulnerability in his voice shredded her. She turned her head and her gaze met his. That same raw emotion was there in his face and he bent to kiss her, their tongues playing as his hips started a small, pulsing beat. She broke the kiss with a groan, dropping her head between her arms so she could brace against the longer, stronger thrusts he was now giving her. She closed her eyes, giving herself over to the sensation of his cock sliding in and out of her, the sound of their flesh slapping together, the smell of sweat and arousal.

When he reached an arm around her and found her clit with his fingers, she shuddered as he strummed her in the same rhythm as his thrusts. This orgasm took her by surprise, sending her trembling and shattering and clenching just moments before he locked up behind her, groaning and shaking until they both slid onto the bed in a warm, satisfied heap. He was hers. She was his. And she'd never been happier in her life.

He had to get off Eva. The poor woman must be suffocating under his weight. But when he lifted himself up and settled in next to her, she gave a little whimper.

"I wasn't crushing you?" he asked as he plucked tissues from a box on her nightstand and took care of the condom.

"No." She turned her face toward his and he felt a little jolt of pride at the loopy, satisfied expression on her face. She snuggled in beside him and he wrapped an arm around her, rolling to his back and dragging her half onto his chest.

"This okay, then?"

"Very." She put her lips to the center of his chest, kissing him softly and making his heart feel like it was going to burst.

"You make me very, very happy, you know that?" he asked.

"Me, too."

It was at that tender moment that Sean's stomach gave an aggressive growl. He laughed, bouncing Eva's head on his chest. "Guess that funnel cake is not holding down the fort anymore," he said.

"I can see what I have in the fridge." Eva's voice had a hazy dreaminess to it that said she was still in a post-sex fog.

"Nah. Let's just order something. That takes less thinking and no cooking."

"Genius." She stirred and he let her go, admiring the line of her back as she sat on the edge of the bed and stretched.

Rolling to his feet, he found enough garments to make himself decent in front of a delivery driver and put them on while Eva did the same and then he had Yelp show him the delivery options in her area. "Pizza good for you?"

"Very. What do you take on yours?" There was a sly expression on her face.

"Ooh. Is this going to be the first relationship hurdle? What is your stance on pineapple? Let's have it."

The expression on her face said it all. Wrinkled nose, narrowed eyes, pure rejection. That's it. He was definitely in love.

He laughed. "No conflict, then. I'm not a fan. What about meat?"

She considered this. "Pepperoni and sausage, definitely. Not a big fan of meatballs on pizza. That just seems weird."

"Okay, we continue to agree. Here's the big one—anchovies."

"Hard pass."

"Olives? Mushrooms?"

"Thumbs-up to both."

"We're going to do just fine, then." He held his phone up to his ear without dialing. "Hi, yeah. I'd like a double Hawaiian with extra anchovies." She swatted weakly at his arm and he laughed, then dialed in earnest, ordering them a pie that they would both appreciate.

"How would you feel about a beer?" she asked.

"Excellent." Following her downstairs, he watched as she pulled two bottles from the fridge, opening them and handing him one, then tapping it with her own.

"Here's to great sex and pizza compatibility," she said.

"That is definitely something I can drink to."

Nineteen

The next Tuesday was the second to last class in Sean's self-defense course. Eva showed up twenty minutes early to make sure the room was ready. She hadn't seen Sean since Sunday, the morning after the fair, and she was practically buzzing with excitement to be with him again.

She hadn't expected to find Darren there, scrolling through his phone with a scowl. Her feet took immediate root on the floor. "What are you doing here?"

He looked up at her, his eyes dark with rage that set her nerves on high alert. Then he went back to scrolling.

"Darren. I asked you a question." On one hand, she was glad that there was no audience of students for this interchange. On the other, his silent presence was getting more unnerving by the moment.

Finally, he held up his phone. "Just enjoying the comments on the latest video of you with your *boyfriend*." He looked down at the screen and began to read in a sarcastic, high-pitched voice as if he was mocking a teenage girl. "OMG, these two are #goals. Look at the way they look at each other. I need a man that looks at me that way." His gaze lifted from the phone and his expression was almost bored. "I can't believe you're embarrassing yourself this way, Eva. It's ridiculous."

She forced her spine to straighten. "I can't believe you give a shit, Darren. You can leave any time."

He scoffed. "You've got to be kidding me."

"No, not kidding. Door's right there. I suggest you use it." Eva turned and pointed at the doorway, willing someone to come through it and end this farce.

But when she turned back, Darren had moved closer. She started to step back, but his hand shot out, grabbing her wrist. "Enough's enough, Eva. You've played your little game to make me jealous, but that stops now."

Eva stared pointedly at his fingers. "There's no game. Take. Your hand. Off me."

"Or what?" Then his tone shifted from challenging to coaxing. "Come on, Eva. We were good together. We can be again. You've got to be trying to make me jealous. I can't believe you are choosing that lunkhead over me."

Anxiety crawled up her spine and twisted her stomach, but she forced herself to not show it. "Darren, I would choose rancid cheese over you. I would choose explosive diarrhea over you. And once and for all, take your hand off me."

He didn't. Instead, he escalated, grabbing her other wrist. "What are you going to do about it?" How had she ever let this man into her life, her bed?

She took a deep breath, centering herself, feeling her feet

grounded the way Sean had taught her. "I'm going to give you one last warning. You don't want to test me on this." Her heart was pounding, a strange humming in her ears. Stress? Shock? Rage? Maybe all of them at once.

"Why, because your boy toy taught you some slow-motion tricks?"

"Jesus, but you're a fool," Eva said, twisting her wrists out of his grip with the speed and ease of practice. Then, for good measure, when he went to grab at her again, she stomped on his foot, then brought her knee up sharply, stopping just shy of his groin. He froze. "Don't you *ever* lay hands on anyone unwilling again. Ever."

Hoots and clapping from the doorway startled her. A small group of students stood there, one of them holding up a phone.

Well. For once, a recording of her and Darren was a good thing.

She called to the student. "Madison, you want to forward that recording to me, please?"

The student nodded, tapping her phone and giving Eva a thumbs-up.

Darren straightened and sneered. Seriously, she was getting tired of the sneering. "What, so you can advertise how you assaulted me?"

"No," Eva said. "So I can forward the evidence of *you* assaulting *me* and me needing to defend myself to the dean. You grabbed me. I asked you multiple times to let go. You didn't. I broke the hold and when I saw you were going for me again, then I bruised your instep. This is all on you."

Finally, a flare of panic flashed across Darren's face. "I have tenure," he said, but his bravado was slipping.

"Good for you. Let's see how well a system that's designed to protect academic freedom will protect a predator from the consequences of his actions. Get. Out."

When Sean arrived, the class was in an uproar. Eva stood in the center of the floor, surrounded by chattering, excited students.

"What's going on?" he asked, pitching his voice so it would boom above the din.

Eva, previously absorbed with a student, looked up and Sean took in a bunch of things at once: she was pale, her eyes looked enormous and he had never seen her look *relieved* to see him.

"Professor Perry grabbed Professor Campbell and it was so cool. She did everything you taught us," one young woman gushed.

Rage surged through Sean and he fought the urge to run his hands over Eva, to check for himself that she was really okay. "Everything?" he asked, one eyebrow shooting up. He'd taught them some fairly drastic things like eye gouging and throat punching.

Eva raised her hands as if she was seeking control over the situation. "Not everything. I just broke his hold and stomped on his foot to keep him from trying again."

"And showed him she could have nailed him in the balls if she wanted to," crowed another jubilant student. The small handful of young men who'd been taking the class grimaced and seemed to hunch a bit.

"Jesus, Eva." Sean shouldered his way through the students and wrapped his arms around her, dimly aware that the excited chatter had changed its tone a little. Coos and titters and even one whispered, *"Oh, my God, I knew it!"* He didn't care. He just cared that Eva was safe and well. She clung to him like a life preserver and it was as if something in his heart cracked open.

Easing up on his grip, he palmed her cheeks and tilted her head up at him. "You weren't hurt?" She shook her head, lips folding into her mouth. "Okay. I think we need to cancel today's class."

"Oh, heck no. I think tonight just proves how much this is needed," she said, her blue eyes blazing.

"Whatever you want." He took a deep, shuddering breath. "What are you going to do? This can't keep happening."

She shook her head and pointed at a student. "Madison got video of the whole thing. I'm sending it to the dean."

"Excellent. For once, this generation's impulse to record everything is going to do some good." Reluctantly letting go of Eva, he stepped back and addressed the class. "Okay, everyone. Let's take five minutes to get the excess adrenaline out of our systems. Everybody go outside and do one lap around the building. Fast walking, running, whatever." He tapped his watch, starting a timer. "And, *go.*" The students streamed out and then they were alone.

"Wow," Eva said, her eyes going wide. "You could have been a coach or something if you wanted to." He was happy to see that her normal color had returned to her face.

"Are you sure you want to hold the class tonight?" He had

to be sure. If Eva wanted anything, he would give it to her. The anger that had flooded his system left him feeling jittery and like he wanted to sweep her up and carry her away to someplace safe.

She gave a brisk little nod. "Absolutely. Let's show these kids how it's done."

The next morning Eva had her second meeting with the dean about Darren Fucking Perry. That was how she thought of him now, like *Fucking* was his middle name.

"Thank you for coming in," Dean Treadwell said, motioning Eva to a chair. "I can't tell you how sorry I am that this happened to you."

"It wasn't your fault," Eva said, feeling a tiny rush of relief. There had been a small part of her that was afraid that the dean would blame her instead of Darren, to take his side, to say she'd overreacted.

"Maybe not, but Professor Perry is employed by this college, and his assault of you happened on campus. I can't help but feel responsible for things that happen here, on my watch."

"Okay." Eva wasn't sure what to do with any of that. It was almost more exhausting to have Dean Treadwell take responsibility for Darren's actions. Another woman having to deal with his shit. Great. It was bad enough that she'd had to think nearly constantly about her own safety. Knowing that so many other people were involved only made it worse.

The dean steepled her fingers in front of her, elbows resting on the desk. "Obviously, I can't fire him outright since he does have tenure. But I can and will place him on administrative leave and ban him from campus pending a full investigation. I am confident that the resolution of this unfortunate event will be that Professor Perry will no longer be employed when all is said and done."

"Oh," Eva said, feeling a little light-headed. She'd hoped for a reprimand. She hadn't even known to hope for this.

"I'm going to ask you again. Will you be pursuing legal action against him?" the dean asked, her normally stern features softening.

"I... Yeah. I think I will," Eva said. She didn't know the first thing about finding a lawyer or filing a restraining order, but she would figure it out. Krystal would help her. And Sean would support her. She swallowed hard, the reality of her support network almost making her weak in the knees.

"Good. Now. Is there anything else I can do for you?"

Eva, feeling a little numb by now, shook her head. "No. Thank you. Thank you for believing me. So many times things get flipped around in situations like these."

The dean stood and moved around her desk. Reflexively, Eva also stood. The dean extended a hand to Eva to shake, saying solemnly, "Those of us who know, well. We know. And these things often only escalate."

"Oh." Eva felt like all the air had been pressed out of her lungs. The *dean*? She knew? Maybe from personal experience? This was getting surreal.

Dean Treadwell released her hand and stepped back. "Thank you again for coming to see me, Professor Campbell. I won't let you down on this."

And with that unmistakable dismissal, Eva practically fled to the sanctuary of her own office.

That evening, walking Timmy and Luther with Krystal, Eva asked, "So I know securities law has nothing to do with this, but do you know anyone who can hook me up with a restraining order?" The jokey tone she was trying to convey fell absolutely flat, and Krystal shot her a sideways look, immediately on edge.

"What happened?"

"Darren. Darren happened. He showed up where we hold the self-defense classes yesterday evening and put me in a position where I had to give him a demonstration of exactly how much I'd learned."

"Are you fucking kidding me right now?" Krystal said, fury flashing in her dark eyes.

Eva shook her head. For the first time since it happened, she felt the urge to cry. "I wish I was."

"Did he hurt you?"

"No. He just grabbed me and didn't let go when I told him to." Then, suddenly, she was crying.

Krystal's arms wrapped around her, rocking her gently, her next words low in Eva's ear. "That's scary enough. A person who will do that will usually do more than that."

She sniffed, pulling back a bit and wiping her eyes. "Yeah. A kid got video of it and the dean is going to fire him. So I've got that going for me, at least."

Krystal squeezed her again. "That's not nothing, but watch yourself. This kind of situation is where things often escalate."

"I know." Eva groaned, then crouched to pat Timmy, who'd shot her what looked like a worried expression at the unexpected noise she made. "Don't worry, doggaloo. Everything's going to be fine."

Timmy looked unconvinced. Eva straightened up and they continued their walk.

"To answer your question, though, I do have a classmate from Georgetown who's a family attorney. She can hook you up, I'm sure," Krystal said.

Eva breathed a sigh of relief. "Thank you. That's one less thing I have to think about, then."

Krystal patted her arm. "You sure you don't want to stay with me? I'm guessing your smoking-hot fireman can't exactly be around twenty-four-seven."

"No, he can't. He's on a shift now as a matter of fact."

"I don't like it, but you're grown. So that's all I'll say about that. How's that going, anyway?"

Something like a real smile tugged weakly at Eva's mouth. "Great, actually. I'm meeting his family this weekend."

"You're meeting. Your *fake* boyfriend's. Family." Krystal's tone was bone-dry.

"Oh, news flash. Not fake anymore," Eva said, a glow of pleasure spreading through her. The one and only bright spot in this entire situation was Sean. Beautiful, generous, loveable Sean was really hers. Lending her his strength and helping her to find her own.

Krystal stopped walking, Luther shooting her a nervous look. "Shut the front door. Why didn't you *lead* with that good news?"

Eva shrugged. "I don't know? The whole situation is so weird and chaotic in a way, but also sweet and lovely. He's... well, he's just great." *I think I'm falling for him*, she didn't add. Because that felt too big and too scary and too, well, *true* to say to anyone but him.

Twenty

"Ready to face the chaos?" Sean asked when she opened her door to him on Saturday afternoon. He felt keyed up and anxious, happy he was going to get to spend time with his family, but also nervous. The elder Campbells had been unpleasant, sure. But they were also very, well, quiet.

The Hannigans were decidedly not.

"Ready!" she said brightly, stepping out of her house and locking her front door.

He took a minute to appreciate the way her silky blue blouse draped over her incredible figure, the way it made her eyes even more intense. "You look pretty," he said, giving her a tender kiss and holding her hand until they got to the truck.

"Why, thank you. You look awfully handsome yourself," she replied.

It was a little absurd how proud that compliment made him. He wanted to shout to the entire world that this amazing woman had chosen him. For now, though, he'd settle for showing her off to his family.

"Any progress on that restraining order?" he asked her as he pulled out of her neighborhood.

"Yeah. I've contacted a family attorney who's a former classmate of Krystal's. She's filed something or docketed something and I'll have to go and testify, which I can't stand the idea of, but it will hopefully help."

"Good." He still wanted to find Darren and pummel him until his own mother wouldn't recognize him, but that was not an impulse he would ever be proud of.

"So what do I need to know about your family before I meet them?" she asked.

He laughed nervously. "I should probably have told you to invest in earplugs. There are a lot of us, almost as many children as adults, and it's basically mayhem."

She chuckled. "Well, that'll be a total change from my family, that's for sure."

"Yeah. It really will." Not to mention, his entire family was going to *love* her, which would be a one-eighty from the situation with him and her parents.

"What are your parents like?" she asked.

He lifted one hand and ticked off his parents' qualities on successive fingers. "Intensely Catholic, which I think you already know, very traditional, very bonkers about being grandparents. It's kind of their entire identity now."

"Oh. How many grandchildren are there anyway?" Her voice had gone a little faint.

He grimaced. "Ten."

"Ten grandchildren?" Now her tone was incredulous. *"Ten?"*

"Yeah. Maeve and Erin have three each. Bridget's an over-achiever with four. Jury's out whether or not Caitlin and Nicole will ever have them but they say no, at least for now. My folks originally seemed to think that being gay automatically meant they wouldn't have any kids, but they seem to have gotten the memo that it's a possibility, so they're still hopeful for more."

"Oh, my God," Eva said, looking a little pale. "I suppose I should have figured that people from a family of five would also have large families themselves, but it just didn't occur to me that there would be quite that many."

"Sorry. Should have warned you earlier. The rug rats are a handful, but they're all good kids." He shrugged. He'd never really thought about it. As the youngest, he'd always been a part of that big family and the way it had grown had seemed perfectly normal.

Her stare seemed to bore into the side of his head. "It's not that there are that many of them. It's the idea that for your parents having ten grandchildren *isn't enough.*"

She sounded so horrified that Sean had to laugh. "What's that quote about excess?"

"Oscar Wilde. 'Moderation is a fatal thing... Nothing succeeds like excess.'" Her voice still had that faint quality about it, though, and Sean was beginning to worry. Now that he could see his family through her eyes, he could acknowledge that it would be overwhelming for her.

"You okay over there?"

"Yeah. Yeah. I'll be fine."

"Don't worry. Uncle Sean will protect you from the ankle biters."

Her hand landed on his thigh, warm and comforting. "I have no doubt that you will."

Eva truly hadn't been prepared for the chaos that faced her when they entered Sean's parents' home. It was a solid red brick structure on a quiet street and it looked tidy, comfortable and lived in from the outside.

But inside? Inside, the foyer and hallway was an instant wall of noise and movement. It seemed like kids were everywhere. Kids in their early teens, kids in grade school and one preschooler who seemed hell-bent on making the most noise of any of them. Sean made a megaphone with his hands around his mouth. "Everybody *out!*" he hollered and the majority of them swarmed toward what Eva presumed was the backyard.

"Thank God. Now I can hear myself think," he muttered. One of the remaining teens slouched over and raised a fist for Sean to tap. "Uncle Sean. Saving the day as usual," he said.

"Aidan, my man. Make sure the kids aren't tearing up Granny and Pop's backyard?"

"On it," the kid said, and loped out.

Sean took her hand and led Eva to a large sitting room in the back of the house where it seemed a hundred people waited for them. "Sorry we're late, guys. Eva, this is my family. Family, this is Eva Campbell. My girlfriend."

The word *girlfriend* suddenly seemed absurd and wrong and too young for her and Eva felt the weight of all of those eyes land on her. She gave a weak little wave. "Hi. Nice to meet you all." Even though she hadn't met any of them yet.

Sean gave her hand a little squeeze as the man who had to be his dad got to his feet and came forward, hand outstretched. "Lovely to meet you." There was a faint haze of an Irish lilt in his voice.

His handshake and greeting was followed immediately by Sean's mother. "So sorry you had to face the chaos of all our grandbabies. I heard Sean hollering at them. Best to have them out back where they can run around to their hearts' content." Her voice was pure Boston, with its flat vowels and dropped r's. She gave a brisk little nod to her only son, her pride evident on her face. "But didn't Sean tell us you're a teacher? You must be used to children and their hijinks."

"I'm a college professor," she said. "The students are a little calmer by the time they reach my classroom."

Mrs. Hannigan beamed. "What an accomplished young lady." Eva nearly laughed. She still did occasionally get called *young* by people older than she was, but it was still odd at her age. "Call me Susan," Sean's mom commanded. "And that's Dale." She indicated Sean's dad. "And then we have my oldest, Erin and her husband, Daniel, Bridget, who's next and her husband, James, Maeve and Michael, and Caitlin and Nicole."

"There'll be a quiz later," the woman Eva barely remembered was Caitlin quipped. She was tall and with her dark hair and green eyes could have been Sean's fraternal twin. In general, the family resemblance in the room was strong, but it seemed strongest between them. Or maybe it was just because she knew Sean was closest to Caitlin out of all of his sisters.

The others gathered in what amounted to an odd, informal sort of receiving line and Eva shook hands, murmured,

"Happy to meet you" what felt like a dozen times and felt quite dazed by the entire Hannigan experience.

If there was truly a quiz later, she was going to flunk it.

After making sure everyone had something to drink, Sean's mom—always the mistress of ceremonies at every family gathering—urged everyone out into the spacious backyard. Sean stayed at Eva's side until she and Caitlin had a good conversational head of steam going, then moved to help his dad with the grill.

"First grill of the summer's always an event," his father noted with his usual verbal economy.

"Right, Pop." Sean clapped his dad on the shoulder, feeling like everything was absolutely right in that moment. His best girl was chatting animatedly with his favorite sister, his nieces and nephews were tearing around, playing some variation on tag of their own invention, and the rest of his family surrounded him, chattering, maybe bickering a little, but always being there for everyone else.

He could give Eva this. She, whose loving heart had been cursed by cold, indifferent parents, could have the gift of his family's noisy, rough-and-tumble affection. The idea bloomed in his chest with a strange sort of tenderness. He imagined another cousin, a redhead, joining the melee on the lawn. Heck, maybe a couple of them.

"How long have you and Eva been together?" his dad asked, surprising him. His father rarely inquired after his children's personal lives.

"Not long, but I really think she's the one, Pop."

His father peered sideways at him. "If you're sure." It came

out clipped and musical. His father's native Irish accent always grew more intense when he was emphasizing something.

Sean blinked. "What do you mean *if I'm sure?*" He was
falling in love with her.

No, he wasn't falling. He'd fallen. Splat. Into a giant bouncy
castle of happiness. The emotion was so huge he felt like he'd
need to run around with the kids to burn off the energy it
gave him.

His father considered the coals in the grill. "You've never
been impulsive before."

Well, this was true. He'd plotted his life out very intention-
ally from a young age. "Okay, yeah, things are moving a little
quickly, but I don't think that's the same as being impulsive."

"Is she Catholic?"

"No." It would figure his father would ask him that.

His dad turned to face him fully then. "She seems like she
might be a little bit older than you, son."

Dammit, why did his dad have to be so negative all the
time? "So?" He tamped down the belligerence that this conversation had rising in him. He'd nearly always had his dad's
quiet approval before. Why couldn't he be at least neutral, if
not outright happy for Sean?

His dad just shrugged, turning back to the grill and me-
thodically flipping the burgers. "I just thought you might have
different goals in life. You know, different stages and all that."

Wow. That practically counted as a major speech from his
dad. "We're not that different in age. We get along. We have
similar outlooks, similar interests. We're fine."

At that point sixteen-year old Saoirse ran up to him and

insisted he come help organize a game of Red Rover. "You okay with the grill on your own?" he asked his father.

"Yup."

Well, that was fun, Dad. Let's do it again sometime. He shook off the oddly bitter feeling and went off to make sure the teenagers were adequately distributed among the younger kids in the parallel lines that were forming in the yard and especially to ensure that baby Ryan, only four, didn't kill himself bouncing off the older kids.

All the while, a jagged pain had replaced the warmth in his chest, and he wondered if his loving family really did live up to that idea he'd had just a few minutes before.

"Oh, my God, Sean, you are just as bad as the kids," Caitlin bellowed, laughing as the Red Rover game devolved into what appeared to be a game of "Everybody jump on Uncle Sean." He roared and chased and was so incredibly adorable that Eva felt herself turning into a human heart-eye emoji.

"You have any kids, Eva?" Caitlin asked.

As someone who'd been ambivalent about having kids as a younger person, Eva'd always been more than a little uncomfortable with that question. The simple answer of "no" seemed to give a lot of people license to freely express opinions on her personal life. Usually negative ones like, "Well, that's just selfish." At best was the unnecessarily sympathetic, "Oh, but you're still young, you have time!" Which might be comforting if she wanted to parent children, but now that she'd passed the age of forty, she knew she definitely didn't.

But it wasn't like she could say, "None of your business" to Sean's favorite sister.

"No. Just a dog. Timmy." She dug in her pocket for her phone and brought up a photo to show Caitlin, who leaned over and cooed appreciatively.

"Aww. Sweet-looking pup."

"He's the best boy," Eva said, stuffing the phone away again with relief. It had been a risky gambit. Some people had the gall to tell her that she was sublimating an as-yet unfelt desire for children by having a pet.

Eva really wished those people would get a different hobby and leave her alone. But Caitlin didn't seem to be the type of person to berate her about being childless. And she didn't have kids, either.

Yet.

At that moment her wife, Nicole, wandered over. The two of them looked at each other with a sort of private intensity that made Eva feel like she was intruding. She felt sure that if Sean's parents were different people, or if Caitlin and Nicole were a woman and a man, that they'd have shared a sweet little *hi, you* spousal kiss. So she looked away, back at Sean, who had one nephew riding his back and was dangling a niece from her ankles. He looked a little like King Kong, truth be told.

"Your little brother is absolutely never going to grow up," Nicole observed, taking a sip of her drink as she followed his progress among the youngest generation.

"Hey. He's a grown man with a very responsible job," Caitlin said, her spine stiffening, though her expression was teasing. "Nobody talks smack about my little brother but my sisters and me."

Nicole, a slight, pretty blonde, who looked like a daffodil among the tall, dark-haired Hannigans, put the back of her hand to her forehead. "And here I thought I had sister-in-law privileges."

Caitlin patted her wife's arm. "Maybe in a couple of years. It's a gradual thing, I think. Not that any of my sisters' husbands ever tried to tease him."

Eva's gaze swept across the brothers-in-law. None of them were small men, but also none of them came close to Sean's towering height and impressive musculature.

Nicole, possibly coming to the same conclusion, snorted and said something about patriarchy and big dogs. Eva glanced sideways to see if Caitlin would take issue with this as well, but she just sighed and rolled her eyes.

"I've told you before. Sean wasn't always the big, tough guy. He was little when we were kids. Bullied by other kids. And he was sweet."

He's still sweet, Eva wanted to interject. But it felt wrong to talk as if she, after knowing him for such a short time, knew him better than his own sister. But this enormous, tight-knit group was intimidating, as kind and welcoming as they were. She wasn't sure she could see her way clear to fitting in with the Hannigans without being overwhelmed by them. She looked back at Sean, now rolling on the grass, swarmed by kids and roaring like a bear. He wasn't her Sean right now, the strong, protective firefighter. The man who made everything inside her light up like a Fourth of July firework. This Sean was the youngest brother, the goofy uncle, the good son.

Did she really know him at all? Or was she only fooling herself?

Twenty-One

They ate at the dining room table—well, the adults did. The kids picnicked outside. Sean made sure to seat Eva between him and Caitlin, since he'd noticed them talking before.

He wanted Eva to like his family so much it almost hurt.

She seemed pale, though. And a little more reserved than usual. Watchful and quiet. Well, he supposed that would make sense. His family was large, opinionated and overwhelming even to him at times.

Right now his oldest sister's husband, David, was jawing on about something in local government he considered wasteful. Sean didn't know what it was and didn't want to know. There was no accounting for taste and his and Erin's couldn't be more different. Then Dave said something about how the county needed to reduce the budget by ten percent. No reason given. He had a way of saying bullshit so definitively it was like he was slamming it down on the table and trying to make it true by sheer force of the kinetic energy he put behind it.

Sean tamped down the irritation his brother-in-law always brought out in him. "Dave, do you even know what's in that budget?" he said quietly, feeling his family's faces turn toward him.

Dave waved a fork. "Eh, libraries and crap. Nobody uses libraries anymore. Why should we pay for them?"

"When did you last go to the library?" Eva asked and all eyes swiveled to her.

Dave, speaking slowly and carefully as if he was talking to his youngest kid, said, "I said nobody goes to them anymore."

Eva's chin lifted, two scarlet spots on her cheeks. "No, what you mean is that *you* don't use the public library and assume that everyone's like you. I think you'll find that if you actually go to one of the local libraries, the parking lot is already half full on Saturday morning with people waiting for it to open up. I know this because I've seen it. Because I *do* use the public library," Eva said quietly but firmly.

Dave opened his mouth again, but Sean cut him off. "You also haven't used emergency services, have you? Maybe you want fewer fire stations? Spread 'em farther out so it takes twenty minutes instead of five to get to your house?"

Sean's brother-in-law stared at him and Sean stared right back. Did Dave think that because his sister was the eldest that Sean was afraid of him? What a fucking joke.

"Now, let's not talk about messy things like politics when we're having a nice meal," Mom said in that *pouring oil on troubled water* voice. Problem was it might well be pouring oil on a grease fire. And Sean knew damn well how much of a disaster that would be. Especially for Eva.

But Dave just gave one more hard look at Sean and, not for the first time, he wondered if his boring middle-manager brother-in-law had been a schoolyard bully like the ones his sisters had protected him from when he was a child.

He strongly suspected he had been.

Eva kicked herself for chiming in. Who was she to insert herself into a family argument the very first time she'd met everyone? Granted, ignorance like Sean's brother-in-law had displayed always irked her. Not to mention the condescension he'd shown her. Conversation flowed around them now, broken off into little groups instead of one central, uncomfortable conflict, and she relaxed a little.

Sean nudged her gently. "You okay over there?"

She turned a smile his way, hoping it didn't look as forced as it felt. "Sure. Everything's fine."

His eyes narrowed with concern. "Hey, I know this has got to be overwhelming for you." He leaned over and whispered in her ear, "And Dave's an ass. Always has been."

Her smile grew a little more genuine. "Usually at least one in every family."

He glanced around the crowded table meaningfully. "And with this many people, it's pretty much statistically guaranteed in this case."

She laughed a little then, though she felt bad it was at the expense of his family. Because mostly they'd been perfectly nice and welcoming.

On her other side, Caitlin murmured, "Good going standing up to that bully. None of the rest of us have ever liked him much. Though he does have his moments and I have to admit he's a really good dad."

Well, okay. That was an interesting consensus. She looked down to the end of the table where Sean's mother sat, placidly chatting with his two middle sisters. Dave still glowered a bit, but Erin appeared to be telling him to get over himself, which made Eva want to laugh.

Nicole leaned around Caitlin. "You're doing great, Eva. This crowd is pretty intimidating to walk into."

Wow, was it that obvious she was feeling awkward and nervous? She had to work on her game face. She thanked Nicole and polished off her potato salad. "Do you want more of that, dear?" Mrs. Hannigan—no, Susan—asked.

"No, thank you. It was delicious but I'm full."

Susan beamed at her, then at her son. "She likes my cooking. I like her."

"Who wouldn't, Mom?"

Eva had to admit Susan *was* a great cook. She was starting to feel a little like Sandra Bullock's character in *While You Were Sleeping* with this big family cheerfully nattering away as they finished their meal and easily folding her presence in as if it was the most natural thing in the world while she was kind of awkward and kind of charmed by it all.

Maybe she could get used to this.

After the meal, Sean and Eva pitched in to help clean up. Eva was just polishing his mom's counters with a dish towel when Aidan came in from the backyard. "Uncle Sean, the kids are bouncing off the walls."

Which meant the younger kids had gotten hopped up on the first popsicles of the season and needed to run around until they fell down.

"You bring your soccer ball?" he asked the kid, who grinned.

"What do you think?"

Sean thought the kid never went anywhere without it. If he couldn't be dribbling it, weaving in and out, he'd be practicing fancy kicks and stunts. He practiced so long and hard he was actually getting really good at it.

"Round up the kiddos and we'll take them to the elementary school soccer field for a pickup game."

"Yeah!" Aidan gave a fist pump.

"But don't play so hard you make the little ones cry again," Sean said, leveling a finger at his nephew. "You know how good you are and this is a friendly, not a real, competition."

"Honestly, Saoirse's getting really good. She's going to be captain of the girls' team next year, I bet." Aidan said. The cousins were the same age and went to the same high school, as their mothers were the infamous "Irish Twins" of the family and had to live near one another, get married within months of each other and get pregnant for the first time nearly simultaneously.

"All right, you and Saoirse will be the captains and I'll decide who's on each team." They'd learned from rough experience that the traditional "Assign captains and let them pick their teams" would lead to tears as well. The whole thing was a massive balancing act, given the kids ranged in age from sixteen to four.

"You got it, Uncle Sean."

"Okay, then. You go get the kiddos. I'll let the adults know what's going on so they can come and watch if they want and we'll get going in five."

It was more like fifteen minutes before the massive herd of kids and the smaller clutch of adults streamed out of his parents' home and down the street toward the soccer field. Aidan, for once, wasn't bouncing or dribbling the ball, just carrying it casually between his hip and forearm. Sean suspected this was because some girl had informed him that his constant antics weren't "cool." Girls were probably also the reason he was sporting that floppy haircut. Sean shook his head, swinging a pair of orange cones from one hand.

"How does this work?" Eva asked, walking next to him. "It seems like this is something they've done before."

Sean nodded. "If it's just the kids, it's two teams of four. We only use half the field, hence these to make up the second goal." He gestured with the cones. "The nine oldest kids all play and the odd one out acts as a sub for either side."

Her eyes went wide. "You really have this down to a science."

He shrugged. "They're really active kids and they like to run around. All of 'em except Ryan play soccer in school. It makes sense. Sometimes some of the adults want to play, then we just readjust the size of the teams and make sure talent and age are equally distributed."

At that point little Ryan ran back from where he'd been walking with Aidan, the cousin he hero-worshipped. "Uncle Sean, I'm big enough to play now. See, I can kick—" His little foot flailed out, almost connecting with Eva's shin.

Ryan would get trampled on a soccer field. Not to mention the older kids would get frustrated with him.

"Hey, buddy. Sorry, but you know the rules. You have to have played in school for a year first."

Ryan's face fell and his lower lip trembled. "But Uncle Sean, I'm not a baby anymore!"

Sean handed the cones off to Eva and scooped Ryan up onto his hip. "No, you're not a baby, and that's why you have a very important job."

Ryan's pouting only intensified. "What's that?"

"You have to help me referee."

Watching Sean take this tiny child so seriously was so adorable, Eva's heart was just about to burst into a shower of spangly, glittering confetti. This was the Sean she knew, the protective, in-control Sean. For his part, Ryan appeared to be giving Sean's statement Very Serious Consideration.

"Do I get to blow a whistle?" he asked.

"I don't have one, buddy. But you get to ride on my shoulders and help me keep a lookout for fouls."

"That sounds like a very important job, Ryan," Eva commented. The little boy's eyes went from her to Sean, as if he wasn't sure what to make of the newcomer.

"Eva's right. Two pairs of eyes are better than one. Can you tell me what the off-sides rule is?"

Eva couldn't have defined the off-sides rule with a handbook and a map, but Ryan excitedly babbled something about players getting between the defenders and the goal.

"Almost, bud. The important thing is that those players don't have the ball. If they do have the ball, then it's okay."

Ryan seemed to be mulling this over, nodding sagely as if he'd been called upon to approve this rule. Eva had the strong feeling that he'd be watching his siblings and cousins like a hawk for any infractions, eager to tell the big kids that they had done something wrong.

They reached the little field and Sean put Ryan down, promising to return for him and taking the cones from Eva. He jogged down the field, placing the cones at the halfway point of the field, functionally making a second goal. Jogging back, he stopped by the existing goal frame, the kids clustering around him. "Okay. Here's how it's going to go. Aidan and Saoirse are the team captains. On Aidan's team—Kathleen, James and Regan. On Saoirse's team—Brianna, Quinn and Luke. Nora's the first sub for either team. Ryan's my assistant referee." He dug in his pocket for a coin. "Heads, Aidan's team gets the kickoff." He flipped the coin in the air, caught it and slapped it on his arm. "Tails. Saoirse—you're on." Sean grabbed Ryan and hoisted him up to have the little boy sit on his shoulders, then put two fingers in his mouth and gave a short, shrill whistle.

Saoirse, a lanky, coltish girl with a broad grin and a mane of thick dark hair, had a quick strategy session with her team. They spread out on the little field, all watching their captain as she squared up to the ball and kicked it.

All of the kids clearly knew how to play, and Eva was impressed by how often the older kids passed to the younger ones, involving them in the game even though they weren't as skilled. Sean, with his long legs, only had to stride up and down the sidelines, using his two-fingered whistle to make calls and resume play. Ryan, solemnly discharging his duties, would point a small finger and holler, "Off sides!" with great gusto whenever he thought one of his elders was out of line. As she watched, Sean's middle sister Maeve wandered over.

"How are you enjoying our chaos?" she asked.

"It's different to what I'm used to, but it's fun, too. And your kids are charming."

"Yeah, we won't send 'em off to the workhouse anytime soon," Maeve said with a sly grin. "Sean's so good with them," she noted as he called a substitution and Nora darted on the field to replace Luke.

"He is. He's teaching a self-defense class to some of my students, so I knew he was good with young people, but obviously they're not children." But he was good with kids. And obviously adored them as much as they adored him. The potato salad that had been so delicious only a half hour before turned to a rock in her stomach as she thought again about their age difference and what it could mean.

"Yeah," Maeve said, looking at her brother with obvious fondness. "He's going to be a great dad someday."

Twenty-Two

Eva had gone quiet again. After the soccer game she'd seemed to retreat into herself and Sean, figuring she was overwhelmed by his family, cut their visit a bit shorter than he normally would if he'd been on his own. She looked out the window as he drove her home. "Penny for your thoughts," he said softly, wondering if he really did want to know the contents of her mind.

"Just mentally sorting through the day," she said, turning to face him and giving him a wan smile.

"My family is a lot, it's true. Maybe I should have introduced you to them a little more slowly. Dinner with Caitlin and Nicole first." Of course he should have. He gave himself a hearty mental kick that he'd been so boneheaded.

"No, they're great. And the kids are awesome."

The grin that split his face probably could have been seen from Mars. "They really are. Ryan's shaping up to be a handful, but I know what it's like to be the youngest and the littlest and always striving to keep up."

"You're really great with them," Eva said. "It's clear you really like children."

"Yeah, well, not all kids. But my nieces and nephews? I guess it's different when you are part of their family. When you're a part of their development. It's been wild to see them growing up. I mean, I remember when Aiden and Saoirse were born, you know? I held them when they were only hours old." It seemed so long ago and he'd been so young, those tiny, new lives in his arms. Sometimes he almost felt like he'd grown up alongside the oldest two.

"Your face gets kind of dreamy when you talk about it," she said.

Did it? "Yeah, well. Kids are a miracle, right?"

"I suppose so." Her voice sounded very far away.

"Don't you like kids?" he asked, wondering what was draining all the energy out of her. Yeah, his family was a lot, but she seemed unusually wan, her normal vibrancy all but gone. *She'll get used to them*, he reassured himself.

"Oh, sure. I'm like you. I like kids I know. But I don't have much chance to be around them these days, you know? My friends' kids are more grown up, more independent. When we were all younger, the kid basically came along for the ride for just about any event unless the other parent could watch them. Now they watch themselves."

He chuckled. "And in my sisters' case, the older ones often get hired to babysit the younger ones."

"I'm glad to know they get paid. I had friends growing up who were expected to watch their younger siblings for free. That always seemed unfair to me."

"Yeah, my sisters are pretty fair-minded people. They don't see the logic in making more work for a kid just because of an accident of birth order. But they'd know, wouldn't they?" Somehow, they'd gotten back onto more firm conversational ground and Eva was starting to sound more like herself. He pulled up in front of her house and turned off the truck, sliding his hand into her hair and gazing down into her face. "Wanna fool around?"

Eva's emotions ping-ponged through her, ricocheting from elation to lust to outright fear. Elation and lust were normal. The fear came from Maeve's simple statement. *He's going to be a great dad.*

It was so *positive*, that statement. Not he *might* be a great dad. He *would* be. Inevitable.

But that was possibly just a sister expressing her desire that her brother have children. It said nothing about what Sean wanted. Their relationship was so new. They'd barely had a chance to get to know each other. Asking him whether or not he really wanted kids seemed like too much of a reach. Something too serious for this early stage of the relationship. They needed to be sure if this would work in the long term before they had that kind of conversation.

So she took the coward's way out and didn't ask. "Yeah. I do. Let's go in. But I have to let Timmy out back first."

That cocky, crooked grin reappeared, warming her from the top of her head to the tips of her toes. "Of course."

She let them in, toeing off their shoes in the front hall, and Timmy's usual wiggling, whining gladness at seeing her made her smile, especially when he transferred some of his joy to Sean. "Hey there, buddy," Sean said as he crouched to pet the dog and get his chin licked. "Glad to see you, too."

They took the dog to the fenced backyard and watched as he ranged around, sniffing and finally lifting his leg, returning to the back door at a run as if he wanted nothing more than to be with his humans. "You're a good, good boy," she told him as he trotted into the kitchen to noisily lap at his water bowl.

Despite what some people said, her life without kids was good. It was full and meaningful and enough for her. Maybe it could be enough for Sean, too.

She locked up and returned to the living room where Sean waited for her. "Everything all set?" he asked, his eyes looking huge in the shadows cast by the only lamp she'd lit.

"Yeah." Her voice felt scratchy, hoarse. He reached out and reeled her in, one hand at her waist, the other sliding around to cup the back of her neck, the gentle friction of his fingers against her skin making her shiver. He just looked at her for a few breaths, as if his eyes scanning her face could find and catalog everything between them in that moment.

Then he bent and kissed her, so slowly and softly that tears threatened, prickling her eyes. When he pulled back, his pupils were blown wide and an odd, crooked smile tipped the corner of his mouth up.

"Ready to go up?"

She was clearly rattled by today's visit with his family, so Sean was going to go as slowly and as tenderly with her as possible. He followed her upstairs, mesmerized by the sway of her hips in front of him, seeing their life together spooling out ahead of him like a movie trailer, highlighting all the best bits of who they were when they were together. The banter, the trust, the simple delight in each other's company.

When they reached her room, she flicked on one bedside lamp and he gave her another long, lingering, sweet kiss.

Well, not entirely sweet. It was hard to be sweet when he was kissing firmly *and* pushing his erection against Eva's pelvis. She responded to him by kissing him back with the same quiet, determined tenderness, running her hands up his arms, across his shoulders and around the back of his neck, pulling them closer together. He groaned a little, angling his head more and deepening the connection, pulling her hips tighter against him.

If they got any closer, they might actually fuse into a single being. It was nice, though, this new note in their sensuality.

Slowly, his lips still fused to hers, Sean plucked the top button of Eva's blouse free, tracing her collarbones with his fingertip, exploring the newly exposed skin. Then the next button, ranging over the tops of her breasts. The next, her shirt gaping wide enough to slide a hand in to cup that sweet curve and tease the hardening nipple with his thumb. Another, and he could sample the warmth of her belly, then pop open the final two to tickle her belly button, making her gasp and squirm, the friction against his denim-covered cock nearly sending him to his knees.

She leaned back then, breaking the long kiss that they'd shared, her gaze roaming his face. "You seem different tonight. You *are* different tonight."

He touched her forehead, then traced the line of her cheekbone, her mouth, her jaw. "I'm in the mood to be extra gentle. Is that okay?"

"Yeah. It's nice. Different, but nice."

"Well, woman. Let me keep being nice to you." He bent to kiss the side of her neck and she inhaled a long, shuddering breath. Hmm. There was something to this going slowly business. He trailed open-mouthed kisses down the side of her neck, the curve of it as she leaned to give him better access more arousing than her open shirt or the promise of baring the rest of her body to his eyes, mouth, tongue, fingers. She shivered and her breath hitched as he swirled his tongue just above her shoulder where she seemed newly sensitive.

"Mmm. I like learning things about you," he murmured against her skin.

She swallowed hard. "You're a fast learner."

"Praise from the professor. I'm here for it." He pushed her blouse off her shoulders and down her arms, letting it drop to the floor. Then he sent her bra after it, leaning forward to capture the tip of one breast with his lips, swirling his tongue, but not sucking. Teasing with more of the tender lightness that seemed right for tonight. Gooseflesh pebbled her skin, and her breath was shallow.

"Sean?"

"Yes, baby?" he mumbled against her taut nipple.

"Please fuck me now."

Sean's chuckle, his mouth pressed against her breast, sent even more shivers running through her. He pressed one last kiss to her breast, then straightened, whipping his shirt over his head and dropping it to the floor. Hands on her hips, he walked her backward to the bed until she sat on it, the mattress bouncing gently under her weight. Then, with gentle efficiency, he pulled off her jeans and underwear and stripped down to his skin, standing in front of her, his cock curving upward and toward his belly.

God, he was beautiful.

Then he was bending forward, caging her body between his big arms and kissing her, somehow encouraging her to scoot back on the bed until they could both stretch out on the coverlet. She expected him to take charge, to show that bossy side he had in every other time they'd made love. Instead, he rolled off her, his hand sliding down her belly, across her mound, bringing that hand up to his mouth to lick one finger and finding her clit, circling in slow, steady strokes. Her pelvis tightened with arousal, her body chasing the sensations, the friction, the heat.

Then his touch went featherlight and a frustrated growl ripped out of her.

"What?" he said, his expression so innocent he could have won an Oscar. He increased the pressure again, his gaze roaming over her face, making her feel exposed and cherished at the same time. She reached for his cock, but he shook his head.

"Why?" she asked.

"Because this is for you." He leaned forward, kissing her neck again in that delicious, tantalizing way he had before, and alternating his touches until she was practically panting.

"*Sean,*" she groaned and he chuckled, breath puffing against her skin.

"What?" he asked again, still all faux-innocence, then gave

her another one of those brain-obliterating neck kisses, pairing it with a firm, rapid circling of his fingers, and orgasm overtook her, flinging her into bliss, shuddering and sobbing out his name as he drew out the sensations with his fingers until she took a deep breath and relaxed.

"Wow. Thank you," she murmured, rolling toward him. "Now you."

"Now me, huh? How do you feel about being on top?"

She sat up and straddled him, reaching for the box of condoms she now kept on her bedside table. "I feel pretty great about it," she said, unwrapping it and rolling it on with firm strokes.

He moved back so he could rest against the headboard and she leaned forward to kiss him as she guided him inside her, feeling the give of her body around the hardness of his, the stretch, the fullness. "God, you feel so good," he murmured against her lips as she started to move, swiveling and grinding, rising up and sinking down.

"Yes, I do," she said, loving that that made him smile.

They moved together like that for a long time, savoring each other with long, languid kisses and slow movements. Then Sean pulled her to him and rolled them over. "This okay?" he asked.

"Of course," she said, wondering where bossy Sean had gone. But this side of him was wonderful, too, sweet and considerate.

He picked up the tempo, pumping his hips, and she wrapped her legs around his thighs and treated herself to the feel of his smooth, muscular butt under her hands. He came with a soft groan and shuddered to a stop, eyes squeezing shut.

She stroked his face as he slowly relaxed and he smiled dreamily, opening his eyes. Yes. Just this. This cozy bubble of intimacy is all she wanted right now. They had time to figure everything else out.

"I love you, Eva."

Twenty-Three

"What?"

Eva's stunned expression wasn't at all what Sean had been hoping for. "Too soon?" he asked, pulling out of her and grabbing tissues to deal with the condom, his post-orgasm bliss going chilly and hollow.

"Just…unexpected." He felt her eyes following him as he swung out of bed to throw the condom away and wash his hands. When he got back, she'd slid under the covers. For a moment he wondered if he was welcome to join her, but she flipped a corner back, inviting him to slide in beside her.

"I'm sorry. I'm not usually so impulsive," he said as he drew her close. She rested her head on his shoulder and he stroked her hair. He thought about his father's words, his cryptic warning about being in different stages of life. Well, maybe they were. But that was okay. She wasn't that much older than he was and they had so much in common. Despite his self-reassurance, fear tugged at his heart. She might never love him back.

She stroked his chest. "It's a lovely thing to say." But she definitely wasn't saying it back. She met his gaze as if her eyes were heavy, too heavy to lift. "But here's the thing. When you were refereeing that soccer game, one of your sisters told me you were going to be a great dad."

That *but* had frozen the blood in his veins. "Okay," he said cautiously, hoping whatever would come next would enable him to sort everything out, to make everything okay. To open whatever door in her heart was currently closed.

"And you *would* be a great dad. And you should be able to be a dad if you want to be."

Confusion seemed to swarm like gnats in his brain. "What am I missing here?"

Her eyes closed. "Sean, I'm forty-one years old. I'm not having kids. If I ever wanted them, that ship has sailed."

"But women have kids in their forties all the time." And she'd be a great mom. Something stopped him from saying that out loud.

"Yes, but many or most of them have already had kids, which makes it less risky. For me, being a first-time mom in my forties would be risky, both to me and to the potential kid. I don't want to take those risks."

"And you shouldn't have to. But we could adopt."

Her jaw tightened. "That also takes time and a lot of money. And even if we could, by the time we got a child—even if we could, which is far from guaranteed—I would be sixty or more by the time the kid went off to college."

"Okay," he said slowly. "So then we don't have kids." It was a new idea to him, he realized, but he could get used to it. For her.

She studied him, frowning. "Sean, no."

"No, what?"

"You were clearly expecting to be a dad someday. And you should have that if that's what you want."

"But like you said, nothing's guaranteed. I could try to have a kid with someone else and it might never happen." The idea of being with anyone else filled him with horror, but he tried to keep his tone as even and reasonable as possible.

"You'd at least have the chance," she said. "And with me, there's no chance."

"You said one of my sisters said this thing about me being a dad. Why didn't you mention it before?"

A sad little smile slid across her face. "I wasn't sure where we were. It seemed like it might be too early to talk about something as big as having children. But then you told me you loved me."

How had a declaration of love steered them toward this cliff? No, he could see it. Despite how they'd first met, Eva was normally cautious, careful. She wouldn't jump the gun like that. He took a deep breath, trying to contain the shattering feeling of imminent loss, to contain the shards of himself that threatened to explode.

"Are you breaking up with me?"

Oh, God. Sean's voice, so deep and so strained, was going to rip her apart. She couldn't say the words she thought she should. To say, *Yes. I release you. Go find a wonderful woman who's younger than I am, someone who will give you babies and en-able you to be what you were meant to be,* who *you were meant to be.*

She forced the next words through a throat tight with emotion. "I'm saying let's take a break. Pull back. You need time and space to think about what you really want."

He cradled her cheek in one hand. "What if what I want is you?"

You won't. If you take time and reflect, you'll realize that being a father is important to you. The very fact that he'd gone through the various arguments—that she wasn't necessarily too old, that adoption could be a possibility—he might not have thought about it consciously, but subconsciously he'd seen that future for himself. He'd expected it.

And if they stayed together, if she didn't set him free, one day he would resent her for denying him that future. She couldn't face that.

"You say you want me, but what if I'm not enough?"

He drew back, cupping her face in his big hands, his eyes searching her face. "How could you ever not be enough?"

She swallowed hard around the lump in her throat. No. She wouldn't cry. If she cried, her resolve would break. "Please."

"Is it that easy to leave me?" There was a hint of anger in his eyes now. The kind of anger that came from hurt.

"No." The word came out in a choked almost-sob as if he'd been throttling her, not cradling her face. "It's incredibly, horribly difficult. But I need you to take the time and really examine what you want. It's crucial. I can't stand the idea of you not thinking this through, or of you thinking I'll change my mind and ending up resenting me."

His expression softened. He ran a thumb over her lower lip,

blinking a couple of times, his gaze focused on her mouth as if he couldn't bear to look her in the eyes anymore. "Well." His voice cracked. "If that's what you need. But what if I only want you? What if I decide that being a father means less to me than having you in my life?"

"Take at least a month," she said. "Think about it. And if you need more time—"

"I won't." His eyes closed and his entire body stilled. "What about the last self-defense class?"

Oh, *shit*. She'd never let her students down before and she wasn't about to start now. "We can do that, I guess."

"Okay." He heaved in a huge breath, then turned and got out of bed, finding his clothes and yanking them on roughly. Eva sat in the middle of the bed, her knees drawn up, the covers pulled to her chin, feeling foolish and lost and yet very certain at the same time. Because morally, this was the right thing to do.

Emotionally, it was wrecking her. He might have said he could go without being a father in a moment of panic, but first he'd trotted out all the reasons why he thought they could have kids. He definitely wanted them. And when he thought about everything with a little distance, he wasn't going to come back to her. Wasn't going to choose her. She knew it in her bones.

Pulling his shirt on, Sean gave one last look around Eva's bedroom, then moved to sit next to her on the bed. He looped a lock of her hair behind an ear, bending to give her one last, soft kiss. "One month," he murmured against her lips, tasting salt. Because there were tears streaming down her beautiful face. "Oh, baby. Don't cry." He pulled her against his chest, her back heaving under his hands.

"Telling someone not to cry is always going to make them cry even more." Her voice was thick and muffled against the cotton of his shirt.

Okay, fair. He knew that. But the abject sobs told him something that gave him a faint hope.

She cared. She might not be willing to tell him she loved him, but this was hurting her. She was hurting herself for him. For what she thought he wanted. And he needed to honor her concerns for him, because if he was being honest with himself, they were valid. He had always figured someday, in some hazy future, he'd have kids. That very afternoon he'd thought about kids. Not just any kids, either. Theirs. She trusted him to give this careful consideration and he owed that to her, to himself.

"Shh," he whispered into her hair. Her crying was easing, her body going limp as if she was wrung out by emotion. His chest tightened like it was his turn to cry, to mourn what had been between them. Eyes burning, he eased away from her and went into her bathroom, splashed water on his face, and brought a damp washcloth out for her.

"Why are you being so nice to me?" she croaked, an echo of their first meeting that made his heart ache.

"Because I love you."

"Still? After all this?"

"Yes. I'll see you Tuesday. And then I'll see you in a month."

Her eyebrows slanted down in apparent panic. "Don't come

back if I'm right, if you decide you do want kids. That would hurt too much."

He didn't respond, just drew the covers up, the ache deep in his chest searing him. Then he left her bedroom and went downstairs. Timmy met him at the bottom, wagging his plumed tail. He crouched to pat the dog and pointed up toward her room. "Up. Go to Eva, Timmy. She needs you." The dog looked at him for a moment, then launched himself up the steps, claws scrabbling on the hardwood.

Sean took a deep breath in, heard her say something to the dog he couldn't make out and left.

Timmy came cautiously into her room. She turned and saw his sweet face, somehow looking worried in the deepening twilight. "Come on, boy." She patted the bed, wondering what he'd do. She'd never let him on the furniture before, but if there was a time to make an exception, it was now.

The little dog loped forward and hurled himself onto the coverlet as if he did it every day, and Eva nearly started to cry again. She'd heard Sean send him up here and it was killing her that he'd still prioritize her comfort after what she'd done. She hugged Timmy's solid little body against her, spooning the dog and heaving a shuddering sigh. Tim twisted his head around and lapped at her salty cheeks.

"Thanks, buddy," she said, wiping her face on the sheet. Her voice was thick from crying, her nose clogged. Her phone rang and she sighed, getting wearily out of bed and digging through her clothes until she found it in her jeans pocket. It was Krystal.

"Eva, are you home?" her friend asked without preamble. Adrenaline shot through her at Krystal's tone. "Yes, why?"

"I just saw what looked suspiciously like your ex's janky old Volvo cruising slowly through the neighborhood."

Shit. Sean didn't have a key to her place, so he would have left her front door unlocked when he left. Eva grabbed her robe off the back of the bedroom door and shrugged into it as she ran downstairs. Holding it closed in one hand and squeezing the phone between her shoulder and ear, she scrambled for the front door and shot the dead bolt, then moved rapidly through her house to ensure that the back door was also locked. "Okay. House is locked up tight."

"Why wasn't it locked before?" Krystal, security-conscious as always, was clearly unimpressed by her lax arrangements.

"Long story." Eva tucked the phone between her ear and her shoulder and tied the sash of her robe in a tight knot, moving to the living room where she could monitor the front of her house through the sheer curtains in the bay window. Her stomach gave a sick lurch as she saw an all-too-familiar boxy, caramel-colored car pull up in front of her house. "Krys? I'm going to hang up now. I might have to call 911."

"Okay. Call me as soon as you can," her friend said.

Eva waited in the darkening room, Timmy looking up at her, his tail wafting back and forth tentatively. She could see Darren come up the front walk, heard the scrape of a key that obviously didn't fit in the lock, then the pounding of a fist.

"Eva, you goddamn slut, if you don't open this door right now, I'm going to break it down."

Heart hammering, Eva called 911. "What's your emergency?" the dispatcher said.

"Someone is trying to break into my home," Eva said, giving her address and being reassured that the woman at dispatch would stay on the line with her.

Several sickening minutes that felt like hours later, Eva saw blue lights bloom through the sheers. Darren had kept up his relentless hammering and verbal abuse as if he could tell she was a scant few feet away. Timmy barked, a shrill, headache-inducing noise that made her want to crumple into a ball and weep.

Only an hour before, she'd been sheltered and treasured. Been told she was loved. Now this.

The cops were apparently talking to Darren because his raised voice informed them he lived here. Rage spiked through Eva and she whipped open the door, keeping Timmy back with one bare foot. "He does *not* live here. He has *never* lived here."

"Eva, honey, are you off your meds? I've lived here for years."

Oh, she saw what he was trying to do. His eyes were practically glittering with malice. She turned her attention to the police officers standing behind him. "Please check his driver's license. It will not show this address. If you want to check with the university, you will also find out that he tried to attack me recently. I believe he's showing up here because he's losing his job. Not to mention the fact that I've filed for a restraining order against him."

"Bitch." Darren lunged for her, but Eva spun sideways and knocked his arm away. Timmy growled, emitting snapping, harsh barks that Eva'd never heard before, and the larger of the two police officers grabbed Darren with practiced swiftness, snapping handcuffs on.

"You have the right to remain silent..."

Twenty-Four

Sean wasn't due at the firehouse until the next morning, but his truck found its way there as if it was a horse bolting toward its barn. His squad wasn't around, but he didn't want to be alone. He crawled into his bunk and let his mind race in fruitless circles for a while. Eva had exposed something he'd taken for granted. Yeah, he'd expected someday he'd be a dad. It was baked into him with every one of his parents' expectations, with his sisters' examples, with his own noisy, chaotic, loving upbringing.

But why did he have to go down that path? Because three-quarters of his sisters had big families? It didn't mean they all had to be the same. He wasn't a wind-up toy to be pointed in a direction of someone else's choosing. He was an adult who could make his own decisions.

Was there some sort of expectation that was in his DNA, or close enough? His conversation with his dad resonated in the back of his mind, discordant. He rolled onto his back,

looping his clasped hands behind his head, thinking about
what his father had said.

She was older than he was. She wasn't Catholic. His dad
had seen it. And he hadn't liked it.

Shit. Yeah. The patterns and expectations of his family lay
out in front of him like the road to Oz. But was that what he
actually wanted?

His gut churned in time with his imagination. He could
see himself being a father. Of having that incandescent moment of holding a newborn—his child—in his arms. The raising of them. The highs of their achievements and the lows
of needing to provide discipline. The long, wonderful road
of bearing witness to creating human beings and watching
them grow up.

Gah. He scrubbed his face with his hands. He couldn't
have that with Eva.

So how did he feel about a future with Eva—just Eva?

The firehouse siren wailed through the building, making
him react instinctively, hopping out of the bunk to head for
the ladder truck before he remembered that he wasn't actually on shift.

Shit. He rolled back into the bunk, facing the wall. Maybe
he was that wind-up toy. Was that all he was good for? Was
that why he was looking for something bigger in his life?

And what was *bigger* anyhow?

Somewhere in his tangled, tortured thoughts, Sean fell
into a troubled, dream-filled sleep, only to be jerked awake
by someone lightly shaking his shoulder. He rolled over to
see Felix standing over his bunk, a puzzled frown on his face.

"Dude. What are you doing here?" his friend asked.

Sean knuckled his eyes and reached for his phone to check the time. Ten minutes until both of them were on the clock. "Didn't feel like going home."

"Didn't you have that thing with Eva and your family? Did it not go okay?" A crease of concern appeared between Felix's eyebrows.

The reality of Eva breaking up with him, of Eva crying, of Eva not being in his life anymore, crashed over him. He'd reset while sleeping, the way a person could. It was like when he was a teenager and his grandfather had died. For days after, he'd wake up in the morning feeling okay, only to have the memory clobber him as if it had happened for the first time all over again.

Sean levered himself off the mattress. He needed to get changed, to be ready for his job. "The thing with my family went fine. What happened after was what sucked."

"What happened?"

Sean shucked his clothes, exchanging his casual weekend wear for his uniform. "One of my bigmouthed sisters told Eva I'd be a great dad. It freaked her out." He headed for the kitchen, Felix keeping pace with him. He needed coffee and a lot of it.

"And why is that a big deal?"

"Because Eva's at an age where she doesn't want to have kids. She said, and I quote, 'That ship has sailed.'"

"And you do want kids?"

Frustration bubbled up in him. "I don't *know*. So Eva told me we needed to take a break so I could figure out what I wanted." The words sliced through him, that horrible fresh pain feeling.

"That sounds sensible."

"I know. I hate it." He'd loved being her solutions guy, her protector. But now he was the problem.

Krystal and Luther showed up while Eva was still standing in her entryway in her robe talking to the police officers, Darren radiating malice from the backseat of their patrol car. Krystal took one look at Eva and slipped inside, telling Luther to find Timmy. Seconds later Eva could hear water running and her electric kettle clicking on. She nearly started crying again that her friend was there to support her.

"I think we have enough, ma'am," the younger officer who'd manhandled Darren into the car finally said.

"Good. Thank you." She closed the door behind them, feeling weak in the knees.

"Girl. Go put some clothes on," Krystal said, coming into the entryway.

"Yes, ma'am." Eva dragged herself up to her room, throwing on the same outfit she'd worn to the Hannigans' and suppressing the urge to weep for what felt like the fiftieth time in an hour. Downstairs she was met by Krystal with a big mug of tea that had, from the smell of it, been doctored with a generous slug of whiskey.

"Sit," her friend said, pointing at the sofa and taking her own seat on an armchair, sipping at her own mug. "What the hell is going on? Where's Captain America?"

"He's going to be a dad."

Krystal's eyes shot to Eva's midsection. "Wait, what? Give me that mug."

Eva, feeling punch-drunk from everything that had happened that day, shook her head. "Sorry. Not with me. But he deserves to be a dad. I think he wants to be a dad. But there's no way I'm going to be a mom."

"So you cut him loose." It wasn't a question.

Eva took a long drink of the hot tea and whiskey. "Yeah."

"What did he have to say about that?"

"That he loved me," Eva said glumly.

"That bastard," Krystal said, her tone arid.

"Krys, I had to do it. He was playing with his nieces and nephews, and his sister said what a great dad he would be. And he *would* be. He deserves to be." As much as she wanted to be selfish, to cling to this wonderful, adorable man, he deserved the autonomy to make his own choices about parenthood the same way she did. If he really did want to be a parent and she didn't, neither of them could have this relationship without one of them sacrificing something huge. She wasn't going to make him make that sacrifice any more than she was willing to sacrifice herself.

Krystal tapped her mug with one fingernail, considering. "Does he want to be?"

"He says he doesn't know. I think he just kind of figured it would happen. You know how some guys can be about that kind of thing. They have all the time in the world. But he ran through all the arguments for having them before he said it wasn't important, which gives me a clue about his real feelings. So I told him we needed to take a break while he figures out what he wants. Which will be babies, I know it. And he was so sweet. I was a mess and he held me and then got Timmy to go up to my room before he left. But he didn't have a key, which was why my front door was unlocked."

Krystal's expression softened. "I'm sorry, hon. You've been through it today."

Pain arrowed through her chest. "I think maybe Sean is the one who's really been through it."

"It's not a competition." Her gaze drifted across the room and she smiled. "Look at those nerds."

Eva followed her friend's pointing finger and found that Luther was curled around Timmy, ostensibly in Tim's doggy bed, which would have been an insubstantial pillow for the larger dog's head. Only a tiny bit of fleece fuzz peeked out from under Luther's belly. Tim sighed and shifted his head, which was lying on one of Luther's massive forelegs.

"At least someone in this house has found lasting love," Eva muttered.

Felix started a fresh pot of coffee brewing as Sean assembled ingredients for a big scramble. Their squad-mates tended to filter in and out of the kitchen and were always hungry, so extra food never went to waste. "So what are you going to do?" Felix asked.

Sean cracked eggs into a bowl. "I don't know. Think, I guess. Envision my life with kids, without them? I have no idea how to do this."

Felix paused, his dark eyes cautious. And when he spoke, his voice was low and patient. "You do realize that if Kevin and I want kids, we'll have to really think about it, plan and possibly move heaven and earth to do it? Whereas you can just drift through life thinking maybe it'll happen someday, then just have sex without birth control, and boom."

Sean paused, an egg poised over the rim of the bowl. Felix was, of course, right. He should have been more thoughtful, more intentional, about something so important. After all, this wasn't just him. This was potentially bringing real people into existence. It wasn't just an item on his bucket list.

He was just set to crack the egg when Thea walked into the kitchen and said, "What's up with your girl?" Instead of cracking it, he crushed it in his hand.

"Shit," he said, swiveling to the sink and washing away the goo and shell. "What are you talking about?"

She picked a few shards of shell that had landed on the counter and flicked them into the sink. "Heard it on the scanner last night. 911 call about a guy who was trying to get into a woman's house. Something about them being professors. Sounded like your girlfriend and her ex. She hasn't called you?" Thea's dark eyes glanced up at him, surprise evident in her expression.

Sean felt hollow, like someone had taken an ice cream scoop to his guts.

"Thea, thank you for your audition for the role of 'bull in a china shop.' We'll be in touch," Felix said, putting his face in his hands and shaking his head.

"What's going on?" Thea asked, her head swiveling between the two men.

"Eva and I are taking a bit of a break," Sean said, amazed at how his voice came out levelly. He yanked the utensil drawer open, silverware crashing. Okay, so maybe he wasn't so level. Grabbing a fork, he whisked the big bowl of eggs into a froth and then poured them into the hot, buttered pan. Looking up, he saw Felix and Thea were both looking at him as if he'd sprouted horns. "What?"

"You just nearly whipped those eggs into outer space, that's what," Thea said. Then her habitually sarcastic expression softened. "I'm sorry about the break, dude. That's rough."

"Thanks." Sean avoided both pairs of eyes that seemed to be boring through him and dragged a spatula through the liquid egg mixture. "Will one of you make some fucking toast?"

"I'm on it," Felix said. Without a word, Thea got butter and jam from the fridge and set them on the big family-style table that dominated the room. She got silverware from the drawer—much less violently than Sean had—and instead of her usual dump-it-in-a-pile technique, actually set three places. "Here, my friend," Felix said, setting a cup of coffee next to the stove.

Somehow, his friends taking care of him made Sean feel worse. It felt like a wake. Because the thing he'd worried about most—Darren trying to get at her in her home—had happened and Eva hadn't called him.

Twenty-Five

Tuesday evening came all too quickly for Eva. Her literature class on Monday had been an absolute shit show, too, so she was feeling like a total failure as an educator and a human being by the time she dragged herself into the room where they would hold their last self-defense class.

And it might be the last time she ever saw Sean again, too.

She would *not* cry now, though. She absolutely wouldn't. She felt bad enough that he'd shouldered the burden of her emotion—quite literally—last time they'd seen each other. She took a deep breath before she reached the door and stepped inside. Sean was the only one there and seeing him caused a twist of pain to rip through her body.

He looked up from his phone and his face went still and expressionless. The pain intensified and she fought the urge to wrap her arms around her waist, to protect herself from the tide of grief inside her. He'd been so open before, so unguarded and warm. Now he looked about as warm as a block of ice in January.

"I heard about the thing with Darren," he said, still without affect.

She blinked, shocked. "How?"

"The thing about emergency services is we kinda tend to know what the other branches are doing. Thea heard it on the scanner and told me."

"Oh, God. I'm sorry. I never meant to blindside you. I didn't know..."

"Yeah," he grunted. "Everything okay with that now?"

She swallowed hard. "Um. I'm not sure. But he's going to lose his job and he was never good with money, so I don't see him being able to keep his condo for much longer. I expect he'll eventually move in with his mom in Indiana."

"Good." He returned his attention to his phone and Eva felt like she'd been dismissed. She retreated to a far corner, dropping her bag to the floor and doing her best to ignore him. Or at least give the appearance of ignoring him. Pain seemed to radiate off him in waves, battering her. Well, yeah. She should be battered by his pain. She was the one who caused it. Twice now.

He's going to choose having kids over you and that's the right choice for him, she reminded herself, reaching for her own phone. But before she could even open an app, the first of their students arrived in a small group. She tucked her phone away and straightened up, her "welcoming professor" expression automatically masking her sadness.

Or maybe it didn't. Because the students stopped just inside the door, looking from her to Sean and back to her as if they'd just heard that mom and dad were getting divorced. She stepped forward, words of welcome forming in her throat, but Sean stepped in front of her. "Here for the self-defense class?" The students nodded. "Good." He returned to his phone. Swiping right on some younger women who could give him the family he'd always expected he'd have?

Stop it. That's beneath you, she thought. But was it? She felt petty, restless and angry. At Sean, at herself, at Darren, at life.

"One hour. Just one hour," she told herself. Then it would all be over.

With a harsh sigh, Sean put his phone away. It was time to get this over with. He half considered making one of the students his assistant this time. Would Eva even care? His shock had hardened into anger since Thea told him about Darren's attempt to get into Eva's house and subsequent arrest. He'd thought when Eva had suggested a "break" that meant she would welcome him back. But she hadn't even cared enough to let him know she'd been in danger?

Yeah. Maybe her "break" was just a way to let him down easy. Or a display of cowardice he hadn't thought she was capable of.

He looked around the room. The students watched him expectantly. He forced himself to look at Eva. Her face was pale and her eyes were huge. Yeah, if he suddenly used someone else to demonstrate, it would seem odd. He beckoned Eva over to him and some of the tension in her flooded out. Had she read his mind? She seemed relieved.

"Okay. Today we're going to cover some of the most difficult kinds of holds to break," Sean said. Was he describing self-defense or his life? He moved behind Eva, feeling stiff and robotic. Bending over, he wrapped his arms around her chest, pulling her to him as he trapped her arms at her sides. The familiar scent of her shampoo flooded his nostrils. *Damn.* His body, apparently not having gotten the memo about the breakup, flooded with desire. He forced himself to keep talking, telling Eva what to do to get free of his grasp even as he only wanted to hold her more tightly. When it came time for him to walk around the room and comment on the students' technique, his mind was relieved at the respite from having to be near her.

His body was having none of it.

He'd never experienced such a total split between mind and body. It was exhausting. But what to come was even more exhausting. He asked Eva to lie on her back on a padded mat and he straddled her. Now his mind was defecting entirely as it flooded with images of her naked, her gorgeous hair spilling out over the pillows and her expression glowing with sated passion. The image was at odds with the way she was now. Her tight, pale face looked miserable; her hair was contained in a long braid.

Her clothes were most certainly on. As they should be. Because he might be touching her, but she wasn't really here. She was gone.

Eva was in hell. The gorgeous man who had held her, cherished her and fucked her senseless was looming over her and all her brain could do was present her with images of him doing ridiculously filthy things to her body on a loop.

Not to mention he was wearing gray sweatpants that rode deliciously low on his hips and hugged his butt like a lover.

She struggled to maintain focus as he held her wrists to the mat and instructed her how to twist her hips and hook one of his legs with hers, a complicated maneuver that would have required all her concentration on a good day.

To say that today was not a good day was a masterpiece of understatement.

She struggled for a while, trying to master the move. Sean was like a Terminator, relentless and seemingly possessing an inexhaustible supply of energy. Finally, her body surging with pent-up frustration, she managed it, getting free and scooting away. Sean blinked, then hopped lightly to his feet, turning to address the class and ignoring her hauling her weary carcass to her feet, feeling sweaty and wrung out, like a discarded rag. This was not the Sean she'd spent weeks with. This was not the man who told her he loved her, who was always happy to see her. This was some stranger inhabiting his body, who walked like Sean and talked like Sean, but was absolutely not Sean.

It was worse than having him not in her life at all, somehow, to be able to see him and touch him and know that everything was different. That he was different.

Well, in just a little while it would all be over and he would be out of her life forever. That thought wasn't comforting, either, but at least maybe she could find a little corner of peace in her misery. She hung back as he worked with the students, noticing that they were still looking from him to her, their expressions concerned. She'd always accompanied him as he moved around the room to issue corrections or compliments, ready to redemonstrate the move that he'd just taught her. But she couldn't bear to be that near him now, to feel the warmth radiating off his body, to inhale the smell of his soap and skin. If she could, she would flee the room this instant, running for home and the comfort of curling up on the sofa and burying her face in Timmy's fur while she cried.

"Hey." She started, realizing she'd completely zoned out. Sean was next to her, his eyes scanning her face, his eyebrows drawn together. Pain twisted in her chest, because this was an echo of the real Sean. *Her* Sean. The Sean who would check in on her, make sure she was okay. The Sean who cared.

She swallowed hard around the lump that was forming in her throat. "Sorry?" Her voice was a tattered husk crackling in the quiet room.

"Are you okay?" The question seemed forced out of him, as if he didn't want to be asking it. As if her Sean was in there somewhere, trying to take control from the Terminator.

She shook her head, trying to clear her thoughts. This wasn't one of her media classes where they dissected metaphor. Sean was Sean. He was angry and hurt and it was her fault. "I'm okay. It's just been a really bad week." The noise level around them rose and she realized that Sean had closed out the class, that the students were grabbing their things and heading for the door.

She couldn't be alone with him again. She was too raw, too weak. She'd ask him to come back, for everything to be okay between them again. But it was too soon and that would only delay the inevitable heartbreak.

So she did the most cowardly thing she had ever done. She said a swift goodbye and left.

"Well, that's it, then," Sean muttered to himself. For a moment there Eva had seemed like her old self—vulnerable and warm. But she'd left so fast he could have sworn she had rockets for shoes. It was clear she wanted nothing to do with him. He gathered up his stuff and walked out to his truck, driving home, feeling the beginnings of what was bound to be a rager of a headache.

Once inside, he grabbed a beer from the fridge, popped the cap off and treated himself to a long gulp. He felt hollow and empty, lonely in a way he'd never experienced before. His phone rang in his pocket and he pulled it out—Cait wanting to FaceTime. He considered for half a second if he wanted to take the call or not, but yeah. Cait was going to hound him if he fobbed her off. He tapped the icon to answer and Cait's face came up on the screen.

"What the hell, baby bro? You look like shit."

Ah, sisters. "Good evening to you, too."

"No, seriously. What happened? Are you sick or something? You look pale and like you haven't slept for a week. You're sporting serious luggage under your eyes."

To tell or not to tell. If it was any of his other sisters, he wouldn't say anything for fear of it getting around the rest of the family like wildfire. But Cait was better about privacy. And dammit, he did need to talk to someone. "Eva broke up with me."

Cait blinked at him for a long moment. "Excuse me? The woman who was clearly besotted with you three days ago has *broken up with you*? Make that make sense."

"One of our bigmouth sisters apparently told her that I'd be a great dad. And she doesn't want to have kids. Says she's too old."

His sister seemed to ponder that for a little while. "Do you want kids?"

"I don't know. I guess I kinda always figured I would have them. At some point. She said she wants me to think about it. Hence we're on a break. But then she had an issue with her ex and the cops got involved and she didn't call me. So it feels like more than a break. It feels permanent." The word seemed to ring in his head like a closed vault door. Permanent. Done. Over.

Cait appeared to think about this. "What would you have done if she had called you?"

"I—I don't know. Gone to see her? Something. I could have done something."

Caitlin closed her eyes and sighed deeply. "My beloved baby brother, I'm going to say this as gently as I can. Get your head out of your ass."

He laughed, startled. "Sugarcoating the hell out of the message, as usual."

"I'm serious. If she was half as besotted with you as she seemed, her cutting you loose to figure out what you wanted had to have been hard as hell. Then her ex does something scary enough to warrant calling 911 and you're upset that she didn't make it about you? I know you have a white knight complex going, but that's extreme."

He thought about the way she had burst into tears before he left her house the last time. Yeah, she had definitely been upset.

"Do you think it's okay to not want kids?" he asked.

"What kind of a question is that? Of course it's okay. Don't give in to Mom and Dad's brainwashing." The force of her denial was like a breath of fresh air rushing through his confused thoughts and feelings. She knew exactly what he was going through in a way that few other people could. The fact that she could so easily give him permission to step off the path he hadn't even consciously known he was on made the tension in his shoulders ease.

"Are you and Nicole really not planning on having any?"

"Answer's still no, pal."

Despite Cait's previous denials, that surprised him. "So probably no more grandkids for Mom and Pop, huh?"

"Do you even hear yourself right now? They already have *ten*. The quota has been met, then exceeded, then overachieved."

"Eva did think that them wanting more was a little extreme." At the time, he'd thought it was a joke. But what was normal for his family wasn't the norm for everyone.

"The woman is emphatically not wrong. And I know you love being their favorite uncle, but being a father is a whole other thing. So having established that she was letting you go for your own good, are you going to figure out your situation and go get her back?"

"You seem to have made my mind up for me."

"No, I think it's the conclusion you're going to come to when you finally have some time to think clearly. I could be wrong. But you seemed crazy about her. And you guys seemed good together."

"We were." He wanted to believe his sister was right. But she'd only met Eva for a few hours. Doubt still sat in the center of his chest like a brick.

Twenty-Six

On Friday Eva met her new lawyer, Rena, at the courthouse. The district attorney had declined to press charges against Darren, but one of the police officers had said he could and would testify about the incident at her house in support of a restraining order. Rena, waiting for Eva on the courthouse steps, had warm brown skin and flawless makeup. Her hair was in twists and she carried a hot-pink briefcase. She had a firm handshake and a dazzling smile.

"You let me know if you see the bad guy," she said. "I doubt he'll be foolish enough to try anything at the courthouse, but I've seen stranger things happen."

A shiver of nerves made Eva's belly clench. "I really just never want to see him again," she said.

Rena gestured to the courthouse door. "Well, let's make that happen for you."

Going through the security line and into the waiting area outside the courtroom doors, Eva constantly scanned the small crowd. She spotted Officer Contreras, who soon joined them, but couldn't find Darren anywhere.

"Don't be nervous," Rena said reassuringly. "This will all be over soon. It's a very routine hearing with a very high likelihood that we'll get what we want."

"It's also just a piece of paper," Officer Contreras said. "So don't count on it to keep you one hundred percent safe."

"Cynical but correct," Rena said, drumming her nails on her briefcase.

At that point the door to the courtroom where their hearing was scheduled swung open, and Rena led them inside.

"What happens if Darren doesn't show?" Eva asked as they took seats.

"Then we win by default."

Eva waited, the tension ratcheting higher and higher with each passing minute. Then her name was called. The three of them rose and Rena waved Eva and the officer to seats at one of the tables in front of the rows of seating. "Permission to approach the bench, Your Honor?" she asked smoothly. Her assurance in this ritualized setting was soothing. The judge beckoned her forward and she said a few quiet words to him.

He peered at Eva, thick white brows beetling over his eyes as he gazed at her over steel-framed reading glasses. Then he glanced around the courtroom and said in a clear, commanding voice, "Is Darren Perry in the courtroom this morning?"

Eva didn't want to look back, didn't want to see the man who'd made her feel unsafe in her own home. The judge barked Darren's name again, making her jump in her seat. Then he slammed his gavel down, muttered, "Default judgment entered. Get paperwork from the clerk, Attorney Gibson," scribbled something on a piece of paper and asked the bailiff to call the next matter.

Eva exhaled, feeling light-headed and, well, lighter.

The next half hour or so went by in a blur. Officer Contreras shook her hand and went off to continue his day. She and Rena waited in the clerk's office for her official documentation, and then when they had it in hand, walked out into the summer sunshine. Eva glanced down the courthouse steps and froze. Darren was at the bottom, looking up at her, his expression unreadable.

"Rena?" Eva asked. Her attorney followed her gaze and saw Darren. "That's him. What is he doing here?"

The attorney laid a comforting hand on her arm. "Probably trying to score psychological points. He knew he wasn't going to win in that hearing, so he's being a cheap little shit about it."

Darren turned his back and walked off down the street. There was defeat in the sagging line of his back and for the first time, Eva thought with relief this ordeal might finally be over. "Is *cheap little shit* a piece of professional vocabulary?" Eva asked.

"In my line of work? Yes."

At work Sean set the smoke alarm off with the toaster. "Christ, you've been distracted lately," Felix said as they opened windows to purge the room of the smoke. "How embarrassing would it be to have to be the source of our own callout? Even worse, Station 31 would have to come out to rescue us." Station 31 was the nearest station to theirs and a longtime source of friendly rivalry in charity fundraising.

"Sorry," Sean said, retrieving the blackened bread from the appliance and throwing it away.

Felix folded his arms across his chest and glared. "Will you go back to your girl and tell her you want to be with her forever and that way we can have our competent squad-mate back?"

"I want to." He did.

"But?"

"But I'm still not sure if she'd want me back. What if her 'take a break and think about whether you want kids or not' was just a different way of saying, 'it's not you, it's me'?"

"Then you find out that it's over once and for all. What's going on with you? You're not usually a coward."

"Gee. Pull your punches, why don't you?" First Cait, now Felix. He guessed he was fortunate to have family and friends willing to be frank with him, but he felt more like he was getting kicked while he was down. Besides, Felix hadn't seen Eva hightailing it away from him like he was on fire. "I had to see her Tuesday for the last self-defense thing. She clearly didn't want to be around me."

"Maybe because she's hurting, too," Felix said. "Having to be around someone you want but can't have can be an in-credibly painful experience."

Well, true. Wrapping himself around Eva had previously been the sweetest pleasure, even in the context of the class. But Tuesday evening? Agony.

It was at that moment the alarm went off, and Sean and

his squad hustled for the garage bay. The practiced routine of donning his protective gear was soothing. Pants and boots, suspenders, straps, hood, jacket. Grab the rest of the gear and move rapidly to the truck. The 911 dispatcher over their headsets informed them it was a house fire as Thea swung the big truck out onto the road, siren blaring and red lights flashing.

In minutes, they were in front of a large suburban home, hooking up hoses to the nearby hydrant and getting to work in suppressing the blaze. It seemed small now, but could double in size every minute if they didn't work quickly. The battalion chief approached Sean and Felix. "Hannigan, Lewis, there is apparently a small child who is unaccounted for. I need you two to go in."

In seconds Sean and Felix had their masks and tanks on, regulators snapped into place and helmets restrapped to their heads. Flashlights strapped to their jackets showed a short way through the hazy smoke as they moved quickly through the unfamiliar building. In a small room in the back, they found a little body on the floor, probably passed out from smoke inhalation. Sean scooped the kid up and they moved back toward the front door.

There was a roar, a booming sound, and Sean hunched his body around the child, feeling a heavy *crack* against his helmet. Instinctively, he raised his arm to shield the kid and something hit him on the back of his shoulder. Bright pain bloomed and his arm dropped uselessly at his side. Felix helped him through the door. Adrenaline surged through him as he located an EMT on standby with an oxygen tank. He staggered a little as he handed the kid off and the EMT's partner pointed at his limp right arm.

"Injury?" she asked.

Felix unstrapped Sean's helmet and peeled off his mask. "Yeah, looked like he got something heavy to the shoulder."

"Can you move your arm?" the EMT asked as Felix returned to the rest of the squad.

He tried and sickening, grinding pain ripped through his shoulder. "No," he gritted out. "Think something's broken."

The EMT led him aside and seated him on a gurney. "Stay with me, Hannigan." He realized he knew her.

"Caroline." His teeth chattered.

"Yeah. That's me. Stay with me, Hannigan," she repeated. "You're going into shock." She produced a penlight and flicked it at his eyes. "You hit your head." It wasn't a question but he nodded anyway. "Possible concussion, too. Easy now." She grabbed a big pair of scissors and started to cut his jacket and oxygen tank straps, the flashing lights and noise continuing around him, overwhelming.

Call Eva. He didn't know if he just thought it or said it aloud as Caroline peeled the cut fabric off him. Then everything slid away.

Eva let herself into her house with an exhausted sigh. Even without a confrontation, dealing with the emotional overload of the hearing was overwhelming. She trailed upstairs, changed out of her court clothes and into shorts and a T-shirt and went back downstairs. Timmy danced around her feet, his toenails making tap-dancing noises on the hardwood floor.

She crouched in front of him, massaging his rib cage until he crooned and leaned into her. "Good boy." Getting to her feet, she checked his water bowl, then wandered into the living room and lay down on the sofa. She had thought she would read for a while, but it wasn't long before the book slid to the floor and she was asleep.

She dreamed that she was looking for Sean, searching long, gleaming corridors filled with doorways. The dream splintered and she jerked awake, reaching for her ringing phone before she even registered consciously that that was what had awakened her.

"H'lo?" she slurred.

"Eva. It's Cait. Caitlin Hannigan. Sean's sister."

Eva snapped fully awake. Something in Caitlin's voice combined with that frantic dream alarmed her. "What's wrong?"

"Sean's going to be okay. But he got hurt at work. House fire. Something fell on him, gave him a concussion and a broken shoulder."

Eva's hand flew up and landed on her sternum. She leaped to her feet, her suddenly pounding heart drumming against her palm. "Oh, my God." She wanted to go to him, to be near him, to reassure herself that he really would be okay.

But she had no right to any of that. "Did…did he tell you we broke up?"

"Yes."

"And you don't hate me for it?" She knew how close he was to this sister.

Caitlin sighed and Eva heard footsteps. When she spoke again, her voice was much softer. "No. It sounds like you did it for the right reasons. I love my brother, but he did need that wake-up call. Our parents can be a little overwhelming with their expectations and he's never really bucked them in any meaningful way. It makes it hard for him to figure out what he wants apart from those expectations sometimes. Anyway, he's still in surgery, but if you want to be here when he wakes up, I think he'd want you here. And I think that would be a good thing."

"You do?" Eva's voice cracked with emotion.

"I do. We're all here, but I'm the only one who knew about the breakup, so it won't seem odd to anyone else if you're here. Suburban Hospital Center. The waiting room outside the surgical department on the third floor."

"I'll be there as soon as I can take my dog to the neighbor's house."

Eva practically flew to the hospital, her heart pounding and her ears ringing. Finding a parking spot in the garage, she practically ran to the elevator when her phone chimed with a text from Caitlin.

He's out of surgery. Room 518.

Fidgeting, she waited for the elevator and then hated every single second it took for the doors to slowly open, then slowly close while she jabbed at the button, knowing her multiple pokes wouldn't do any good, but desperate to do *something* even if it was pointless. Finally released, she raced for the hospital's front doors and quickly took stock of her surroundings, locating another elevator that thankfully operated a bit faster, whisking her up to the fifth floor. When she emerged, she hustled down the corridors, feeling a disorienting sort of déjà vu thanks to her dream. Rounding a corner, she was brought up short by the crowd that was Sean's family in the corridor. Or not all of them. It was just Sean's parents and his sisters and Nicole. Presumably, the husbands had been left to take care of the kids.

Her steps slowed as the Hannigans turned to look at her. Suddenly, she felt out of place, an interloper. Cait stepped forward, her hands outstretched, and gave Eva a quick hug. "You have the right to be here," she whispered fiercely in Eva's ear.

But did she?

Cait drew back and gave her a reassuring smile. "We were just arguing about who got to go in and see him first. The nurses don't want us crowding him and getting him agitated, and that'd be bound to happen with all of us in there." She led Eva back to the group, who seemed to be taking Eva's presence as natural, not as an intrusion. Her shoulders relaxed a little.

"I can go in whenever," she said. "I don't want to put anybody out."

To her surprise, Susan shook her head. "No, you should go in first, Eva. He should be awake any minute now."

"Oh." Eva didn't quite know what to do with that. Her nerves reasserted themselves, making her stomach flutter and her breathing quicken. But Susan was opening the door to the room and gesturing her in.

She peered around the door frame. Sean, big and solid, lay on the hospital bed, an IV drip in his arm and a nasal cannula on his upper lip. She moved forward almost without think-ing, taking in the bandage on his shoulder, the arm strapped to his chest by a high-tech sling. As she moved closer, she could see he was pale, with dark shadows under his eyes. But his breathing was deep and steady and the monitors beeped in time to his heartbeat.

Closing the last few feet of distance, she laid tentative fin-gers on his left hand, needing to touch him but not wanting to hurt him. "Sean?" she said softly. His eyes remained shut. She'd thought she'd lost him when she sent him away, but she hadn't thought about losing him completely. That near miss stretched in front of her like an abyss, terrifying in its permanence.

She swallowed around the lump in her throat. "Sean, I'm going to be a coward right now and tell you what I should have before. I'll tell you again when you're not just out of sur-gery, but you deserve to have all the information. You deserve to know that I love you, too. That I love you enough to let you go if I can't give you what you need. But I do love you."

The big hand underneath hers turned, grasping her, and his beautiful green eyes opened. "Baby, don't cry."

Twenty-Seven

Sean couldn't be totally sure that he wasn't dreaming. The last thing he'd remembered was having his gear cut off him, his shoulder screaming in agony. Waking up to the sounds of a hospital hadn't disoriented him much—he'd been in enough of them for various reasons for years—but he hadn't expected Eva to be there, talking to him.

Telling him she loved him.

He was pretty sure he hadn't caught all of what she had to say, but he'd caught that. It was better than whatever drugs they had pumping through his system, that confession of love. He could get through anything with her. And now here she was, tears streaming down her face. He moved slowly to wipe them away, aware of the anesthetic still fogging his brain and making his motions clumsy. She clasped his hand and kissed it, smiling through the tears.

"You love me, huh?" His voice was rusty.

"You weren't meant to hear that until later," she admit-

ted. "It's a lot to lay on you right out of getting your shoulder put back together."

"Nah, it's the best thing I could possibly wake up to," he
said.

She gave him a watery smile and he wished he could pull
her close, but the wires, IV line and the fact that his right arm
was currently strapped to his chest all made that impossible.
He settled for a simple request. "Kiss me?"

She leaned over him and gave him the softest, gentlest kiss
of his life. One he knew he'd never forget. "Your family's in
the hallway. They're going to want to see you, but they're
limited in how many people can come in at once. Who do
you want to see first?"

"I don't care, as long as you stay. How many people are
they letting in at a time?"

She grimaced. "I don't know. Let me go ask your parents."

"Are the kids here?"

She shook her head. "And your brothers-in-law aren't here,
either."

"Good. That means we can get the visiting and worrying
out of the way a lot faster."

Eva wiped the remaining tears off her face and straightened her shoulders, giving him a little nod. "I'll just go talk
to them to see what we should do," she said and slipped away
from his side. When she opened the door, he could see the
worried faces of his family and he wanted to be cowardly, to
pretend to slip back into sleep and not deal with the tide of
emotion that was about to crash over him, visiting restrictions or no visiting restrictions.

Eva led his parents into the room and stood by his bed as his mother wept and fussed and crossed herself. His dad, laconic as usual, mostly just stood by and looked from him to Eva, then finally put his arm around Mom and told her that she'd fretted enough and Sean needed to see his sisters and get some rest.

His older sisters paraded through in a bit of a blur of similar quasi-motherly noises until it was time for Cait and Nicole to come in. "Saved the best for last," his favorite sister said softly. "We won't stay long. You look like shit."

He chuckled. "Peak Cait."

She shrugged. "I gotta be me. Is there anything we can do for you?"

He shifted, already sick of the hospital bed. "Mom and Dad are going to want me to move back in with them while I recover."

Cait grimaced. "Yeah. Well, you're definitely not going to be on your own until you get the use of your right arm back. And you're for sure not sleeping on our pull-out sofa. That'd just do you more harm than good."

"You can stay with me," Eva said.

The offer had been utterly spontaneous, spoken without thought. But when everyone looked at her, surprise evident on all three faces, she said, "It makes sense. My summer schedule is light. I have the room. And I want to."

She maybe should have said that last part first.

Sean reached for her hand and squeezed it. "You sure?"

Eva nodded.

Caitlin glanced at the closed door. "You know I'm the biggest cheerleader for your relationship, but this is kind of a big deal. You haven't had a chance to have the kid talk yet and I don't want either of you to get hurt."

Sean sighed and groaned, a deep rumble in his chest. "Not for nothing, Cait, but you're channeling Mom. Go away now, willya?"

She chuffed out a laugh and patted his cheek with a gentle palm. "Fair enough. Don't have the kids talk when you're still high on pain meds, though, okay?"

"Cait." His voice was a growl.

She raised her hands in surrender. "Fine, fine. I'm going to take my wisdom and my fabulous wife and we're going to go home."

"Get some rest," Nicole said as they gathered their things to leave. "I'm glad you're doing so well." She shot a shy smile at Eva. "I'm also glad you came. Let us know if either of you need anything."

"Thank you," Eva said, a little in shock from the events of the afternoon, then even more shocked when Caitlin stepped forward and pulled her into another strong hug.

"Thank *you* for loving my exasperating little brother," she murmured in Eva's ear, making her choke with laughter.

"Thank you for calling me. This means everything to me."

Cait gave her one last squeeze. "Good." She pulled back and held out her hand for her wife to take and the two women left the room.

Eva took a deep breath and scanned her surroundings,

wondering what she should do. Feeling like she *should* do something.

"What's up?" Sean said.

"Just feeling like I should be useful," she admitted.

"Come over here and hold my good hand. That'll be useful."

She dragged a plastic chair to his bedside and sat, weaving her fingers into his, cherishing the familiar feel of his calloused palm against her skin. Something she hadn't thought she'd ever experience again.

"What've you been up to?" he asked, shifting a little then wincing.

"Are your pain meds wearing off?"

"Don't think so. It's just not comfortable being all strapped in like this."

She grimaced. "No, of course not. But I'm sure it's necessary."

"Yeah." He heaved a sigh. "You didn't tell me what you've been up to, though."

"Well." She thought about her morning and how different it felt from now. "I did get a restraining order against Darren."

He squeezed her hand. "Good. Did the asshole put up a fight?"

"No. He defaulted, in fact. Showed up after the hearing just to be a cartoon villain by making his presence known outside the courthouse, but I think I'm truly done with having to deal with him for good."

Sean's eyelids drooped. "Good."

Guilt surged through her. She should have put him off, not actually told him about the hearing. She should have protected him just now, the way he would have protected her. "Sleep," she said, lifting his hand to her mouth and kissing his knuckles. "I'll be here."

Discomfort and unfamiliar light woke Sean. He groaned and looked around the sterile hospital room, remembering the night of disturbed sleep, of nurses' rounds and medication, of Eva's pale, worried face as she took in the latest data from the latest medical professional.

Hospitals were no place to get better; that was for sure.

He rummaged for the bed's controls that would lift his torso and looked around the room. Eva was curled up in a vinyl upholstered recliner in the corner, covered with a cotton hospital blanket. His heart felt like someone had reached into his chest and squeezed.

She loved him.

That alone was better than a full night's sleep.

Untangling the blankets with the hand that wasn't strapped to his body, he carefully levered himself to a sitting position. He was only on an IV at this point and he could wheel that into the bathroom to relieve himself.

God, just sitting up was exhausting.

He sat and just breathed for a few moments, admiring the baby blue rubber-adorned socks someone had placed on his feet, then carefully shifted upright, his good hand on the IV stand for balance. He took one step forward, then another. Okay so far. Moving slowly but with more assurance, the wheels on the IV stand squeaked and Eva started awake.

"Sean! What are you doing?"

"I'm going to take a piss. It's fine."

"You should have woken me up."

"I apparently did," he said, his voice dry.

She struggled out of the recliner, almost tripping over the blanket as she got to her feet to come over to him. "I mean before you got out of bed." Her hands hovered around his left arm as if he was about to topple over.

"I'm fine. I just have a full bladder." He tried to give her a reassuring grin, but what went across his face was probably more of a grimace. Her brows drew together and he patted her shoulder. "Hover if you want, but I have to piss." Stepping carefully, he went into the bathroom and took care of his needs, finding dealing with life one-handed to be incredibly awkward and difficult. Though he had to admit being in a hospital gown helped. No fly to deal with.

And yet, it was going to be okay. Because Eva loved him. And he was going home with her. Emerging from the bathroom after washing his hand and splashing water on his face to make himself feel marginally more human, he found Eva talking with a nurse.

"They're discharging you this morning," Eva said, her face alight with the most radiant smile. It lifted a tiny bit of his fatigue, that smile. Because it appeared she was as happy as he was that he was going home with her.

As it turned out, they did need Caitlin's help in the form of getting clothes from Sean's apartment. Everything he'd worn on the upper part of his body had been cut off him by the paramedics, and as much as it might be a kind of stripper or beefcake calendar fantasy to have him exit the hospital in just his firefighting pants and steel-toed boots, it wasn't exactly practical.

Caitlin arrived with a giant duffel bag full mostly of workout wear that was easy to slip on and off with only one hand. She'd also raided his bathroom for necessities like his toothbrush, deodorant and razor.

He rubbed his chin as she gave them the rundown of the inventory. "I don't think I'm going to try to shave left-handed. Guess I'm going to get to grow a beard for the first time." Eva blinked, confused, and he grinned at her. "They aren't allowed on the job. Can't have one and get a good seal on the oxygen mask."

Comprehension flooded through her. "Oh." She had so much to learn.

Caitlin commented that he looked a degree less like shit than he had the day before, gave him a sisterly peck on the cheek and left. Eva helped him dress, assistance that he grumbled about but accepted. For her part, Eva was glad to have a nurse show her how best to get a T-shirt off and on Sean without moving his arm. She marveled at the smoothly competent way the nurse explained how he should rest his elbow on something and work the shirt onto the injured arm first, moving it up high enough on his biceps so he could use his left hand to thread it over his head and on completely. Then the sling went back on, carefully immobilizing his arm against his torso.

Then there was a period of time where they did nothing, waiting for Sean's discharge papers. "Hurry up and wait," he grumbled. Finally, another nurse came in with the papers, a follow-up appointment and instructions for care so his surgical incision didn't get infected. At last, with more grumbling from Sean, the nurse made him sit in a wheelchair while Eva scurried out to the garage to get her car and pull it around to the front entrance of the hospital, weighed down by the giant duffel Caitlin had brought.

Finally, Sean transferred himself into her passenger seat, ratcheting it back to accommodate his long legs and carefully managing the seat belt. Eva shut the door and rounded the car, sliding in and pausing for a moment to catch her breath.

"You okay?" he asked.

She nodded. "It's just been a bit of a whirlwind." In truth, she was starting to worry she'd been too hasty, offering her home to a convalescent Sean. But he grinned at her, weary but apparently happy and she remembered every kind thing, every thoughtful gesture, every concerned action, then buckled her seat belt and headed for home.

Twenty-Eight

By the time Eva had pulled up in front of her house, Sean had fallen asleep. What woke him was the lack of sound when she cut the engine, the quiet echoing in ears that had grown used to constant noise. He blinked and rubbed at his eyes, then let Eva open his door for him, getting slowly out as she retrieved his bag from her trunk. He felt imbalanced by the arm that was strapped to his chest, tired and generally not himself. He followed her inside, wondering why the house felt off.

"Where's Timmy?" Normally, the little dog would be bouncing and prancing around both of them, eager for attention. But Eva'd been with him in the hospital since yesterday evening.

"Krystal took him for me. He's having a playdate with Luther. She said she'd keep him until we got sorted."

Sean realized she was already rearranging her life to help him. "You don't have to do that. I can help. I can feed him, walk him—I only need one hand to hold his leash. Maybe only one finger."

"Okay. But later. You need to get to bed. You look like you're about to fall over."

"Then you need to come with me. I think you got even less sleep than I did in the hospital."

"Yeah, but I didn't have a serious injury and surgery be-forehand."

He stepped forward into her space, cupping her cheek. "It's not a competition. Krystal can keep Timmy for a few more hours while we sleep. Then we can both go get him when we've had some rest."

Her expression melted into something he couldn't quite read. "Dammit, Sean, I'm supposed to be taking care of you."

"Come on upstairs. We can take care of each other." It felt right to be with her. To be here where they'd made something special between them. They still needed to talk about kids, but he knew how he felt now. Somehow, in those days apart, he'd been able to unstitch the expectations he'd unwittingly absorbed from his own feelings and priorities.

They climbed up to her room and stretched out on top of her covers without conferring, as if they'd already agreed, Sean on his back, Eva on her side. "How do you feel?" she asked.

"Sore," he admitted. His head throbbed and his shoulder ached.

"Do you think you can sleep?"

He yawned, his jaw cracking. "Mmm-hmm."

The last thing he registered was Eva's hand coming to rest on his good shoulder, warm and comforting.

★ ★ ★

Eva only slept for an hour before her eyes popped open and she was instantly awake. She'd rolled away from Sean in her sleep and now she cautiously turned to see how he was doing, careful not to wake him up. She needn't have bothered. He was obviously deeply asleep, his massive chest rising and falling with his breath, his face slack and peaceful. She slid out of bed and crept downstairs, grabbing her keys and her phone and slipping out of the house. Krystal was home with the dogs and Timmy pranced and whined and generally behaved as if he hadn't seen Eva in weeks.

"Thanks for taking care of this silly creature," she told her friend.

"My pleasure. I think Luther appreciated the company." She rested her hand on her dog's massive head and he looked soulfully up at her, drool trailing from his jowls.

"I left Sean fast asleep, but I better get back in case he wakes up." The need to be there felt like a line tied around her heart, towing her back to be with him.

Krystal flapped a hand. "Go take care of your heroic fireman. I'll see you later."

She thanked her friend again and she and Timmy fast-walked back to her house. Creeping upstairs, she reassured herself that he was still asleep. Good. His healing body would need the rest. Going back to the living room, she grabbed a pen and paper and sat down to make a grocery list. He was going to need fresh, healthy food and lots of it. It felt good, purposeful, to be able to take care of him.

Her phone rang. "Is this Eva?" a vaguely familiar voice asked.

"Yes, who's this?"

"This is Felix—we met at the county fair."

"Oh, of course. How are you?"

"Better than Sean is, that's for sure. His sister says he's recuperating at your house."

"He is. He's asleep now, as a matter of fact."

"Good. Is there a good time for some of us to swing by? We've had a slow few hours and made up some chili and soup and stuff if you have room in your fridge or freezer." The reality of Sean's life—so many people ready to step up and support him, to support both of them—made tears push at the backs of her eyes.

"Oh, gosh. I was literally just making up a grocery list because I figured he was going to need a lot of food as he recovers."

"You're not wrong. He's a big guy and can put it away even at the best of times. We figured you might want some help."

"That's so sweet of you. Really any time today would be fine. I'm not going anywhere. But if you want to actually talk to Sean, you might want to give him a few hours. He seems like he's going to be napping for a while."

They arranged for a time for the firefighters to come over to Eva's and she looked off into space for a long time after they ended the call.

Sean drifted awake slowly, aware of pain before he was aware of anything else. His eyes slid open and he realized where he was. Eva's bedroom. The aches in his body didn't disappear, but they somehow seemed to recede, to become less important.

Eva was somewhere in the house and she and he were going to make a go of it.

Voices filtered up from downstairs. Was that *Felix* he heard? Carefully, he levered himself up and got to his feet. The next few weeks of sleeping exclusively on his back were truly going to suck. He went to the bathroom, emptied his bladder and washed his hand and, awkwardly, his face. It wasn't just sleeping on his back that was going to suck.

Maybe Eva would give him a sponge bath. That would improve his mood.

He moved slowly downstairs, finding not just Felix in Eva's little living room, but also Thea and a bunch of the rest of the squad. "Hey," he said, his voice raspy.

"Hey, sleeping beauty," Thea said, but her voice didn't have its usual irreverent snap. Her skin was pale and her eyes looked too big for her face. She was trying to smile but it was more like a grimace.

"Hey yourself," Sean replied. If he asked Thea what was up in front of the rest of the guys, she'd clam up. But maybe he could talk to her later. Something was definitely wrong.

Eva moved forward through the little crowd. "How are you feeling?" she asked, her eyes scanning his face.

"Like something heavy fell on me and I was cut open and reassembled. But with more sleep. What are all you reprobates doing, invading my girlfriend's house like this?" he asked with mock severity. It felt so good to be able to call Eva his girlfriend again.

"Hush. They brought food," Eva scolded with an affectionate grin.

"Mike and I made chili, Ray made his matzoh ball soup, and Thea made stuffed shells," Felix said.

"And thank goodness I had extra room in my freezer," Eva said. Then she turned to the entire group. "But honestly, thank you all so much. It will help a lot, I'm sure."

Sean hadn't thought he was hungry, but mention of his squad-mates' best dishes made his stomach rumble.

"Ah, well. That's our cue. We'll get out of your hair and let you feed the big guy," Felix said, winking at Sean and waving everyone toward the front door. "Let us know if we can do anything else while he recuperates. We can deliver more food, drive to doctor's visits, physical therapy appointments, you name it."

The memory of handing the small child off to the paramedic hit him. "Wait, before you go—how's the kid?" Sean asked.

Felix stopped and turned. "Kid's right as rain, ya big hero. The EMTs got her on oxygen and despite some smoke inhalation, she'll be just fine."

"Good." A family losing their home—as Sean was sure was the case here—was bad, but homes could be rebuilt. If the family was whole and together, that was the important thing.

The squad cleared out and he and Eva returned to the living room, sitting on the sofa, Eva putting several inches of distance between her and his good side.

"You don't have to treat me like I'm made of glass," he said, wrapping his left arm around her shoulders and pulling her against him.

"You only had surgery yesterday," she said, settling against him with a rigidity that said she wasn't comfortable with their usual dynamic. He hated that. But he also had to acknowledge that he'd feel the same way in her shoes.

He rubbed her arm, satisfied to feel her relaxing a little into him. "We'll get there. I believe in us."

A week later, after an exhausting day of student conferences, Eva let herself into her house to the most delicious smells. She closed her eyes and inhaled deeply, settling her back against the door and feeling her shoulders relax. Sean's squad must have delivered another round of food for them. They'd been great with their offers of help. And Sean had been a surprisingly good patient, taking all the doctor's restrictions in stride.

But it was still really exhausting.

She pushed off the door and detoured through the living room, noting that Timmy was sleeping on his dog bed, apparently having already been fed and walked. She dropped her bag on the couch and trailed into the kitchen, finding Sean stirring whatever it was that smelled so good on the stovetop.

"Did your coworkers give us *more* food?" she asked.

He turned, his face lighting with the most beautiful smile. "No. I made this."

"You *made* something? How?" Chopping things one-handed might be possible, but she didn't think he'd had the time to learn those skills. With his non-dominant hand, to boot. And the stew in the pot definitely had things going on that would require chopping.

"Well, Ray came by and helped. And drove me to the grocery store. But I found the gumbo recipe and decided on the seasoning and, well." His face went frustrated. "It was my project."

She moved to his left side, rubbing his arm and resting her head against his shoulder. "It smells wonderful. Thank you." She had witnessed how hard it was for him to limit himself from his usual abilities, and as much as she wished he would rest, she couldn't fault him for wanting to get back to normal.

He set the spoon on a small plate and bent to kiss her. "Welcome home. How was your day?"

"Exhausting. But it's done now and much better to see you and smell this deliciousness."

"Super. Go get changed. Timmy's all set and this just needs to simmer for a bit."

She examined his face for strain or other signs that he was doing too much, but his easy grin was undimmed and his color looked good. "Okay." She went up to the room she'd stopped thinking of as hers and started thinking of as theirs and changed into a T-shirt and shorts, a now-familiar thrill of pleasure running through her at having him there.

When she got back downstairs, Sean was just opening the oven door and she could smell cornbread. "Why don't you let me get that out," she said, grabbing a pair of oven mitts and stooping in front of the hot oven to get the pan out.

"I could've done it," he grumbled, but there was a tiny smile on his face.

"Yeah, but hot things and only one hand is a recipe for a nasty burn."

"Tell me about it. I'm around you one-handed all the time."
He waggled his eyebrows expressively as she put the hot pan
on a trivet.

"Very funny," she said, but she was happy to see him starting to come back to normal.

"Taste this and let me know what you think." He offered
her a soupspoon of gumbo. She took it, blowing on it to cool
the lavalike mixture, and took a taste.

"Oh, wow. I shouldn't be surprised that you can cook,
since your squad-mates definitely can, but this is next level."

"Thanks." There were spots of color on his cheekbones
above the short beard he now sported.

She caressed his chin. "That's starting to get soft," she commented. "Does it still itch?"

"Nah. But I'll be glad to be able to shave again."

She shot him a lascivious smile. "I don't know. I'm kind of
interested to see how it'd feel in…interesting places."

He heaved a huge sigh. "Get better faster, shoulder."

Twenty-Nine

"I have a good feeling about this," Eva said while they sat in the waiting room. "You've been a model patient."

Sean shot her an amused look. "Am I the valedictorian of shoulder injuries, Professor?"

"Absolutely. One hundred percent."

A nurse came out and called his name and he stood. Eva remained seated. "You're not coming in with me?"

"Of course. If you want."

He reached for her hand and held it as they were led back to the exam room. A few minutes later, after a light tap on the door, the surgeon's assistant came in to help Sean out of his sling and shirt. His shoulder still ached and was stiff, but it no longer felt hopeless as it had in some of the early days after his surgery. He was instructed to rest his arm on a table the assistant wheeled over to the exam bed. Then they waited again. Eva paced a couple of restless steps, then seemed to realize that wasn't productive and sat in a chair.

"You're nervous," Sean said.

She shook her head. "Not nervous, just don't like not knowing what comes next."

"That's what this visit is for."

At that moment a light tap on the door preceded the entrance of Dr. Liu. Petite and no nonsense, she walked briskly into the room and proceeded to examine his surgical scar. For the first time, he was allowed to move his arm a little, which felt both wonderful and weird.

"Good news. You can stop wearing the sling," the doctor said. She made a referral to a physical therapist and gave him some initial gentle exercises, together with a stern warning against "overdoing it," a phrase she repeated several times.

Sean didn't mind the scold. He could begin to move more naturally again, to not always feel oddly unbalanced.

The doctor gave them a printout of next steps and congratulated Sean on his recovery progress, then hurried out, presumably on to save the next person's joint.

"Okay, then. You're a free man," Eva said. Sean followed her out of the medical building. He'd been thinking for days about the speech he was about to make. When they were both in her car and she was about to put the car in Reverse, he stopped her with a hand on her knee.

"You asked me to make up my mind about whether or not I want kids before coming back to you. But well…"

She turned beautiful, sad eyes to his face. "Yeah. Neither of us counted on this happening. But you're going to be okay." Her face looked so resolute, so brave.

"Yeah. I'm going to be okay. And I still want you more than I want anything else."

"You do?" She blinked at him.

"Yeah. Kids are great. And I have a ton of them in my life. I don't need to be a dad." He shushed her as her eyes went misty and she started to shake her head. "Listen. As far as having kids went, I was coasting, assuming. Which is the wrong way to think about bringing people into the world. If a person's going to be a parent, they should really *want* that, not just assume it'll happen."

"Okay." She swallowed hard, her eyes huge.

"Even before the accident, I knew you were everything to me. I don't need to be a dad," he repeated, hoping the message would sink in. He lifted his right hand, the hand that hadn't been able to caress her for too long, and cupped her jaw. "I just want you and the life we could have together. I love you."

Her eyes closed then, tears spilling from between her lashes. "Really?"

"Really." He kissed her, willing his lips to make her believe what he had said. "Let's go home."

Eva pulled up in front of her house and turned off the engine, glancing over at Sean's truck, which Felix and Thea had delivered in the early days of his recuperation and had sat unused ever since.

"You'll be driving again soon," she said. The doctor hadn't cleared him for that quite yet, but it was coming. Despite what he'd said, a corner of her still harbored leftover worries.

Stop catastrophizing she scolded herself. Even before his declaration, Sean had been as attentive as he'd always been, still sweet. He hadn't turned into any of her horrible exes. He'd cornered her in the bathroom a few times, growling a few of the filthy things he'd like them to do when he was feeling better...

That gave her an idea.

"Why don't you go up and take your first proper shower without the shower sling?" she asked.

He sighed and ran a hand through his hair. "That sounds pretty great, actually."

She leaned over and looked him in the eye. "Then you towel off and get into bed. Lie on your back. Wait for me."

His pupils expanded. "Are you taking a page out of my book?" he asked.

"Maybe." She let the tiniest of sly smiles curve her lips.

"Well, then. Yes, ma'am." They got out of the car and if he was walking a little oddly, she didn't comment on it, just licked her lips as she opened the door.

"In you go. Get clean and get horizontal." She was a little amazed at her own boldness.

He just winked and hustled for the stairs. She followed more slowly, smiling at the sound of the water turning on, of the rattle of the shower curtain rings. Rummaging in her chest of drawers, she came up with a square silk scarf, which she folded carefully and laid on the bedside table. As she was considering what else she might pull out, the water stopped and the shower curtain sounded again. After a mere minute Sean emerged from the bathroom, clean and naked and sporting a rampant erection. She breathed a huge sigh. He looked almost like the old Sean, though he still held his right arm a little oddly.

"C'mere," she said, taking up the scarf. He came forward willingly and she twirled her finger to get him to turn around. Then she softly bound the makeshift blindfold over his eyes. "This okay with you?"

"Honey, you can do whatever you like with me," he said, his blindfolded, bearded face looking unfamiliar to her somehow. Like a sexy stranger. She moved around him then, putting her hands on his hips and urging him gently backward until he sat on the bed.

"Lie on your back," she said.

He did. "You going to tie me up, too?"

"Thought about it, but that would be a bad idea with your shoulder."

He pouted extravagantly.

"Later," she reassured him. "After you're fully healed."

He shifted, his cock bobbing. "Sweetheart, we have all the time in the world."

He couldn't have known in that moment, that was the most perfect thing he could say.

Sean waited, the blindfold heightening his other senses. The soft rustling sound of Eva moving. Was she taking off her clothes? The gentle breath of air that kissed his skin as, presumably, she moved beside him. The slight dip of the mattress as she climbed onto the bed. Anticipation zinged through him; his cock ached.

Her hand closed around him and he almost shouted, his hips jerking.

"Shh." Her breath tickled his ear. "No moving."

What? Not possible. But he set his jaw and struggled to remain motionless as she began to gently work his cock. Much gentler than she knew he liked.

Oh, this woman was going to be the death of him and he was going to enjoy it.

She gave him a squeeze and then the quickest flicker of her tongue over the head made him groan. She chuckled and he shut his eyes tight, fighting for control. A few more licks and he was wound tighter than a piano wire, his hips begging to thrust, to move, his butt clenched hard. Then her soft, wet mouth enveloped the crown and paradoxically he relaxed, his body practically melting into the mattress. He hadn't thought she'd be into this, hadn't ever even considered asking her. But now that she was offering it to him, it felt like the most precious gift.

It also felt fucking amazing.

She alternated soft mouthing with more concentrated suction and his body wound up again, tense and straining. "I'm going to come if you keep doing that."

Her response was to hum a languid, "Mmm-hmm," and suck harder, one hand working the lower part of his shaft, the other hand cradling his balls. He was a goner. He came, helplessly bucking and groaning and she stayed with him, finally caressing his softening penis as he took a long, shuddering breath. He felt her stretch out beside him, her bare skin against his, and the blindfold was tugged away from his eyes. He blinked, looking at Eva's grinning, beautiful face.

"Welcome back," she said.

His response was to kiss her long and deep. When he pulled back, there were tears standing in her eyes. "What's wrong?"

She shook her head. "Nothing's wrong. I'm just happy."

"You cry when you're happy?"

She shrugged one shoulder. "Sometimes. Don't you? Crying isn't always about being sad. Sometimes it's just being overwhelmed."

He stroked her cheek with his thumb. "What's overwhelming?"

"You. Being here. Choosing me. It's still a little scary sometimes. You could change your mind. And that would hurt a lot."

"I could," he admitted. "But can you believe me when I tell you I know I never will? I meant it when I said I loved you. And I mean it now. Being with you is everything."

She kissed him again and he looped his left arm around her, tugging her onto his chest in a way that hadn't been possible for weeks. It felt good. It felt right.

Eva squeezed her eyes tight shut, breathing in the familiar scent of Sean, feeling his chest rise and fall under her cheek. A tear squeezed out and she ran her hand across his chest, hoping to distract him from her—she didn't even know what it was. Gladness? Relief? Because for whatever reason it was only now that she realized Sean wasn't going anywhere.

They could have this. This life. Together.

She snuggled closer to him, her skin to his, but his hand—his right hand—skimmed over her cheek. "You're crying again," he said.

Her head shot up. "Don't overdo it. Rest that arm," she commanded.

He laughed and pulled her down against his chest again with his good arm. "I love you so much, you worrywart."

She laughed, too, her tears spilling helplessly down. "I love you, too, you bossy man."

He growled then, making her laugh again. "You made me come. I need to settle the score."

She lifted a finger to rest on his lips. "No. You've made me come so many more times than you have. Rest. Besides, like you said that one time, this is for you."

"Bossy."

She settled her head against his shoulder. "Turnabout is fair play."

"Okay. Just this once."

A tiny thrill of nerves zinged through her stomach. "I have something to ask you."

"Shoot, beautiful."

She took a deep breath as the nerves intensified and she lifted her head to look him in the eye. "How would you feel about moving in for good?"

"Here?"

"Here."

One corner of his mouth kicked up and he stroked her hair. "I'd feel like the luckiest guy in the world."

Thirty

A little less than a year later Eva was in her university office grading yet another batch of final papers. Her phone buzzed on her desk.

Sean: Know what day it is?

Eva racked her brain for a few seconds. No?

Sean: Come outside. I have something to show you.

With a small smile, she got to her feet and walked out to the quad. Scanning the green lawn, she found him standing under a tree a short way away. Timmy was on a leash, seated by his side, his tail thumping as he spotted her. She walked over, confused. "What's going on?"

"I wanted to give you this." He handed her a book. It was

the same book Felix had recommended to him around the time they'd first met.

"But I have this book," she said, confused.

"Open it."

Maybe he'd gotten her a signed copy? She went to open it, even more confused that the paperback didn't seem as flexible as it should. But when she lifted the cover, she realized it wasn't a book at all. It was a box made to look like a book. Inside the box was another box.

A small box covered with black velvet.

Her entire world seemed to slow and spin, her mind unable to process what was going on, the enormity of it. Sean took the little box out and dropped to one knee. "It's been exactly one year since you and I first talked under this tree. So I wanted to bring it full circle and choose this time and this place to ask you to marry me. Will you?" His voice had a wobble to it and his hands shook as he cracked open the box to reveal an oval sapphire that sparkled in the spring sunshine.

Her hands flew to her mouth. They'd talked about getting married, but she had no idea he'd move so quickly. *This is real. This is really happening.* "Yes," she choked out, realizing that he had tears in his eyes. She cupped his cheek. "Are you crying?"

He grinned, eyes shiny as he slid the ring onto her finger and stood. "Yeah. You might say I'm overwhelmed."

"I know what that feels like," she said and he bent to kiss her, both of them laughing when Timmy tried to wriggle in between them to share the embrace. "You brought Timmy to propose to me?"

He cupped the back of her neck and looked down at her, a dazed expression on his face. "Well, I had to ask for his blessing, so it felt like the right thing to do. We're a family, after all."

★ ★ ★ ★ ★

Acknowledgments

This book is dedicated to my husband, the man whom the internet knows as "Mr. B." Why am I mentioning you here as well? Because without you it's highly unlikely this book (or any of my books) would exist. I am so fortunate to have you in my life. You're my support in all the ways that matter. Plus, you're really funny and cute.

Jayce Ellis, for your friendship and your help with the original chapters and proposal for this book. Your insight is invaluable and I love you to pieces.

My agent, Katie Shea Boutillier. I've benefited so much by having you in my corner and I look forward to many more books in our future.

Jason Gibson, M.D.—your patience and help saves my butt with medical issues every time. My butt and I both thank you.

John, Stacy, Errin and the rest of the team at Harlequin Afterglow and HarperCollins—thanks so much for being so patient and accommodating to this new-to-traditional-publishing author! It's a privilege to work with such a talented team.

Suz Brockmann, JoAnn Ross, Emma Barry and Karen Booth—thank you so much for reading an early version of this and having such nice things to say.

To all my author and reader friends on social media and in person. I am made both a better author and a better person by your insights and friendship.

You—yes, you! Authors wouldn't write without readers and the fact that you decided to read this book means the world to me. Thank you.